PRAISE FOR TH

T0244780

"Filled with emotion and well-researched details of the period, *The Paris Escape* transports the reader to World War II in the very best way. The evolution of Laura and Henry's relationship from dubious travel companions to romance touches the heart, and the addition of David to their small circle pulls at the heart strings even more. *The Paris Escape* is breathtaking World War II fiction, and book clubs will enjoy it immensely!"

—Anita Abriel, Internationally bestselling author of *The Light After The War*

"Social expectations and injustice collide in this breathtaking love story, taking readers through a heart-pounding journey that explores the deeper meaning of family."

—Cynthia Ellingsen, bestselling author of *The Lighthouse Keeper*

"An enthralling read, blending the pace of a thriller with a romance that is heightened by the urgency of impending war. Dreams and innocence are met with danger around every corner, loyalties lead to desperate choices, and trust is shattered even while hope and heroism struggle to emerge from an ever-changing landscape. Readers will enjoy this fresh WWII tale and see themselves in the story in a way few books of the genre achieve."

—Camille Di Maio, bestselling author of *The Memory of Us*

"James Tucker brings an era and a lost world to crackling life and fills it with richly imagined characters whose stories and secrets entangle in such a way that the reader cannot help but follow them into the tale. Perfectly paced and tense as a wave about to break. You can't put this novel down."

—Marya Hornbacher, Pulitzer Prize–nominated author of *Wasted*

The
PARIS
ESCAPE

ALSO BY JAMES TUCKER

Buddy Lock Mysteries

The Holdouts (Book 2)

Next of Kin (Book 1)

The PARIS ESCAPE

A NOVEL

JAMES TUCKER

This is a work of fiction. Names, characters, organizations, places, events, and incidents are either products of the author's imagination or are used fictitiously.

Published by Lake Union Publishing, Seattle

www.apub.com

Amazon, the Amazon logo, and Lake Union Publishing are trademarks of Amazon.com, Inc., or its affiliates.

ISBN-13: 9781662520150 (paperback)
ISBN-13: 9781662520167 (digital)

Cover design by Mumtaz Mustafa
Cover image: © Richard Nixon, © llinda Simeonova / ArcAngel; © sftravis, © sommai damrongpanich, © Everett Collection / Shutterstock

Printed in the United States of America

For M, A, and E

Live all you can; it's a mistake not to. It doesn't so much matter what you do in particular so long as you have your life. If you haven't had that what *have* you had?
—Henry James, *The Ambassadors*

PART I

1

He noticed the wealthy men gazing at Laura Powell as she sang in the ship's lounge. They probably imagined kissing her small nose, which turned up slightly at the tip, or touching her slender figure through the little black dress she wore. To them she must have seemed flawless. But they didn't know her as he did.

Her audience tonight had seen only surfaces: the shoulder-length blond hair that brushed the right side of her face as her voice held them in a kind of trance; her creamy skin and chocolate-colored eyes; the string of pearls around her neck. They couldn't guess that although he and Laura were traveling together, he disliked her, and he was certain that she despised him.

I'm not going to sit here like a worshipper, he thought as he left their table. *She doesn't deserve it.*

Out on the promenade deck he lit a cigarette. Salt filled the air in the middle of the Atlantic, and even in summer the night was brisk. He looked to the horizon and observed a yellow disk that was different from the moon's pale shimmer. Perhaps another ship, or worse: a U-boat, one of Germany's deadly submarines. Yet he repressed his fear. Since the Great War, no U-boat had attacked a passenger ship. A moment later the light flickered and disappeared, and he imagined a submarine plowing through the deep, toward the *Île de France*, which was carrying them from Manhattan to Le Havre. He gripped the railing and readied himself for impact.

But the ship continued forward, unhindered, just as it had for the previous three days. He shook his head.

You shouldn't worry, he told himself. *There won't be another war. Everyone remembers the last one all too well.*

To his left, a diminutive man approached. As the figure drew close, he saw that it was a boy of perhaps ten or eleven, dressed in a suit much too large for him. In the lights over the deck he could see the flicker of the metallic pins used to shorten the coat sleeves, the dirty white shirt and maroon tie, the tangled and dusty hair and the face dim with grime. The boy's eyes fastened on Henry's Cartier Tank watch and his gold cuff links shaped like apples.

Golden apples, he thought. *Tempting for a boy from steerage.*

"Hello, Mister," the boy said in a high, clear voice. His accent was unplaceable, neither American nor English, possibly German.

"Good evening," Henry said.

"Are you from New York, sir?"

"No."

"But you went to school in New York, or was it Boston? I hear it in your accent." When Henry raised his eyebrows in surprise, the boy moved nearer. "Your cuff links, sir. May I have a look at them?"

Shifting his cigarette to his left hand—to hide his wristwatch—he held up his right sleeve and cuff. The boy peered at the link as if he were a jeweler. Slowly, maybe involuntarily, his small hands reached up to the golden apple. His index finger stroked it gently, as if it were magic and by touching it his wishes would come true. When at last he withdrew his hand, there were smudges on Henry's cuff. At this point Henry realized the boy wasn't from steerage but was a stowaway or had in some other manner short of paying the fare gotten himself onto the ship.

Henry was about to say good night and return to the lounge, when a white-haired man and woman walked out onto the deck.

This starchy couple had been at the table next to the one he'd shared with Laura. The man wore a dinner jacket, and his wife a simple midnight blue gown, a matching blue jacket, and, around her neck, thick silver chains. The jacket was decorated with a dazzling pin in the shape of a dragonfly. Over the past hour this older woman had several times looked at him severely when he laughed too loudly. Now she saw the boy.

"Young man, you don't belong here, do you?" she said. "Did you climb over the turnstiles?"

Her focus on distinctions made Henry's chest smolder, for his own origins were modest. He cleared his throat and said, "The boy is with me."

She glared at him, knew he was lying, but turned away. Her husband said, "You'd better return to the bar. Your wife is becoming friendly with the band."

Henry smiled to mask his anger. "She isn't my wife. In fact, her father—my employer—has forbidden us any physical contact."

The old woman's mouth fell open, and the gentleman's eyes narrowed. As if in silent agreement, they turned and hurried away.

"Thank you, Mister," the boy said.

Henry looked down and recognized in the boy a chance to play Robin Hood. "You're good with your hands, aren't you?"

The boy nodded.

"You might have had my cuff links if I'd been careless."

"Maybe I still could."

"Probably not," Henry said. Of course it was wrong, what he was considering, but his chest still blazed with resentment toward people like the old woman and Laura, people who'd been given so much money that they looked down on those who hadn't. He asked the boy, "Did you see the handsome pin the old lady was wearing?"

"Oh yes, sir."

"Do you think it's valuable?"

"Yes, valuable and rare. It was made in the twenties by Lalique, if I'm not mistaken."

"I see," Henry said, not sure if he should believe him. "Perhaps we should have that woman's pin. If you get it for me, you'll have five dollars for your effort."

The boy's eyes widened in dramatic fashion as he appraised Henry for honesty. Then, with a slight bow, he left in pursuit of the older couple, who'd walked a dozen yards along the teak planks.

Henry took out his platinum cigarette case and moved closer to the railing. He was beginning to be cold, but the stars and moon glowed with an intensity he'd never seen, even in the woods and fields of Minnesota. He'd been born and had lived in Saint Paul, except during his years as a scholarship student at Harvard, where he'd read English and French literature. As he leaned on the railing, he grew calm and welcomed the growing distance from home, the place of ever-present reminders of his parents, who, less than a year ago, had been struck by a car in an evening snowstorm.

The postman had discovered them the next morning, covered with a blanket of white, and Henry had been left with nothing but debts and the job he'd obtained from Laura's father on the glowing recommendation of his college dean, a former classmate of her father's. And while the shock of that loss couldn't be lessened by travel, he yearned to remove himself from his own life, to see the world and to learn what more he could become. Ahead of him, still unknown and unseen on this arctic night, he hoped to find new life in the Old World, in the City of Light, where he could leave behind American expectations and inhibitions, where he might become someone else, if he wanted.

Behind him, a door opened, and the sound of Count Basie's "One O'Clock Jump" drifted out into the night air. He was disappointed to catch the scent of Laura's Chanel perfume, its allure and expense obvious from the morning he'd met her only a week ago, at the train station in Saint Paul when they'd departed for New York. Not only then, but tonight, she seemed an obstacle to what he might learn in Paris, and the new experiences he wanted for himself. He couldn't know—not then and not for some time—how her search for freedom might echo his.

2

"I looked around, and you'd disappeared." Laura's voice was her instrument: rich, in the middle range, and she enjoyed its smoky, almost hoarse tone, which belied her youth and impressed those who heard her sing. The ocean air cooled her hot skin, but she sensed her heartbeat racing with adrenaline after her performance.

Finely dressed in his dinner jacket, he turned to her. "I needed some air."

"And *I* need a cigarette." With a gesture of familiarity that she hoped would annoy him, she plucked the cigarette from his fingers and lifted it to her mouth.

His eyes narrowed, just a little, as he watched the orange tip brighten when she inhaled, but he didn't complain. She knew he wouldn't—he was a gentleman, or at least he pretended to be one, pretended to be part of her social circle.

She surveyed the empty deck. "Lots going on out here, I see."

"More than meets the eye," he replied in a clipped voice.

She gave him the cigarette and watched his lips go where hers had just been. It was like kissing him, she realized, and rubbed her own mouth as if to remove any trace of his own. He was handsome—she'd admit that to anyone. His brown hair, worn a little too long; his slightly dark complexion; his broad shoulders; and his flat stomach couldn't fail to make an impression on a woman. His nose was a bit crooked, the result of a youthful fight, but it kept him from being pretty. He never raised his low voice and always seemed calm—a trait that made her want to disrupt his peaceful demeanor. God knew she was sore at him. Wasn't he taking advantage of her father by going on this trip? He didn't strictly need to go to Europe and didn't deserve all her father had given him, notably the job as head of European sales for the family firm, Powell Manufacturing & Munitions.

He speaks French and is good at his job—so what if Dad mentioned his abilities at the dinner table?—but he's also a hanger-on, she thought, gripping the railing. *And I don't need a chaperone.*

Chaperones, she knew, were for prep school girls and tottering spinsters, not for competent twenty-three-year-old women such as herself. Part of her even wished that he hadn't been in the lounge when she'd sung. Whenever her eyes caught his, she felt herself flush, and she turned away and tried not to glance at him again—efforts that had failed. For a moment, she worried he'd report her singing—a blatant violation of her parents' demands—and her father would make her return to Saint Paul.

But Henry wouldn't report her behavior, she realized. For this was Henry's chance, just as it was hers, to escape from a constricting life at home. Her father's gift of a European tour had only three conditions: that she agree to marry an eligible man promptly upon her return, that Henry make further connections and sales on behalf of her father's armaments business, and that Henry, as her chaperone, ensure that she remain out of all kinds of trouble. These didn't seem overly burdensome for either of them, even if she regarded her marriage to an eligible man as something abstract that would take place in a vague and distant future. And, of course, she'd eventually succumb to her father's demands, as she always did. And Henry? He'd do whatever her father asked, or he'd lose his job. And in the summer of 1938, in the midst of the Great Depression, there were no other jobs to be had.

No, she sighed, correcting herself, inhaling the bracing sea air, noticing how well Henry's jacket fit around his shoulders. No, there was a fourth condition that her father had implied to Henry, and her mother to her: nothing would happen between them. It didn't need to be said that her world was separate from his, and in no way would those worlds ever blend.

She smiled now, recognizing how silly this last condition had been. Her mother must have understood how impossible such a thing would be, as she hadn't bothered to explain why Henry would be a terrible choice. *He's not one of us,* her mother would have told her, if she'd needed to explain. But it would have been wasted breath, for Laura knew her own mind, and a dull business type would never be right for her. It was the dull business types who'd been courting her that she most wanted to escape.

At the notion of escape, she realized that she hadn't told him the good news. She said, "A man came up to me after I sang."

Henry shrugged. "Who?"

"Louis Bellegarde," she replied, "the owner of Café la Pomme in the boulevard Raspail. He's asked me to audition."

"Congratulations," he said flatly.

His failure to appreciate her success piqued her. "I knew you wouldn't understand," she told him.

In the dim lights of the deck, she saw his expression darken. He said, "You know almost nothing about me."

She considered a sharp reply but decided not to argue. Why spoil her happiness at singing in Paris, even if it was only for an audition?

Thirty feet away, she noticed an older couple was standing by one of the suspended lifeboats. A boy stood near them, practically up against them, and she saw the man draw back. The boy embraced the woman, bowed toward the older man, and turned in the direction of Henry and herself, a flash of metal disappearing into his pocket.

Henry rested an arm on the railing and again faced her. "You won't care, and you clearly don't need it. But I asked this boy to deliver a gift for you."

"Right." She laughed. "A gift. Out here?"

He nodded. "But you shouldn't wear it until we're in Paris."

Now she believed him. Her eyes widened. "It's stolen?"

"Yes."

"Just now?"

He gave her a sly smile. "We've taken it from that nasty old biddy who was sitting next to us in the lounge."

"Her dragonfly pin?"

"The very one."

"You've surprised me," she said, an unexpected warmth forming in her chest. "I didn't think you could."

Though he must have felt her gaze, he kept his eyes averted. A suspicion formed in her mind that she didn't, in fact, know him all that well, and that part of him remained hidden from view. She wondered what he was hiding and if it would interest her. Likely not, she decided. But one never knew.

The three months of their European tour, beginning two days from now in Paris, would reveal whatever he might be hiding, or if he was like her other beaux, well mannered, unimaginative, and terribly, vexingly dull. She hoped, for her sake, that he wasn't as dull as the other men she'd known. For it wouldn't hurt for them to get along with some measure of civility, even if they never became true friends.

A moment later, the boy returned.

3

As the boy drew near, skipping across the teak deck, Henry saw his eyes alight on Laura and her strand of pearls, her large pearl earrings, and the silver bangles at her wrists. When Henry held out his hand for the old woman's pin, the boy firmly stuck his fists into his pockets and shook his head. "I can't eat unless you pay me."

Laura looked up at Henry. "Are you paying for it with my father's money?"

Ignoring her, he withdrew the sterling-silver money clip her father had given him on the occasion of his graduation from Harvard. *Go Far,* it read. He withdrew a five-dollar bill and held it in the air. The boy reached for the money, and Henry raised it beyond his grasp.

As the boy began to object, he said, "Let's see the pin."

The boy took his hand from his pocket and held it between them. In his palm lay a dragonfly pin of sapphires embedded in platinum, its wings of delicate silver and its eyes of diamonds.

Laura breathed deeply when she saw it. "How beautiful."

"Deal?" Henry asked.

"Deal." The boy's voice was light and clear.

Henry took hold of the pin, and the boy reached for the five-dollar bill, each believing he'd gotten the better deal. With the money, the boy knew he could eat well all the way to Le Havre. For Henry, the pin was a reprisal against the officious couple.

He held out his hand, the pin glowing under the lights, for Laura. She took it, her elegant fingers touching his palm in a way that wasn't as unpleasant as he'd expected, and slipped it into her clutch bag.

"Thank you," she said, her eyes meeting his for the first time since her performance. "That was charming."

"You're welcome." Her gratitude seemed to be authentic, but her assumption that he wouldn't pay for the pin with his own money galled him. No further discussion with her was necessary or desirable tonight. He turned to the boy and saw that he was staring at them. Henry asked, "Do you live aboard the ship?"

The boy shrugged and averted his dark eyes seaward. "Not usually."

"Then where do you make your home?"

"Sometimes in London, and Paris, and New York."

"Houses all over the world?"

"In a manner of speaking, yes, sir."

He noticed the boy's accent had disappeared. Now the boy sounded like him. In fact he realized the boy was imitating his accent and wondered at this diminutive chameleon and what he knew and had seen. Probably all kinds of horrors.

"Where are you staying, in Paris?" the boy asked them.

Henry hesitated to give out this information—an open door for the boy to walk through. Looking over at Laura, he saw her usual expression soften. Her eyes seemed to be studying the boy, to be creating a vision of him without the dirt and grime on his face, without the ill-fitting clothes. "We'll be at the Crillon," she said at last.

The boy's eyes widened. "Yes, I've been there many times," he offered excitedly. "There's a view of the place de la Concorde and the giant obelisk from the rooms on the south side of the building, if you don't know."

She stared at him, a faint smile on her lips. Saying nothing, she touched her pearl necklace as if to assure herself that it remained around her neck.

Henry thought the boy hadn't heard of the hotel until a moment ago. "If there's an emergency, you can find us there," he said, though he immediately wished he hadn't. For his plan to travel without hindrance had now been threatened by a dusty little boy he happened to like and even to admire. Even stranger, he didn't expect Laura—the high-and-mighty-former-debutante Laura Powell—to speak to a street urchin, let alone to tell him where they were staying. Perhaps there was a minuscule portion of her heart that wasn't proud and hard as stone.

"Thank you, miss," the boy said. "May I have your name?"

"I'm Laura Powell. And this is Henry Salter."

The boy gave one of his little bows, this time with genuineness, and offered Henry his hand. "How do you do?" piped the clear voice.

After the briefest hesitation, Henry took the boy's hand. It was small and delicate but strong. The boy's coal black eyes held his. "How do you do?" Henry said. He let go and saw that Laura was shivering visibly in the cold.

"We must return to the lounge," she said to the boy, "but would you tell us your name?" The boy watched her and said nothing. She bent down until their eyes were level. "Please, tell me your name."

He glanced up at Henry, who nodded, before focusing on her. "I'm David Stein."

She offered her hand and smiled. "How do you do, David Stein?"

"Hi, Miss Laura."

She stood up. "Now we'll have to say goodbye. I hope you can find somewhere to be warm."

Henry gave the boy an appreciative nod. "Good night, David."

"Yes, sir. Good night."

David watched Henry pull open the door to the lounge and step with Miss Laura into the sounds of a piano, a brush on a snare drum, and a man's pleasant voice. This was the most perfect couple he'd met—so rich and glamorous and kind. He thought if they could replace the family he'd lost in the fire, his original family, he'd be happy. Instantly he began to hope for this impossibility, to think of when he might see them again. Laura's hair glimmered briefly, brilliantly in the lights, before the doors swung closed and he was alone on deck, surrounded by a world of endlessly dark water.

The spray lofted over the deck, and his teeth chattered. As he walked toward the stern, where there was an air duct he could climb into and then down to the lower decks, he noticed a faint yellow light rolling in and out of the swells. He closed his eyes and opened them again, thinking his hunger had made him see things. But the light remained.

Another ship, he thought, *or a submarine.*

As he climbed into the large duct, he imagined walking into l'Hôtel de Crillon and being greeted with embraces by Henry and Miss Laura, the most beautiful woman he'd seen.

4

Two days later, Henry and Laura climbed down from the train into the crowds of the Gare du Nord in Paris.

Laura watched as Henry directed the blue-uniformed porters to load carts with her seven pieces of luggage—two of them empty. These were Louis Vuitton steamer trunks, wardrobes, and footlockers, all with the brown *LV*-monogrammed canvas and leather trim, brass nailheads, beechwood slats, and stamped hardware. The porters worked quickly, surely expecting a large tip from what they assumed was a wealthy young couple. But she kept her eyes on her bags, not letting herself be distracted by the thickly humid heat under the station's high-peaked roof.

In her peripheral vision, she noticed other travelers staring at her beauty and clothes, at her obviously expensive luggage. Pushing against her were dirty men, women, and children who resembled little David Stein. She held her purse against her chest and kept her composure.

"Who are they?" she called to Henry.

"Refugees," he answered. "All trying to get away from the Nazis. Three years ago they passed the Nuremberg Laws against Jews and Roma. And remember, this spring Germany annexed Austria in the Anschluss. So even more people are trying to get away from their awful Third Reich."

The great number and condition of the refugees led her to question her idea that war might be avoided. Now she had the sense of Germany pushing thousands of people across the Continent, toward Poland and France and Spain or across the channel to England. And why were they fleeing? What could be so terrible about living in Germany? She'd read some of Hitler's statements in the Saint Paul newspaper, of course, a paragraph here or there, but she'd believed that he was like a loud-mouthed figure in a theater, that his words had little effect, even upon Jews and others he deemed undesirable. But now she began to reconsider. Was terror much closer than she'd imagined?

They had to use three taxis: the first carrying them and the second and third following with their luggage. Laura turned around to be sure the other portions of the caravan hadn't changed course and made off with their clothing and shoes and books, but the driver looked at her in the rearview mirror and said, "*C'est bien*, madame. For guests of l'Hôtel de Crillon, there are no difficulties."

They rolled down the windows in the back of the large Citroën and saw the buildings lining the rue La Fayette gleaming white in the late afternoon sun. The city was alive, the leaves of plane trees adding a skirt of green to the buildings in the square de Montholon. Many people strolled by: children with their dogs, and mothers and nannies pushing infants in prams. Sidewalk cafés had filled with people drinking wine, whiskey, and coffee.

Here—so far from her mother and her friends and the expectations of her social position—she wouldn't have to worry about marriage or children. Her life, once like a train that couldn't deviate from tracks laid years earlier by parents and circumstance, was no longer bound by anything but common sense, and perhaps not even that.

In the hotel lobby, she watched Henry walk a little uncertainly across the black-and-cream-colored marble checkerboard floors. At the front desk, he asked if a package had arrived for him from Bergdorf's in New York—a navy blue cashmere overcoat he'd ordered.

The clerk shook his head. "Perhaps in a week or two, *oui*?"

They followed the bellhops to the lift that took them to the third floor of the hotel, where they'd been given adjacent suites.

Henry didn't look at her.

She said, "Fifteen minutes and then a walk? Something to eat?"

"Sure," he replied softly. "Fifteen minutes."

As the bellhop opened the door to her rooms and she walked inside, she stopped and stared at the breach of propriety that would have alarmed her parents.

In the wall between their suites, two connecting doors were closed flush against each other.

She studied the door on her side of the wall. The lock appeared to be set. She reached for the door handle and pulled, but the lock held, and the door remained closed.

After the bellhop brought her luggage into the room and she gave him a tip of a few francs, she stood alone, her eyes on the door between hers and Henry's suites.

A lovers' door, she thought. *If I were to unlock and open it, nobody would know.*

She shook her head with a mixture of interest and disapproval. Turning from the door and toward the windows, she saw the Egyptian obelisk in the place de la Concorde and remembered how David had mentioned that it could be seen from the hotel. *How did he know?* she wondered, smiling at the boy's wiliness. *Had he seen the obelisk and guessed that the Crillon afforded a view of it? He couldn't have gotten inside the hotel, could he?*

Looking briefly at a tourist map, she appreciated her father's choosing a hotel in the center of Paris. To the west of the Crillon ran the avenue des Champs-Élysées, which led to the Arc de Triomphe, and to the east lay the gardens of the Tuileries and the Louvre. Her heartbeat sped up, and she sensed her growing excitement at being in the great city she'd read about since childhood.

Fifteen minutes later she'd changed into an emerald green sundress and white heels. Her right hand held a pair of sunglasses. As she stepped into the passageway, she found Henry waiting for her in a tan linen suit with a blue-checked shirt and a navy blue necktie.

She nodded and considered complimenting him on his appearance but said nothing. Nor did she refer to the lovers' door—that was a thing never to be mentioned.

As they walked out of the hotel, out into the still bright evening, she put on her sunglasses and heard a familiar voice that wasn't Henry's. She halted and looked to her side.

"Who—" she began.

Several yards away, she saw David Stein, wearing the same ill-fitting suit and maroon tie, being dragged away from the hotel.

5

A black-coated doorman gripped David's upper arm.

Barrel-chested, with a bushy mustache, the doorman flushed red with anger. He raised a thick hand and slapped David across the face.

David cried out, and tears streamed down his cheeks.

The doorman called for the help of a truncheon-wielding policeman, who was standing nearby in the avenue Gabriel.

Repressing a feeling of panic, Laura hurried toward them, Henry at her side.

The mustachioed doorman ignored them and spoke to the police. *"Il s'agit d'un garçon de la rue. Je pense qu'il a dû entrer dans l'Hôtel de Crillon. Il va m'entendre celui-là."*

The policeman, in his tan uniform and his black cap with gold borders and a golden fleur-de-lis, grasped the truncheon with both hands, looked at David, and chuckled. *"Tu ne séjournes pas dans cet hôtel, n'est-ce pas, mon garçon?"*

David's high-pitched voice, now in English: "Yes, sir. Yes, I'm staying here with my Aunt Laura and my Uncle Henry. Here they are, monsieur. Just trying to get up to our room to bathe. I was attacked by a gang that ruined my clothes and hurt me bad."

The policeman, who didn't seem to understand English, smiled at David and shook his head as if he'd heard this lie many times before. *"Tu penses que je suis stupide?"* he began. *"Tu penses que je ne sais pas que tu vis dans la rue? Que cet hôtel t'est autant étranger que mes propres enfants?"*

He spoke so quickly that Laura couldn't follow anything except the last bit: Aren't you as much a stranger to this hotel as my own children?

"But the view of the obelisk!" David shouted, again in English, his dark eyes nervously fastening themselves on hers. "From the rooms on the third floor. I've seen it myself, monsieur. Anyone can tell you it's true."

For a moment the policeman hesitated. And in that moment Henry intervened.

He took off his tan suit coat, at first giving the impression that he was preparing to fight. "David," he said, "I told you not to leave the hotel. Do you see what happens when you disobey?"

The face of the mustachioed doorman faded from red to pink. He squinted in confusion. "This boy?"

"My wife's nephew," Henry replied in a cheerful, magnanimous voice, darting a quick glance at her to see if she was upset by his effrontery. "*Le neveu de ma femme.* Doesn't always mind, as you can see. So he's ruined his clothes, and I'll have them taken to Charvet and made right. Here, David, put on my suit coat until we get up to the room, where you can bathe and put on something proper."

David took Henry's coat with his free hand and held it close to him, at the same time attempting to wriggle away from the doorman. The lower part of the coat dusted the flagstones.

Henry winced. "Watch the hem."

"I'm sorry, Uncle Henry," he replied, lifting the coat higher.

Laura glanced at the policeman, who'd watched this exchange. Despite her worry, she forced herself to smile at him.

He knows we're lying, she thought, *but he can't object. We're claiming our nephew, and if he asks for a passport or other papers to prove the relation, our last names would be different. Papers would prove nothing.*

In heavily accented English, the policeman said, "We have homes for boys like this one. No need for your *charité.*"

She shook her head, playing along, though unsure why. "There's no charity, except what I've agreed to," she assured the policeman. "My sister asked us to bring her son on our tour. Dear Katharine isn't well, and she's always wanted David to see the world."

The policeman nodded to the doorman, who released David. The boy put on Henry's tan suit coat over his own filthy one and moved toward her. She took his hand and pulled him in the direction of the hotel doors.

From the corner of her eye, she saw Henry withdraw his money clip, pull out a note, and hand it to the doorman. "Sorry for your trouble," Henry said. "A misunderstanding."

"Thank you, monsieur. Not sure the misunderstanding is mine."

"All the same," Henry told him, then followed them into the grand lobby.

6

Laura indicated that nothing should be said until they were within her suite. Once she'd closed the door and the three of them stood in her room, she faced David.

In the soft yellow light, she observed his filthy shoes and suit. He smelled, but not too badly. "I see you've found us," she said.

His dark eyes widened. "I'm sorry, Miss Laura. Didn't mean to make trouble. Really, I didn't. Thought I could walk into the hotel and wait outside your room if you weren't here. But the doorman got me. I could have fought him off, could have kicked him and punched his nose, but I'm too good mannered, you know I am."

"Yes, your manners are admirable," Henry said as he took his suit coat off David and used his hand to brush off the dust. "Did you run through the five dollars I gave you?"

"*Gave* me? It wasn't a gift, it was a trade. You got the Lalique pin. Don't you remember giving it to Miss Laura?"

She nodded. "Of course he does. But I don't want you to steal anything else, all right?"

"Yes, Miss Laura," David said. "I won't steal, unless I have to."

She surprised herself by laughing. "Then let's hope you don't have to."

"Yes, ma'am."

"And I have a question for you. Can you tell me how you knew Lalique made the pin you . . . obtained . . . for me?"

The boy tilted his head, as if surprised by her question. "Yes, I can tell you. I saw the old woman wearing it."

"You saw it pinned to her jacket?"

"Um, yes."

"But how did you know it was from a Paris jeweler? How do you know Mr. Lalique's work?"

"Oh, that's not so difficult," he explained in his clear voice. His expression had softened with relief that she'd asked him an easy question. "My father was a jeweler, Miss Laura. He had a shop in Berlin, on the Kurfürstendamm, where he sold Lalique and Van Cleef & Arpels and Gariod and Boucheron—all the best things. He kept them under the glass cases that I cleaned every morning before the store opened. Sometimes he told me about the pieces and who made them and how to tell the jewelry of one workshop from another and how you could know well-made pieces from the other kind."

She silently regarded him, believing that he wouldn't harm her but might steal from her.

He has good reason, she thought. *He's from the world I glimpsed at the Gare du Nord, having lived on the streets without money or food or protection. Now he's standing in a suite at one of the finest hotels in the world amid furniture upholstered in cream-and-pale-blue silk. Should I help him? Can I trust him?*

Almost unaware that her casual attitude had vanished and her voice grown calm, she asked, "What happened to your father, David? Why aren't you working at his store?"

His typically animated expression turned blank. His voice dropped and softened. "He died, Miss Laura. From a fire in our store. My mother and my sister Rachel were in our apartment on the floor above. The Geheime Staatspolizei, the Gestapo, boarded up the windows, and they couldn't get out. The fire got them too." His eyes watered, but he visibly restrained himself from crying. "*Arisierung,*" he said finally, giving the German word for Aryanization.

She crouched near the floor, her face lower than his, and touched his arm. "I'm very sorry, David. It's terrible what happened."

Henry said, "The Gestapo started the fire?"

David looked up at him. "Yes, Mr. Henry."

"But where were you?"

"I was coming home from chess club after school."

Henry sat down on the sofa, took a cigarette from his platinum case, and lit it. He leaned forward and put his elbows on his knees. "So you saw the fire? You saw the store and the apartment burning?"

"Yes."

"But the Gestapo didn't catch you?"

"No, Mr. Henry. I ran fast. I ran until I couldn't run anymore."

"What happened after you ran? What did you do?"

David lowered his eyes. "I couldn't stay in Berlin, because I had no papers, not even Jewish papers. I was scared, but knew I had to go away. So I rode on the backs of lorries at night until I was in France, and then to the coast. A ship took me to America."

"America," Henry echoed. "Why not stay there? Wasn't it safer?"

David shook his head. His voice cracked as he looked bravely at Henry. "America didn't want me. Nobody wanted me." He wiped his eyes.

"Jesus," Henry muttered. After a moment, he said: "My parents were killed not long ago, but it was an accident. I think about them, and I miss them. What's happened to you is much worse, David, but Laura and I would like to help you."

She appreciated how Henry's words echoed those she'd been forming in her head. David's story had made her eyes sting with the beginning of tears. Managing to nod, she considered how they might quickly find him a better situation that didn't entail his living with them at the Crillon. Her opinion of Henry shifted, too, as she noted his willingness to help this resourceful but filthy boy.

David blushed at their kindness.

She almost placed a hand on his shoulder before she remembered his soiled clothes and lifted it away. "Why don't you come with me?" she told him. "We'll run a bath. With fresh clothes you'll feel better. We'll have dinner brought here—the three of us will eat together."

7

Laura ran hot water in the claw-foot bathtub. After showing David how to work the taps, she gave him soap and put a white towel on a cabinet by the tub. "Wash up, and take your time," she told him from the doorway. "I'll leave some of Henry's clothes on a chair in the hallway. All right?"

The boy stood—gray with grime and grease and the dust of the streets of New York and Paris and God knew where else—in the middle of the white bathroom, with its white curtains and white towels and white tub. Away from Henry, his bravery and mischievousness dissolved, and he was only a child. He looked up at the chandelier and cried until his face was wet. She bent down and kissed his forehead, though she feared he'd put his arms around her and she'd have to send her emerald green sundress out for cleaning. But after a moment, she knew that for his sake, she must embrace him.

She opened her arms, and he nearly fell into them. She felt, within his oversize suit, his slender limbs that were like the bones of a bird within its wings. His chest shook with sobs as he pressed his face into her stomach. His hands grasped each other at the small of her back and pulled her tightly against him. She touched his head and ran her fingers through his dirty hair.

"It's all right," she told him. "It's all right now. You're safe tonight."

Her words made him cry more loudly, until he abruptly grew silent. He pulled away and averted his face.

He's afraid that I'll abandon him, she thought, her own eyes growing damp. *But what choice do I have? I don't know him, and I'll be in Europe for only three months. How could I take care of a ten-year-old boy? Maybe the policeman outside the hotel was right. Maybe David belongs in a home for orphans.*

As she left the bathroom and pulled the door closed behind her, she asked him to put his clothes in the basket by the door. Although she couldn't see him, she knew that those tears at the corners of her eyes had begun to fall.

"Thank you, Miss Laura," came his crystalline voice.

She walked into the sitting room and put her arms around herself, around her dress, which now needed cleaning. Wiping the dampness from her cheeks, she breathed deeply and then went to the bar in the corner to mix gin and vermouth. Since she'd met David aboard the *Île de France,* she'd thought it was he who needed her and not the reverse. But she admitted to herself that it felt good to be hugged. She decided that when he was clean, she might hug him once more as he went to sleep.

She had her drink and wondered where Henry had gone. And why he'd left her with David.

She set down the glass and stood by the lovers' door, a hand raised to knock.

What if Henry doesn't want to spend time with David and me? No, she thought, setting down the glass. *He must. I'm not going to care for a child by myself.*

Despite the breach of etiquette her knocking would entail, she went ahead and rapped on the enameled white door.

She heard Henry's voice, muffled but clearly his. "Everything all right?"

"Open up, if you're decent."

When she heard his lock draw open, she drew hers. At the same time, they opened the doors, just a crack at first, then wider, and when each saw the other fully dressed, they half smiled.

She saw that Henry had loosened his tie and was drinking from a tumbler. His breath smelled faintly, pleasantly, of bourbon. His hair was unkempt, as if he'd run his hands through it every which way.

He asked, "Are you all right?"

She nodded, stepped aside, and indicated that he should come into her sitting room. "David is in the bath."

As he walked in and stood by the sofa, he noticed her dirtied sundress. Though raising an eyebrow, he made no comment, only took another sip of his drink.

"Maybe he should stay with us for a day or two," she suggested. "Until we can take him to the Red Cross or another organization that can help him."

"All right," he said. "A day or two."

She pursed her lips. "I realize we can't take him home with us."

Henry nodded. "So we'll leave him at the Red Cross?"

She shook her head in confusion. "He's in an impossible situation. I'm not sure what we can do for him, or why we have to decide tonight."

Henry put his free hand in the pocket of his trousers. "Not tonight, but soon," he said. "I don't see how we can change the fate of a German orphan."

Going over to the bar in the corner, she dropped fresh ice cubes into the tumbler, mixed another drink, and returned to Henry. "Why do you care what I decide to do?"

He didn't hesitate, replying calmly: "Because this is the first time you've seemed like a normal human being, the first time you haven't been cold."

She felt her face flush. "How can you say that?"

He shrugged. "I've watched you. You keep all your feelings locked away, if you even have feelings."

Her stomach tightened with surprising pain. "How can you . . . ," she began, then stopped. Turning away, she went over to the windows, her eyes not taking in the dusk or the illuminated obelisk. *He didn't have the same upbringing that I did,* she told herself. *He hasn't been taught to be restrained, to hide most of his emotions. But he's seen me perform—and all the warmth and sentiments I show onstage! How could he say something so hurtful, so untrue?* Again facing him, she said, "You don't think I'm a normal human being when I sing?"

"You're a performer when you sing," he replied. "But I suppose you have moods when you're onstage. The moods of the songs, at least."

She set down her tumbler on the table by the sofa and crossed her arms. "So I have no emotions other than when I'm onstage or talking with David?"

"Sure you do." He smiled, but not a friendly smile. "You show anger, frustration, arrogance, entitled pride, carelessness about what you do and say."

"Oh, only those traits?" she muttered softly. "Are you certain you haven't forgotten any?"

He shrugged. "You asked what I thought."

"When have I done this?"

"When? Many times."

"Give an example, please."

He hesitated only a moment. "We're aboard the *Île de France* in the first-class cabins and lounge, and it's clear you don't think I belong there. Or in this hotel. You arrive in Paris with your expensive luggage, some of it empty for all the things you'll buy, without the faintest idea how you look to everyone else. You're not better than other people, and you're not better than I am. You've just been luckier."

Although she wanted to continue arguing with him, she realized that he was right, that he'd noted a glaring flaw in her character. Her indignation faded away, leaving her with damaged pride and a new uncertainty. She stared at him. "You really think this?"

He nodded. "Most of the time."

"I didn't . . . I didn't realize. I don't mean to be awful. I just don't know how to show the way I feel. You see, I'm expected to behave in a certain way, and when I'm afraid or insecure or hurt, I suppose I cling to the way my mother always told me to act—the way she acts much of the time. You must think I'm terrible. You must. Don't you?"

She saw his expression soften. His eyes ran over her arms, her legs—eyes in which she saw not disdain, but curiosity.

At last he looked up. "I'm here for your father's business. My opinion of you doesn't matter."

"It matters to *me*!" she said with a force that surprised her.

He stared at her, his eyes widening, but he said nothing. Awkwardly, he turned to the telephone and picked up the receiver. "I'll order dinner," he said. "Very soon, David will be finished with his bath."

8

Laura watched Henry tip the steward as David walked into the sitting room.

The steward had set up a table with a white linen tablecloth, a bottle of bordeaux, steamed green beans, pureed potatoes, dinner rolls, and three large helpings of prime rib—the American dinner that Henry had requested.

As Laura stood by the windows, she decided to maintain a friendly expression, despite her quarrel with Henry. She ignored the steward's curious glance at the boy and closed and locked the hallway door behind him.

And David did look odd, she knew, like a scarecrow in clothes that Henry had lent him. He'd rolled the shirtsleeves and trouser cuffs into thick bands. He padded barefoot into the room, a cleaned-up vagrant come to dine on linen and bone china, silver and crystal.

Henry said, "You look like Tom Sawyer."

David questioned him silently. A floor lamp showed his skin to be smooth and tanned and his hair to be darker and curlier than before his bath. In that moment, he looked innocent.

"Come on." Henry broke into an easy smile. "I'm teasing you. Please, join us."

David walked over to the table and sat down, Laura still in her sundress to his left and Henry to his right. Other than her request for

Henry to loan the boy clothing, she hadn't spoken to Henry since their argument.

The silver covers were lifted off the food, and David's eyes widened. He picked up his knife and fork and began slicing the prime rib into large strips that he speared and dropped into his mouth. He ate quickly, three bites for each one taken by Henry or Laura.

She pushed the plate of green beans toward him. "Take some," she said. "You need to eat vegetables."

He did as she asked, interspersing beans with prime rib.

Henry poured David a quarter glass of the bordeaux and diluted it with water. David took it up and drank eagerly.

Laura realized their argument hadn't ended, and she waited for another round. Speaking very little, except to David, she didn't look at Henry. Over dinner and wine, she somehow forgot the main points of contention. Had they been arguing about her attitude or about what to do with David? Or something else she hadn't identified?

At last David's soupspoon dipped more slowly into the bowl. His eyelids began to flutter open and closed, and his shoulders slumped.

She pushed back her chair, stood, and placed her hand lightly on his shoulder. "Why don't I put you to bed?"

He stood and swayed drowsily. "Yes, please."

In her bedroom she pulled back the covers of the large bed and helped him off with the blue shirt and cotton trousers. He stood before her in Henry's boxer shorts, which reached nearly to his knees and which he had to hold up with his hands. When he climbed into bed, she pulled up the sheet and blanket. Then she leaned over, hugged him lightly, and kissed his forehead. He smelled clean, like the lavender soap provided by the hotel. "Good night, David."

He lifted himself, pecked her cheek, and let himself back down onto the bed. "Good night, Miss Laura." He closed his eyes and turned over on his side, toward her.

For a few minutes she sat on the bed beside him, feeling tranquil as she rubbed his bare shoulders and back. Her eyes were drawn to Henry's cotton trousers, which lay on the floor. In one of the pockets David had stuck a dinner roll.

She hadn't seen him take it, but he must be so habitually hungry that he grabbed more than he could eat in one sitting. Not angry, but not trusting him, either, she unconsciously touched her earrings and the strand of pearls at her neck. He hadn't taken these, might not steal from her, but she couldn't be certain. In a way he seemed wild, and in another an innocent child. But she thought, too, of herself, of the change in her preferences. While she remained focused on her wish to sing, her heart had opened a little to this boy, who was alone and without protection or care. Regardless of his true nature, she wanted to give him food, to buy him new clothes and shoes, to protect him from the police, to introduce him to others who'd help him while she and Henry continued their European tour.

When his chest rose and fell evenly, she looked down at him a last time and left the room, closing the door behind her.

9

Henry was having a cigarette when she returned to the sitting room. He'd left the table and had eased himself back into the pillows of the sofa. With legs crossed, he could have been a model in a fashion magazine. She thought he looked far too comfortable in her room.

After standing by the table and pouring another glass of the bordeaux, she sat in one of the occasional chairs to the right of the sofa. "David's asleep," she said.

"Yes? Good. Would you like my room for tonight, and I'll sleep on your sofa?"

"No. I'll sleep here."

He nodded. "All right. But if you need anything, just knock on the doors between the rooms."

"Righto." After she said this word, she knew that snootiness had crept into her voice. Had it always been there and she hadn't noticed it? Had her unquestioning acceptance of her parents' way of living—the redbrick mansion on Summit Avenue, the servants, the interactions with others limited to her own kind at their clubs—led to a sort of blindness? "Thank you," she added. "I'm sure that I'll be safe here, and David will probably sleep longer than I will."

"Okay."

As she sipped the wine, she considered the right way to begin this conversation, but there didn't seem to be a right way. She chose the most direct route she could: "I'm not the kind of woman you think I am."

He exhaled toward the ceiling. "You might not be. Or you might be. It doesn't matter, because our tour will end in a few months, and we won't see each other again."

"It's a . . . a point of honor, I suppose," she continued, "to show you, to *prove* to you, how I really am."

He tilted his head, his expression serious. "Why prove that to anyone, let alone to me?"

She considered the reasons she might want to show him more of herself, but she quickly became lost in a thicket not of reasons but of emotions she refused to confront. Her social and familial training had been to hide unruly emotions, to remain dignified. Without quite realizing that she was remaining within the very bounds she sought to break through, she answered truthfully, "I don't know why I'd like to prove it. I just want to do it."

"Well, that's swell."

"I thought you might appreciate my honesty."

"I told you, I think it's swell you're going to prove things."

She felt as if she were arguing with an empty chair. "That's all you have to say?"

"Yes. That's all."

He has no interest, she thought, *in arguing or in understanding me.*

Disappointment and frustration filled her, but she wouldn't show him either. "Fine," she sighed.

"Fine," he agreed. And stood up. Without looking back at her, he walked out through the lovers' door and closed his side of it.

A moment later she got up, went to the door, and closed and locked her side of it. Turning to the empty room, she at last allowed herself the freedom to say what she was thinking: "Damn him!"

10

She awoke and felt something warm pressing against her.

David's breath made the regular and easy sound of sleep. All at once, she knew that he wouldn't leave, wouldn't go back to the streets—not unless she and Henry put him there. She realized that if she allowed it, he'd stay with her, he'd hold fast to her as he was holding on to her now, as she lay on the sofa in the sitting groom. He'd turn her into his mother, because his mother had died and, as far as she knew, she and Henry were the only people who'd given him kindness since. This responsibility stifled her, was too much too soon, was more than she bargained for when she pretended to be his aunt last night and brought him up to her suite.

She was twenty-three years old, ostensibly on a European tour but secretly, and against her parents' express wishes, hoping to sing in clubs and cafés. Taking on the responsibility for a child would be the end of her dreams, she understood. Her chief role would be caretaker for him, leaving scarce time or strength for herself.

I'm too young, she thought, *to make that sacrifice. Henry may decide that I'm coldhearted, but it's what I must do.*

David grew heavy, and she began to have difficulty breathing. Suddenly, she was hot and perspiring. She looked up at the ceiling, which was turning hazy and pink. Feeling faint, she pulled his arms from her shoulders. He whimpered softly as she pushed him away and sat up.

Then she stood and gazed down at him. His large brown eyes opened and sought her face. She was all that he had, and she decided that before they parted, she wanted to give him the necessities: clothing, and money to see him to wherever he decided to go.

She smiled. "Good morning, David."

"Good morning, Miss Laura."

"Today we must buy you new clothes."

His face brightened. "Really?"

"Yes."

"But my suit . . ."

"It needs to be thrown away. But would you put on your old things, just for a couple of hours, so that we can go out and find you something new and clean to wear?"

"Yes, I will." He stood but, after a moment of regarding her silently, said, "Miss Laura, I can't pay for anything. Maybe we shouldn't go to the store. Maybe we should stay here."

"David, the clothes will be my gift to you. I don't expect you to do anything except wear them. But first I'll order breakfast for you and coffee for me, and then I'll take a quick bath while you eat."

"Won't you eat with me?"

Typically, she didn't eat breakfast. "Just this once," she told him, "I'll have a croissant while you have a big omelet."

After telephoning to order their breakfast, she went to the lovers' door and knocked. When there was no answer, she knocked again. "Henry?" she called. Only silence. As she was turning back to the room, she noticed a scrap of hotel stationery that he'd slid under the door. She bent over to pick it up and read:

Gone to business meeting with Richard Crescent,
of Whitehall.

Will return late morning.

H.

Although she knew her father required him to have this meeting, she felt disappointment. Their conversation from last night hadn't ended properly or with any kind of sympathy between them. This inexplicably unsettled her. And now he was gone when she had surprised herself by wanting him here with her, for his help with David, even for his unreliable and halfhearted companionship.

11

Henry went by foot all the way from the Crillon to a small office building near the place de la République. He dressed the part of a young arms merchant, in a gray suit with chalk pinstripes and peaked lapels, a white shirt, and a plain blue necktie. On his way, he stopped at a café and stood at the counter while drinking two cups of espresso. He was tired. Half the night he'd lain awake, disturbed by his clash with Laura.

With effort, he turned his mind to business as he walked up the hot and narrow rue de Turbigo. This wasn't a wealthy area of town but was not bad. It was away from the streets frequented by tourists and government officials.

The real Paris? he wondered. *Maybe.*

Not far from the place de la République—with its giant bronze sculpture of Marianne, representing the Republic—on the quiet rue de Malte was number thirty-five, narrow and little different from the buildings on either side of it. He guessed there were apartments upstairs and offices on the first and possibly second floors. No signs in the windows, although the blinds were drawn. Standing at the door, he attempted to turn the knob, but the door was locked. He pressed a buzzer by a diminutive sign marked, very simply, Bureaux anglais. English offices, he translated.

After a moment he heard footsteps, and the door was opened by a stout older woman with blue eyes. "Bonjour," she said. *"Oui?"*

"J'ai une réunion avec Monsieur Richard Crescent."

She smiled. "This way, please. Are you Henry Salter?"

"Yes, I am."

"Good morning," she said in a firm voice. After leading him into a large room with several private offices—in which he saw no other people and heard nothing—she brought him to the door of the last office in the row. After knocking on the closed door, she waited patiently.

The door opened quickly, without warning. He started, although the older woman had no reaction. Crescent's name implied that he might be slender and perhaps cunning. But slender he'd probably never been. He was about fifty and bald, with jowls and a domed forehead. His voice sounded like a car driving over crushed rock, though his Oxford accent and demeanor betrayed a British public school education.

"Salter?"

"Yes."

"Please, come into my office, such as it is."

They sat down. On the desk between them, a bottle of Dewar's whisky stood by two glasses of uncertain cleanliness. Crescent poured two fingers for each of them and began speaking of their stated business as if he were in a great hurry, in contrast to their staid surroundings. "We've heard about Powell's new antitank gun, the Arrowhead. How quickly can you build five hundred to a thousand of them?"

This would be an immense order for a machine gun that rested on a caisson and was pulled by truck. Was war closer than he realized? "I'd guess four months," he said, "plus shipping time. Shipping, you understand, must be done . . . quietly. Through Canada, due to the American restrictions."

Crescent drank and set down his glass. He looked at the bottle, as if deciding whether or not to pour himself more whisky, and then turned his massive visage toward Henry. "In the next twelve or eighteen months, we expect Parliament to pass an emergency powers act that will begin our preparation for war. An immense army will form, Mr. Salter." Crescent raised a thick eyebrow. "Is your firm selling to any other nations, perhaps Germany?"

"We'd make your order our first priority," Henry promised, though the prophecy of British conscription worried him. But he silently told himself that such a move would act as a deterrent to Germany—a way of keeping the hard-earned peace after the Treaty of Versailles. "And no," he added, "we've made no sales to any European nations except Belgium and France, and of course to your country. But Mr. Crescent, your schedule is difficult without adding an overnight shift—a significant expense."

Crescent's eyes moved from his empty glass to Henry's face and back again, like black marbles rolling in a field of fat. He opened a slender attaché case, set it on his knee, opened it, and withdrew several papers. "Two originals of our standard contract," he said, handing them across the desk. "You'll see we've ordered one thousand, and we've increased the payment by twenty percent for overtime and shipping costs. But the guns must arrive in England within ninety days."

An enormous order, Henry saw, the largest the firm had ever received. His quick success buoyed him as he read the nonnegotiable contract. At the end of it was the British minister of war's signature. He took his pen from the breast pocket of his jacket and signed both copies for Powell Manufacturing & Munitions. He then kept one of the copies and placed it on the table by his elbow. After finishing the last of his drink, he began to stand.

"Please, Mr. Salter," Crescent said, placing a restraining hand on his arm. "A few more minutes of your time?"

Henry nodded.

"You have facility with languages, no? French, Spanish, Italian, a little German?"

Henry began to ask how the man knew of his success at college, of his mother's being French Canadian, but then said, very quietly, "What do you want, Mr. Crescent?"

"I was sorry to learn of your parents' deaths," Crescent answered.

"Thank you." He wondered how the man had gained this information.

The Oxford voice softened and warmed. "A suggestion, Mr. Salter, while you're here in Paris." Crescent paused, folding his large hands on his desk. "If you hear anything that might be of help to the people of Great Britain, to our goal of understanding the threat of Hitler and his Nazis, would you let us know?"

Henry believed that he understood what the man was asking, but he wanted to be sure. "Anything?" he asked.

Crescent raised an eyebrow, leaned forward over the desk, and lowered his voice. "If your observation uncovers anything of interest . . ."

This request didn't surprise Henry. His buyers in the US Army had asked him to do the same. "But I've no background in what you're asking," he deflected. "I wouldn't know what was important. And why would I send information to you instead of to my own government?"

Crescent shook his head. "The Americans aren't so interested in France. But for us, France is close, across a narrow channel, and we're very interested in what happens here. What you tell us is far more important to us than it would be to the US Army."

Is the business deal for the Arrowheads contingent upon my agreeing to provide my observations to the British? he wondered briefly. *No. No, the deal is signed, and the British need the Arrowheads. This is something else, something separate from Powell Manufacturing & Munitions. This is about me, and only me.* Yet his hesitation remained. "I don't understand why you're asking," he said. "Wouldn't your experts know far more than I?"

"Experts?" Crescent sniffed and poured each of them another whisky. "I need men on the ground, neutral men who can identify arms and munitions and who'll tell me the truth without the bollocks. And if you see nothing, you've no need to contact Levy."

Henry knew that his face showed confusion. "Levy?"

"Ah. He's one of our men in Paris. Loyal to the French but worried they aren't prepared for war, which they're unquestionably not. They haven't been prepared for war since Bonaparte. But that's history. So visit with Émile Levy, all right?"

The image of little David Stein intruded into his silent deliberations—and the way the Gestapo had murdered the boy's family. The Nazi threat had become less abstract, more real, and more terrifying. "I . . . yes," Henry began, without thinking why he'd agreed.

But of course he knew. And the reason wasn't only what he'd learned about David Stein.

Crescent's offer gave him an entrée into the world of shadows, of treachery and secret couriers and unsung heroes. At Harvard he'd heard his classmates whisper of friends who'd been approached by a confidential division of the army. If asked about their plans after graduation, they'd replied vaguely of work overseas for an obscure bank or import firm. At the time he'd been interested only in returning to his life in Saint Paul. But now his family was gone, and while he was conducting business for Laura's father, the British had asked him to communicate with them about *anything*—Crescent's word—that might help with their understanding of the Nazi threat. There didn't seem to be a reason not to let the British know what he learned. He wasn't spying for them, after all. He'd be a friendly observer, an amateur. Yet his heart beat rapidly, and he took out his pen in order to write down the contact name.

Crescent leaned forward. "But this isn't a game, Mr. Salter. People die in this business. So put away your pen and remember the name Émile Levy. He's an editor of the newspaper *La Gazette*." Crescent allowed himself a smile before throwing the whisky into his capacious mouth. "Very good? I'm leaving tomorrow for London, but I'll be back here in Paris around Christmastime, if you're still in France."

Henry shook his head. "I'll be gone by then. I'm sorry."

"Best of luck to you." Crescent smiled. "And thank you, Mr. Salter, for your services."

After shaking Crescent's large hand at the door to the sterile offices, Henry began walking back to the Crillon. Southwest on the rue de Turbigo and then south on the boulevard de Sébastopol. The sun beat on his face and on the top of his head. He felt himself sweating through his dress shirt. He reached up to his neck and loosened his tie.

For a moment he thought he might choke or faint, but he pressed on, increasing his pace. When he came to the square de la Tour Saint-Jacques and the intersection with the rue de Rivoli, he stopped, nearly in a panic.

It came to him then why Crescent must have asked for his help. While he might be able to provide valuable information, he was also more expendable, because he had no family and no connection to anyone except his employer and to Laura. He was in a solitary raft at sea, without protection or even understanding of the dangers under the surface.

He looked around at the many people walking through the park and heading past him on the busy rue de Rivoli. The sidewalks were filled with those going about their lives. Children, their voices bright, accompanied by their mothers. Men in business suits, already perspiring in the summer morning. Women entering the boulangerie and the markets. Pensioners enjoying the summer warmth over coffee at a sidewalk café. Breathing deeply, he grew calm. And in that calm he realized that both he and Richard Crescent had been wrong. The danger of the Nazis remained far away, in Germany. Here in Paris, life was peaceful but lively and full of promise, the only threats imaginary.

Shaking off his concerns, he smiled to himself. Without hurry, he continued strolling through the unfamiliar but beautiful streets in the direction of the hotel.

12

Laura approached the concierge on the main level of the Crillon, David two steps behind. "Good morning, I'm Laura Powell," she said. "I arrived yesterday afternoon."

"Bonjour. My name is Madame Fournier. How may I be of service?"

In her early sixties, Madame Fournier had short hair that she'd dyed. But the dye hadn't taken evenly, leaving her hair a patchwork of gray and brown. Below her forehead were hard blue eyes.

Laura said, "I need to buy my nephew some new clothes. Is there a suitable department store nearby?"

Madame Fournier nodded as she wrote the name Galeries Lafayette and its address on a note card, then handed the card to Laura. "This store has everything your nephew could need."

David nodded to the older woman. "Thank you, Madame Fournier."

Laura placed a hand on David's shoulder as they walked out into the morning sunlight and along the rue Royale, before heading to the boulevard Haussmann.

◆ ◆ ◆

Madame Fournier watched them go, her eyes unblinking, her hands gripping her pen so tightly that her knuckles showed white through the skin. The boy's accent, together with the dark skin around his eyes and his black and wiry hair, led her to the conclusion that he was a Jew and that the blond American woman couldn't be his aunt but was some kind of impostor. Madame Fournier's blood ran hot at this situation, as she'd hated Jews all her life.

One of *them*—a banker with a pin-striped suit—had turned her family out of their apartment in Lyon when her father had lost his job after the Great War. Her father begged for more time and offered his wristwatch and her mother's wedding band and a necklace, with a pendant of a single modest diamond, but the man in the pin-striped suit shook his head and, in her memory, scoffed at their most valuable possessions. She hadn't forgotten her family's sleeping for a week of cold nights in the Parc de la Tête d'Or, until her mother's sister had grudgingly offered them a small room. While she must be careful around l'Hôtel de Crillon, she agreed with many of Monsieur Hitler's views.

Earlier that year, she'd opened her best bottle of wine in her diminutive apartment as she'd read *Le Figaro*'s reports of the appropriation of Jewish property and businesses in Germany. *Arisierung*, the Germans called it. Aryanization. Cutting the Jews from the nation's lifeblood. This glorious decision, she knew, meant no more Jewish doctors or professors, bankers or lawyers, stores or manoirs. Sending these people who deserved no mercy to Dachau—yes, she'd enjoyed reading about this concentration camp—warmed her heart. How she wished for *Arisierung* here in Paris!

But she considered ways that she could do her part in cleansing her city, beginning with the boy Mademoiselle Powell claimed to be her nephew. Madame Fournier's mind, honed into a sharp object by her lost social position and her parents' lost home, began to take aim.

Laura watched David turn round and round as he admired the many floors of the building—which were layered like a cake and filled with decorations—and, overhead, the domed ceiling of multicolored glass that gave light from outside. Then she saw him look down at his black shoes: scuffed, scratched, the leather soles hanging loosely to the uppers. He'd begun to shuffle, she observed, so they wouldn't fall apart.

She led him to the boy's department, having decided to wait until another day to shop for herself. In fact she'd already put in a call for an appointment at Vionnet, to be measured for two evening dresses and, if she chose to obey her mother's wishes, a wedding gown.

He stood in one of the aisles as she searched for trousers, short pants, long-sleeved and short-sleeved shirts, and several suits and odd jackets. She held the shirts and jackets not only to his shoulders but to his face, assessing whether or not the color complimented his features. She found a dozen pairs of socks in blue, black, and tan, as well as new underwear—two large packages of a dozen each.

By this time there were three clerks helping them, carrying the things she'd chosen, following them through the racks and shelves. After a while she decided that she'd found enough and asked for the changing rooms. The clerks led them to a small room with a black louvered door and a single chair. One by one, the clerks entered the room, hung the clothing until the hooks threatened to tear out from the walls, and then lay the additional clothing on the chair, at last backing away and closing the door.

He stood with her in the small room, not moving, his breathing rapid.

Her eyes catching the signs of his distress, she proposed a solution. "Why don't I face the door? You can take off your old clothes and open one of the packages of underwear. Once you've put on the underwear, you can see if the trousers fit you."

"Yes, Miss Laura," he said meekly.

Her eyes near the louvered door, she heard him step out of his old shoes and let his pants fall from his hips to the floor. The package of underwear tore open, followed by the sound of his legs going through the holes.

Several pairs of trousers fit him. Most needed to be hemmed and would be delivered to the Crillon in several days, but three required no alterations. He wore a pair of solid gray as she helped him out of his soiled shirt and handed him new shirt after new shirt, until they settled on ten. Not once did he say he didn't like something or that a collar was uncomfortable.

Before they left, she took him to the area of the store where boys' shoes were sold and bought him four pairs, all of them attractive and comfortable. Returning to the ground level of the store, she bought each of them a raspberry ice, and then they walked out into the midday sunshine—David in his new gray trousers, a blue-and-white striped shirt, and lace-up shoes in the same brown leather as his new belt. Each of them carried two bags filled with new things for David.

As they strolled toward the hotel, she noticed tears in his eyes. "You look like a young gentleman," she told him.

"Thank you, Miss Laura," he said. "But . . . but I can't do anything for you."

Oh! she thought. *How could he think he ought to do something for me?*

She stopped abruptly, set down her bags, caught hold of him, and looked into his eyes, trying to convey the warmth and care she felt for him. "You're welcome, David. But you don't need to do anything for me. I *want* you to have new clothes. We aren't bargaining. These are gifts, yes?"

He gazed up at her, his large dark eyes damp. His free hand made a tight fist. "But why, Miss Laura? Why are you doing these things for me? Why are you taking me into your hotel and buying me so many clothes? *Why?*"

She wasn't sure how to respond. The great conflict within her tied her tongue. A mother would tell her child that she did these things because she loved him. But she wasn't his mother and couldn't say these words. She couldn't say that she wanted him to have nice clothes in case they stayed together, because she also wanted him to have nice clothes for their imminent separation. There was no easy answer. Yet he continued to stare at her, expectantly. "Because," she managed to say, "you should have these things. Because I want to help you." She knew these words were inadequate, but they were true.

"You do?" he asked.

"Yes. You're a young gentleman with your new clothes. Before, when you were wearing the old suit"—the suit they'd left in the garbage at Galeries Lafayette—"you had nice manners, but the suit didn't flatter you. But now you're especially handsome."

He beamed at her and wiped his face. "You think . . . you think I'm handsome?"

"Certainly I do."

"Mmm. You're nice, Miss Laura." He leaned forward, raised both arms, and embraced her. She held him tightly for a long moment and then bent over and kissed the top of his head.

An unexpected warmth filled her as they picked up their bags and continued along the sidewalk. She smiled when she caught their reflection in the window of a café, a boy and a young woman, clean and well dressed and in high spirits, walking in tandem.

13

Laura watched Henry smile and put a hand on David's shoulder. "Would you like a toy sailboat?" Henry asked him.

They'd just finished lunch at an overpriced café in the rue Saint-Honoré, David having eaten his cassoulet as if he were close to starvation. Henry and Laura had ordered salads. She wanted to remain slender in a nation in which butter seemed to be the primary ingredient of every dish. It wouldn't do for her to gain the stage at La Pomme looking matronly. And because she so often walked or stood beside Henry, who was slender and handsome and now sported wonderfully tanned skin from their Atlantic crossing, she must keep up her end of the bargain, as it were.

David sat up very straight in his chair, his long hair ruffled by the steady breeze. "A toy sailboat? Yes, Mr. Henry. But we aren't near the ocean."

"Have you heard of the Luxembourg Gardens?"

The boy shook his head.

She briefly considered objecting to a toy sailboat. It would be impractical and little used. But then she decided that everything had been taken from David, not least his parents and his sister. What harm could come from spoiling him this once?

Later, in a shop near the gardens, David chose a sailboat with a functional rudder and rigging. Its mahogany hull was polished to a high shine, and he ran his hands along its curved shape.

After crossing the place de l'Odéon outside the Palais du Luxembourg, they came to a large octagonal basin. Around the basin and throughout the gardens were those who, due to poverty, illness, infirmity, work, or disposition had remained in the overheated city during the summer. The old and the very young sat on the abundant benches. Groups of women, in light cotton dresses and holding white parasols, strolled the walkways, many of which were lined by horse chestnut trees whose branches formed a canopy that provided patches of shade. Workingmen, relishing the fine Friday, walked in their shirt-sleeves, with the cuffs rolled up to their elbows. And many, many children ran and chattered and played, watched over by their mothers and governesses and sometimes by their fathers.

Laura watched as David, showing no hesitation, carried his new sailboat out of the taxi and into the groups of children gathered around the basin just south of the palais, Henry a few steps behind him. Henry bent down and showed David how to lock the rudder and cleat the mainsheet and the jib. Eyes at David's level, he pointed to the faint ripples on the water that showed the direction of the wind, and he held the sailboat over the water to demonstrate how the wind would strike the sail and propel the boat forward.

She appreciated Henry then, in a way she hadn't before. His kindness made her want to know him better, and she wished that he'd somehow give more of that kindness to her.

David nodded, said he understood, and then took his toy from Henry and with great care locked the tiller straight, pushed down the centerboard, and moved the boom with one hand until he was satisfied with the angle. He then adjusted the sails and set the boat in the water.

For a moment it remained stationary. He reached down and pushed it outward, away from the concrete basin wall to where it might be blown about by the faint wind. The boat moved cleanly through the water until the wind blew against its crisp white sails. Then it turned, and the mainsheet slipped loose of its cleat. The boom and sail jutted outward, perpendicular to the boat, and the sail filled, and the boat moved rapidly with the wind to the east side of the pond.

"See it!" he said, pointing. "It's going. It's going fast."

"Very fast," Henry said. "But go to the other side and catch it before it crashes into the wall."

Laura smiled as David ran, dodging around other people who were walking or playing on the path surrounding the water, between other small boys who were adjusting, setting, and watching sailboats of their own. She felt relief and some pride that David, despite the tragedies of his life, had the resilience and optimism to play like others who'd been blessed with safety and living parents.

"Do you think it will be ruined?" she asked Henry, who'd stepped back from the basin and joined her a few yards away.

He shook his head. "No, he'll make it. He's determined."

David reached the eastern edge of the lake in time to catch the sailboat. With great care, he lifted up the boat, ignoring the water dripping onto his shirt and trousers, and carried it back around the basin to where Henry and Laura were standing. "It's so fast!" he said, his voice and face bright with excitement. "I almost didn't catch it. It's the best sailboat here, the best sailboat on this whole lake!"

Laura laughed and ruffled his hair. "But you're the captain, the one who tells it where to go. Would you like to keep sailing?"

In answer, David returned to the basin, threading his way through the other children, and set his boat in the water. As he watched it and then ran around the basin to catch the boat on the other side, she turned to Henry. "I'm not sure how to think of him," she confessed. "And I don't know what to do with him."

Henry wasn't wearing sunglasses, and in the sunlight she noticed for the first time that his eyes were hazel, their light-brown irises flecked with emerald. They were intensely focused on her. "Do you mean," he said, "what *we* should do with him?"

She nodded and looked at the water. "Exactly. What *we* should do. I'd appreciate your suggestions, if you have any."

"I don't want to be cruel," Henry told her, "but the longer he remains with us, the worse it will be when we send him away. Tomorrow we could take him to the Red Cross."

The image of her leaving David at a grim facility for orphans and lost children made her body go cold. *There must be another way,* she thought. *And tomorrow is too soon.* She firmly shook her head and kept her voice even. "No, his new clothes from Galeries Lafayette won't be ready for another few days."

Henry nodded. "We'll keep him until the clothes arrive, and then we'll find somewhere else for him—somewhere people will care for him."

She protested to Henry, "We can't just leave him, can we? Wouldn't that be the cruelty you're trying to avoid?"

Henry placed a hand on her arm. "Can't you see what's happening?"

She met his eyes and shook off his hand. "Yes, I see just as well as you do. But he's been with us for only a day. He can't be so attached to us."

"Mmm," Henry said. "It doesn't take long to change a boy's mind about things."

She put her hands on her hips. "Should I treat him badly? Is that what you want?"

"No, you should treat him well. But he can't stay with us, can he?"

She paused, her skin hot. "You're not helpful. You're pitiless," she told him, though she didn't really believe this and knew he was being rational. But her anger and confusion and her fear for the boy led her to strike at Henry, for there was no one else. "You think he's an orphan who has nothing and belongs on the street. You think we shouldn't offer him charity for more than a few days. You think . . ."

And then she stopped. David was nearing them, his dripping sailboat in his hands, a white-toothed grin spread across his face. At once they turned to him and smiled.

Henry squatted down. "You did well, David. Really well. You learned how to do it so quickly."

David gently set the boat on the ground, its white sails fluttering in the breeze, stepped forward, and hugged Henry. Whose arms went around him, patting his back, those hazel eyes closed but the face buoyant.

You were wrong to accuse him, she thought. *He nurtures David just as much as you do. Why did you act as if he doesn't? Why act as if your vision of Henry hasn't changed, when you know it has, when you understand that he's nothing like the dull businessman you'd first believed?*

Her mind turned feverishly upon itself, banishing her earlier thinking about Henry and replacing it with a new man who seemed admirable, even attractive—no, that wasn't the right word, she knew it wasn't. He'd begun to enthrall her. She couldn't stop thinking about him, imagining what he was doing when he wasn't with her, wishing he were with her when he wasn't, wanting him to be close to her, much closer. A tremor in her chest and between her legs told her the essential truth, but she mentally pushed that truth aside. They were here in the garden, with David and in the midst of a conundrum.

She recognized anew her impossible bind—her fear of sending David away and her fear of having him stay with them. *But don't blame Henry for your own worries,* she told herself. *He's the only other person on earth who cares for this lonely and remarkable boy.*

14

When Laura raised her hand and knocked on the lovers' door at dinnertime, no answer came from Henry's room. *Strange,* she thought. *He didn't say he was going out.*

Walking quickly to the telephone, she lifted the receiver and waited for the hotel operator. After she was put through to the front desk, she asked, "Has Monsieur Salter gone out?"

A momentary pause. "Not as far as I know," answered a man's efficient, helpful voice. "May I leave him a message?"

He's angry with me, she realized, *for accusing him in the gardens this afternoon. Well, he has every right to be.*

Could their friendship, or whatever companionable feelings he had for her, be salvaged? She hoped so.

"A message, mademoiselle?" repeated the clerk.

"No, thank you," she replied. But then she reconsidered. "Wait. Yes, monsieur. Would you let him know that Miss Powell offers her apologies?"

"Very well, mademoiselle."

She replaced the phone and realized she'd have to dine alone with David. He wandered into the sitting room in a pair of tan trousers in tropical-weight wool, paired with a pink shirt. As she'd asked, he'd bathed, and his hair was damp, but he'd made a halfhearted attempt to brush it with his fingers. *He must have a haircut tomorrow,* she thought. *Then his transformation will be complete.*

But for what purpose, for what end had she worked to transform him? She imagined pushing him out the door of the Crillon, a small valise filled with the clothes she'd bought him and a couple hundred francs, and into the faceless hands of the Red Cross or another institution, where he might be trained to perform some menial task, where he'd be one of many boys, without the special attention of a man or woman who'd protect him. Where would that organization send him? Out to a farm where he'd labor before dawn? Or to a factory, like his namesake David Copperfield? Thrust into such a situation, wouldn't he flee, choosing yet again to be on his own rather than to live communally with those who didn't know him? Yes, he'd return to the *Île de France* or some other ship, she guessed. But could she really let him, once again, become filthy and unkempt and uncared for?

She'd talk it over with Henry, if Henry would speak to her. Very simply, there was no solution that would make anyone happy.

Later that night, after she'd tucked David in bed and sat by him as sleep gathered him in its arms and carried him away, she returned alone to the sitting room. She went to the bar in the corner and fixed herself bourbon over ice, conscious only after she'd poured that it was Henry's favored drink rather than hers. Standing by the windows, cradling the tumbler in both hands, she looked out over the place de la Concorde and sighed. Traveling to Paris was supposed to be a liberating experience, and yet she was in her hotel suite with a boy. She was young, she thought. She might be beautiful or at least attractive to men, and she wanted to go out and see the great city of Paris by night. Shouldn't she be sampling nightclubs and revues, learning from other singers, trying to see Piaf at La Java?

She sensed a change within her—a recognition of something, or the wanting of something. It had been there for days, this new idea that she'd refused to contemplate, let alone act upon. But now, when the wanting related to the man in the adjoining hotel room, her hesitation seemed pointless, like staying in her suite all evening.

Stubbing the cigarette into the crystal ashtray on the desk, she strode across the room. After unlocking and pulling open her side of the lovers' door, she rapped on his door. "Henry?" she called. *"Henry?"*

No response came from his rooms. She tapped her high-heeled foot against the parquet floor. Click, click, click. She struck the white-enameled door again. And again. And again. A fifth time.

Then she heard movement behind the door. The lock on his side of the door was drawn. Rather than stepping back, she remained expectantly on the threshold, hands at her sides, ready for any reaction. Her throat swelled, and she dried her palms on the sides of her dress.

Henry's door opened, and he stood there, his hair damp from the bath. He was wearing a pair of khakis and a light-blue shirt untucked and half-buttoned. In his bare feet, he stood not much taller than she did in her three-inch heels. Their faces were very close, his slightly crooked nose almost straight at such a short distance. She could smell fresh soap on his skin. His face reddened the moment he saw her.

Her chest grew hot, and her throat swelled. Though her breathing slowed, her lungs seemed not to need air.

For a moment neither of them spoke. Her eyes met his, and she didn't turn away. He stared at her. And then he leaned, almost imperceptibly, closer to her. She expected him to speak, but he said nothing. Nor did she step away from him, her heart racing now, the heat spreading from her chest down through her hips and out into her arms and legs. He moved closer still, and she allowed it.

He kissed her gently, his lips brushing hers. A taste of bourbon, the flesh of his mouth firmer than hers. She knew that she must push him away—decency required it—but somehow that wasn't what she wanted or what she did.

The sensation was so pleasant. He tasted sweet but masculine. It was only for a moment, a few seconds, and then he leaned back. When their mouths parted, she opened her eyes, which she hadn't realized had closed.

He looked to the side, at the doorframe, yet he didn't return to his room.

"I'm sorry," she said softly. "I'm sorry for what I said in the gardens."

"Don't mention it."

"But I wasn't gracious. You were right about me, at least some of the time. I don't always think about the effects of what I say, and it wasn't fair to accuse you of not caring for David. I'm trying to be better, due to your . . . comments about me."

Still, they hadn't moved. He was close, so close to her. When she met his eyes, her face and lips tilted upward, near his. She could hear his breath and guessed he felt no calmer than she did.

"I've forgotten what you said," he told her, his voice low. "I've even forgotten what *I* said."

She nodded and looked down, catching sight of the bare skin of his chest. Heat seemed to flood through her entire body, from her shoulders down to her toes. "I suppose that's best."

"I think so."

"All right then."

Neither of them moved. Eventually she brought her eyes up to his. He raised a single piece of stationery between them.

"I received a note," he explained. "I need to meet with a newspaper editor tomorrow."

And the moment—the moment when she'd been suspended in time and when nothing mattered but his kiss—ended abruptly. She gave him a false smile and turned, closing her eyes briefly as she exhaled and walked to the bar in the corner of her room. It was as if all energy, all urgency for going out into the City of Light dissolved in the lost opportunity. He might have kissed her again, but he'd refused, or at least refrained, and instead brought up a newspaper editor. About whom he was talking now, standing in the doorway as if he believed this editor might interest her.

"Good night," she said, moments later, standing with a drink in the middle of her sitting room.

He hesitated, but then said good night and closed his door.

She didn't bother to close her side of the lovers' door. He wouldn't come through it, and she knew why.

"Mother and Father," she whispered to herself. "He's doing what they asked—staying away from me. In the fall, we'll be back in Saint Paul, where he'll find someone else to marry."

She set down her glass on the desk and kicked off her heels. Sighing, she closed her eyes and imagined him marrying.

It won't be me, she thought, and felt a thorn of regret that startled her.

15

The next morning Henry walked to Café des Patriotes, which was midway between the Crillon and the offices of *La Gazette*. Another bright summer day, already warm. He unbuttoned his navy blue suit and loosened his striped tie in order to remain cool. As he passed through the famous streets, lined with whitewashed buildings crowned by black roofs, his emotions churned under his composed bearing. Most of the night he'd lain awake remembering the moment he'd kissed Laura.

Why he'd done it, he couldn't be sure. *I can't be attracted to someone I dislike,* he reasoned. *But that urge, that overwhelming urge to feel her lips, where in the world did that come from? Has it been there for days, and I didn't notice? Or have I been refusing to call it what it is?*

He'd tried to picture it in his mind. Where he'd stood and how. The scent of roses and irises on her skin. How her lips had felt.

Their mouths, he realized upon reflection, had been the only part of them that had touched. He hadn't reached for her, and she hadn't put her arms around his neck. The smallest, slightest point of contact, and yet that connection had yielded a distressing excitement. Kissing her had so distracted him that he'd lost the ability to converse properly. And instead of resuming the contact that had given him pleasure, he'd stupidly brought up the letter from Émile Levy, who'd asked him to meet this morning.

"Why did that kiss distract you?" he said aloud. "You don't even like her."

But she's pretty, he silently admitted. *No, she's more than that.* And he now knew that she was talented, that she could sing, and that her wish to escape her friends and her social milieu in Saint Paul wasn't so different from the way he felt about that very escape in his own case.

Yet he considered her father's implied demand that she was off limits to him and the devastating loss of his livelihood if he violated her father's trust. He knew there were hundreds—no, thousands—of young men who'd take his place, in a nation in which the unemployment rate was nearly 20 percent. "You *can't* like her," he told himself. "You simply can't."

In this questioning mood, so full of uncertainty regarding his feelings about Laura, he approached the tables outside the café and looked at the stylishly dressed crowd sitting in the cane chairs around small tables with marble tops. In the far corner, up against the building, an older man waved him forward.

"Bonjour," Henry said, taking the man's hand, whose fingers were stubby and yet strong.

"You are different from the man I expected," Levy said, in heavily accented but grammatically correct English. "More boyish. Not so old."

He smiled, despite himself. "I'm old enough, twenty-five."

"I am sixty-eight," Levy told him, his eyes hooded by folds of loose gray skin, "and I have seen too much. The Great War . . ." He shrugged. "Life does not move backward." He eased his frail limbs and his hunched back into a chair as Henry ordered a café au lait. Levy asked for an espresso, pulled a package of Gauloises from the pocket of his dark-gray suit, and offered one to Henry.

In a spirit of camaraderie, he took one and used his lighter for Levy's cigarette and then his own. The strength of the Gauloise caused him to widen his eyes and stifle a cough. But he liked the taste and tried again.

Levy watched him appreciatively. "Turkish tobacco, different from American, yes?"

"Yes. Bitter."

The older man gave a surprisingly hearty laugh, his black eyes glistening. "As bitter as I am. You see, *mon ami*, I have an elephant's memory, but most of my countrymen forget. Perhaps they are happier. For me, happiness is something in the past, to be remembered as Monsieur Proust remembered his childhood. I will not ask if you are happy. But I will ask if you will help me."

Henry leaned back in his chair. "Wasn't I to contact you, Monsieur Levy, if I noticed something to do with the German war effort? But as I've noticed nothing, I'm surprised to have heard from you, and so soon."

"Ah, that's the English for you," Levy said, waving his hand to the west. "They dance around the point without ever quite getting to it. But you see, my dear Mr. Salter, I have need of your help, your observational skills, now." He exhaled a cloud of gray smoke. "Don't you see, I can't wait? And it's you I need, not just anyone. Didn't Richard Crescent explain it to you?"

Henry tried to remember what Crescent had told him. "Perhaps not fully."

Levy leaned closer, lowering his voice. "Mr. Salter, you're American, you're neutral, and you're an expert on armaments, munitions. Why else would Mr. Crescent ask for your help?"

Henry set his Gauloise in the ashtray, not wanting any more of it. As he did so, he considered the man's request. Crescent had seemed forthcoming but turned out not to be, while Levy appeared to be entirely open about his motivations and needs. But was he? And did it matter, when helping these men might be interesting or even exciting?

Perhaps not. Yet the fact that Crescent and Levy had asked for his help might mean that the work was more dangerous than they admitted, or that the others who'd done it were dead, or that Crescent and Levy had no resources to fund the work—that it was outside official channels or even in violation of British and French government policy.

For a long while he sat quietly, weighing what Levy wanted against what he wanted. He sipped at his café au lait. "I'm willing," he said at last, "but I've no training in 'observation,' as Crescent referred to it."

"Observation?" Levy said with a raised eyebrow. "That is one part of the work."

When the editor paused, Henry asked, "And the other?"

"I must sell newspapers, so you'd observe, as Richard Crescent told you, and then you'd write a story for *La Gazette*."

Henry stared at him, dumbfounded.

"But it's more than that," Levy continued. "A newspaper article exposing threats against the Republic will embarrass the French gendarmerie into action so that they'll protect us against the Nazis, *n'est-ce pas*? This is the true goal of the British, yes, to have the French do more against the Germans."

Henry crossed his arms. "Crescent said nothing of newspaper articles," he said, eyes wide. "I wrote a few short stories at university, but I know nothing about journalism."

The older man swatted away his misgivings under a plume of smoke he'd blown up into the café's awning. "This isn't Molière you'd be doing. This is writing what you see and hear. It is not so difficult, and you have very good French, even if you sound as if you're from Montréal. And your byline would be a pseudonym." Levy paused and glared at him. "Mr. Salter, will you work for my country?"

Can this be happening? Henry thought, wiping perspiration from his forehead.

Faced with adventure and intrigue—things he believed that he wanted—he hesitated only to demonstrate his independence. Levy's proposal that he write for *La Gazette* made him even more interested in this work. It wove his ideas of adventure with dreams of becoming a gentleman writer. But now he found a more compelling argument for accepting Levy's request.

While still home in Saint Paul, he'd skimmed news reports of the mistreatment of Jewish people in Germany and wished the situation were otherwise, but what could he do? Yet once he met David and learned of his plight, the reality of life a mere two-hundred-fifty miles east of Paris became real. And, for the first time in his life, he could do something to counter the menace from which he could no longer turn away.

"I wouldn't help you every week," he began slowly. "Only when it suits me. If you'd like to request an article, I'll do the investigation and writing. If you don't publish the story, I can sell it to someone else. Agreed?"

Levy smiled. "Yes."

"And pay?"

Levy didn't react.

Henry smiled, aware that with the exchange rate, or even without it, he earned more for his work at Powell Manufacturing & Munitions than did a freelance reporter for *La Gazette*. "I suppose there's no need for pay."

Levy nodded once.

Henry leaned forward. "A final matter. My companion and I are traveling with a young boy named David, a Jewish refugee. I need you to work with Richard Crescent—yes, I know he's back in London—to obtain a passport for David, a passport with my last name that gives his place of birth as Saint Paul, Minnesota."

Levy was shaking his head. "Everyone wants papers for this or that boy. And I'm sympathetic. I've read of the Nuremberg Laws, of the disappearance of Jews and others into the concentration camp at Dachau. But I cannot get the boy a passport. I'm the editor of a newspaper, you understand? Nothing more."

Henry pulled a few francs from his pocket, set them on the table, and stood. "Then you'll have to find another reporter. Adieu, Monsieur Levy."

A wiry arm reached for him, held his sleeve. "S'il vous plaît, Mr. Salter. Another moment, to finish your *café*. Perhaps my contacts in London would help."

Henry sat down, but on the edge of his chair. He worked not to show his relief the editor hadn't let him walk away. "I must have the boy's passport in order to work for you."

"But that will take months," Levy said, palms upward in supplication. "Can you help us now, before the boy has papers?"

He considered refusing until he'd discussed it with Laura. But what if she ignored him after last night's foolishness? At least he'd have something to do in Paris while she tried to sing in a café. And writing for a newspaper might even impress her. "Yes," he agreed. "One assignment."

Levy didn't smile or even nod. The hoods over his eyes rose for an instant and then slid down like a black curtain over a stage. He bent closer and spoke in a mumble. "We understand from a friendly stevedore that the French fascist groups known as the Francistes and the Jeunesses Patriotes bring contraband through Port Lympia, in Nice. So, in the day you are yourself, an American tourist enjoying *la mer*. In the night you visit the port where the Francistes or the JP will be loading their trucks. We need to know what they have and where the trucks are going. Whether they transport ammunition or something else, like cigarettes or whiskey. Perhaps you will discover."

"I'm an American tourist," he said, incredulous. "Won't they notice me as I walk around the port?"

"It will be dark," Levy assured him. "Wear black clothes, not tourist clothes, and do not shave. You will make yourself . . . rougher. Be close to the men. You understand weapons, so report what you see. *C'est bien compris?*"

"Be close to the men?" he asked, taking up his Gauloise only to crush it in the ashtray. "How will I do it? Approach them and ask what they're doing?"

Here Levy spoke in his usual expansive voice. "Did you not play such games as a child?"

"Yes," Henry said, "but now, if I make a mistake, I'll be shot."

Levy nodded. *"Exactement."*

Henry sat a moment longer, thinking about what he was doing, his eyes following the passersby on the sidewalk. His mind told him to refuse, to leave the café and to think no more about his meeting with Levy. But blood rushed through his body, making it tingle with excitement. He turned to Levy. "When do I leave?"

"Tomorrow morning. Early."

16

Henry waited for Laura to return to her sitting room after she'd put David to bed. Lounging on the sofa in his navy blue suit and a tie of navy-and-cranberry stripes, he held a cigarette in one hand and *The Sun Also Rises* in the other. But he wasn't reading; he was lingering in anticipation of whatever would happen next.

Beside him in a stand filled with ice stood the bottle of champagne he'd ordered from room service while Laura had been talking with David. When he saw her, he put the book aside. "Drink?"

She plopped down in the armchair to his right, slouched deep into its cushions, and kicked off her heels. "Yes, please."

When they'd visited the Louvre with David early that afternoon, after David had gotten a haircut at a shop near the hotel, not once had they referred to what had occurred the previous night by the lovers' door. Uneasy brusqueness had mediated between them, and they'd always included David in their conversations so they didn't have to speak directly to each other.

"What was here?" David had asked while he'd still been interested in the museum.

They were standing in the Denon wing near where a painting had long hung. The wall was darker here and in the shape of a rectangle that marked the absence of the museum's most famous painting.

"A portrait called the *Mona Lisa*," he explained.

"What does it look like?"

"It's a portrait of a woman with an unusual smile, and behind her is a lake and jagged mountains."

"Is it a good painting?"

"I don't know. I've wanted to see it. Another time, perhaps."

"I'm not excited by this portrait," David concluded, "but I wonder where it went."

"That must be a secret," Henry told him. "They've moved it in case there's war, hidden it outside of Paris, I'd guess, somewhere the Germans won't find it."

David looked up at him and crossed his arms over his chest, a gesture of protection. "The Germans are coming *here?*"

Henry patted his shoulder. "No, I don't think so. I'm sure the French have moved the painting just as a precaution. When they see there won't be war, they'll bring back the painting and we'll come to see it, yes?"

David had nodded uncertainly.

"Yesterday," he began now, having stood and poured Laura some champagne, "I met with Richard Crescent, from Britain's ministry of war."

She pushed herself up in the chair. "You told me."

He handed her the glass and sat down. "The man asked me to meet with a newspaper editor here in Paris, a man named Émile Levy, of *La Gazette*. They've asked me to observe life here and to report what I see to Levy. If he thinks the information is important, he'll publish it in the newspaper."

"I don't understand. What would you observe?"

"Whatever they ask. And I've agreed." He leaned toward her. "This is my chance to publish an article or two. An interesting idea, isn't it?"

"I'm not sure. When might the newspaper give you an assignment?"

"There's the rub." He grimaced apologetically, hiding his enthusiasm. "The first one is tomorrow."

"What is it?"

"They want me to watch cargo being unloaded in Nice."

Her face reddened. "Nice? How can you go there tomorrow? We're in Paris, and we've seen almost nothing of the city. Have you forgotten that you need to help me with David?"

"I know all of that," he said, more dismissive of her concerns than he meant to be. "It's for two days, and then I'll be back. I'll write the article here, in this room." He pointed at the floor.

She stared at him. "I don't understand. You *have* a job. Why would you become a newspaper reporter while we're traveling? Are you unhappy with your work for my father?"

"I'm not unhappy, not at all. The British ministry of war thought I could be helpful. Perhaps I can do some good."

She gave him a quizzical expression. "So I'm to stay in Paris and take care of David, while you're on the Riviera?"

"You make the trip sound glamorous, but it won't be."

Having finished her champagne, she held her empty glass toward him. He refilled it and handed it to her. She said, "What cargo will you observe?"

"It's nothing."

She cocked her head. "Do you think I'm an idiot?"

"Maybe whiskey," he said. "Maybe ammunition."

Her voice rose. "Christ, Henry! Don't you see they're asking you to spy? Have you considered the danger? When your story is published in the newspaper, we won't be safe. Not you or I or David. You've read about the Nazis. Do you think they'll be gentle because you're American?"

He absorbed her concerns, which were the same but somehow more pointed than those he'd considered that morning at the café with Levy. A cold, hard idea suffused his mind—that he'd made a catastrophic mistake, that he was far out of his depth, that he might fail to recognize a threat until it was too late. Yet he inhaled slowly, then let the air from his lungs. He remembered Levy's description of the work: *observation.* No, it wouldn't be dangerous to watch others. He appreciated Laura's concern, but she simply didn't understand.

Standing, he looked in the direction of David's bedroom. "Please, let's not wake him."

She glared and got up. Carrying her glass with her, she walked in the direction of her bedroom. And then she stopped and turned. "Would you wait in your rooms? We can talk there."

As she disappeared quietly into her bedroom, where David was sleeping, he took his glass and the half-empty bottle of Roederer and went out through the connecting door.

17

As Laura entered Henry's suite, she hoped the scent of Chanel No. 5 that moved with her gave no hint of what she intended—something she herself didn't grasp. She went from one lamp to another and switched all of them off, except for a single floor lamp, which gave a shy glow. She wanted her cream-colored silk dressing gown—decorated with a hand-stitched white egret—to accentuate her subtle curves. Yet she'd retained some armor, for on her feet were high-heeled shoes that matched her gown and dramatically increased her height.

When she saw him staring at her shoes, she laughed nervously. "I don't know you well enough to take them off. I'm not as tall as you might believe."

"I don't mind," he said, his expression guarded.

They sat at each end of the sofa and turned toward each other. Both were silent for a long time.

"I suppose," she said at last, her body growing warm at the thought of what she intended to ask him, "you've had many love affairs."

His face reddened. "Only one, for several months. A young widow who worked as a secretary at my college. Does this surprise you?"

She shook her head, secretly proud of him for having had a lover and disappointed for the same reason. "It doesn't matter. I just wanted to know, since we're traveling together." She waited for him to ask if she'd had a lover or if she were, as her mother would say, *intact*. She'd nearly decided to sleep with her last beau, having wanted the experience and pleasure. Yet he stopped their caresses without explanation. His reticence had to do, she thought now, with fear—that he didn't know how to do it or that he'd make her pregnant. After a week of silent questioning, she grew relieved not to have given herself to him, because she hated his response to her dream of becoming a singer. When she'd told him of her attempts to sing in the few nightclubs of Saint Paul and Minneapolis, he'd smiled and changed the subject, as if he'd been speaking to a child whose attention was easily diverted.

So tonight she wore a silk robe and rested on a sofa with a man who wasn't afraid. Yet she didn't think she was ready for romantic complications. Their kiss last night had been so brief, almost an accident—perhaps it *had* been an accident or a fleeting urge—it may have meant nothing to him. Since that moment she hadn't been able to read his emotions. He certainly hadn't been affectionate. It was best, she decided, that she remember his touch fondly but not attempt to relive it. For a relationship was impossible: her father had forbidden it, and more importantly, she remembered that until very recently, she'd believed that they had nothing in common. But somehow, he must have changed or she'd come to understand him since they'd left New York on the *Île de France*.

These were her thoughts at midnight, when she realized that he'd said nothing for a minute or two. He'd been too polite to ask if she'd had lovers.

For the first time she could say nothing, but her mind was restless. In this secret place, so far from home, she wondered if she might allow him to kiss her again, just for a moment, and forget her ambition and her parents' disapproval. But who knew if he wanted to kiss her?

As he reached for the bottle of champagne, she held out her glass. Silently admiring his suntanned hand, with its strong fingers wrapped around the bottle, she took her full glass and drank deeply, the mineral taste filling her mouth and the bubbles bursting like weightless caviar in her throat. She felt calmer now. "I'm sorry for asking about your . . .

history," she said. "I've become much too familiar. You could ask me strange questions, if you'd like."

His expression showed confusion. "*Why?* I suppose that's what I've been wondering."

"Why?"

He nodded. "Yes."

"Why *what?*"

"Why are we traveling together? If what your father told me is true, you've had many suitors. Why weren't you aboard the *Île de France* with a husband? Why are you alone?"

She felt blood rushing to her cheeks. His questions went directly to her sense of herself, to her independence, to her fear that in some way, she was lacking, that she was undeserving of love.

For these reasons, *Why* was the question she most wanted to avoid.

"I . . . ," she began, and then faltered, went quiet, looked over at him.

18

Laura watched Henry set down his glass and turn to her, raising his hands defensively. "I'm sorry. I shouldn't have . . . it's none of my business. You don't need to share your private life with me. We're touring together, but we're only acquaintances."

She crossed her legs, her free hand holding the robe closed at her thighs. "I'll choose a man when I'm ready to do so."

"Of course," he agreed.

"But you're right that I'm alone," she admitted. "And I'm alone because none of the men I've met have cared about the part of me that matters most."

"Your singing, your performing?" he offered.

"Yes, Henry, that and more. They want me to fit into the mold of the society women in Saint Paul. They want me to be my mother, Henry. But I don't want to be my mother. Don't I have my own life to lead? I mean, something that isn't planned out and foreseen, every inch of it. But that isn't what men seem to want. Women of the mold are predictable: there won't be surprises, everything is settled, and the men can do their business, and the family grows, and everyone is happy, except I wouldn't be happy—not in that mold or that life. No"—she shook her head with finality—"I don't think I could be."

As she spoke, her eyes had moved from Henry to the window and the lights of the place de la Concorde outside. But now she stared at him to see how he'd respond.

He remained attentive, his eyes showing not skepticism but understanding, and perhaps a common frustration with the rules of Saint Paul, and the wish to be free of them, to have a different kind of life, a more daring life. Briefly, she realized that he was the only man who'd listened to her without smirking, without brushing off her dreams and her sense of her family's social life and customs as a very real cage.

"You're right about the mold," he told her. "It's that very mold that I'm supposed to aspire to join, to fit into. I'm glad that we're in Europe, where we can be free, at least for a while. But what will happen when our tour ends? We'll have to return to Saint Paul."

She winced at this idea and put her free hand over her face, her fingers rubbing her forehead. "It will be like death," she murmured. "A living death. And there's no escape from it. None at all."

He was quiet for a moment, and then he said, "But we should live while we can."

She removed her hand from her face, met his eyes. "Yes, Henry. You're right. We should live for a while."

He nodded but then looked down at the drink in his hands. His expression seemed intent, as if he were trying to discern something hidden in the glass.

Her throat swelled, and her chest felt hot, as if she'd gotten too close to a fire. Leaving now, returning to her room, being alone with the bright city outside her window—these were unappealing prospects. Instead, she found herself wanting to remain in his company, in his rooms. After setting her glass on the table beside her, she could think of nothing further to say. She simply stared at him, dumbly. Frustrated by her lack of ability to fill the silence between them, she blurted, "We ought to consider how we could keep David for the rest of our tour." And then she regretted bringing up the subject that had led to an argument the day before.

But he nodded calmly. "For a week or two, anyway. You should know that protecting David was part of my bargain with the newspaper editor. I'll do the reporting, and in return he'll get a passport for David—an authentic American passport. At least then David will be able to get into the United States if there's war."

She stood and faced Henry. "Really? The editor can get a passport?"

"He'd better."

"And if he doesn't?"

"I'm not sure. I need to think."

"Yes," she said, glancing at the light coming through the lovers' door from her suite. "We need to think more about it. But we should stay together, the three of us, until David has a passport."

"Until then," he agreed.

"That means you have to return from Nice."

"You shouldn't worry."

"But I do, Henry. Of course I worry," she said as she walked to the door, hoping he was right. If something happened to him . . . what would she do? The very idea brought a cold emptiness into her chest. She hadn't been prepared, not at all, for any positive feelings toward him. And yet she couldn't deny their presence. His willingness to place himself in danger for an important cause made her heart swell. As he stood and followed close behind her, she quivered with expectation.

Suddenly, she decided to risk disappointment.

On the threshold between the rooms, she stopped and turned. Just as on the night before, their faces were inches apart. Without delay, she leaned forward and lifted her chin until her lips lightly touched his.

Once, and then again.

The contact between them grew unhesitant.

A kiss, and another, and another. It seemed they couldn't move apart. She opened her mouth, and his tongue found hers.

This time, she put her arms around his neck and pulled him close. He placed one hand on the small of her back and another on her side, something that gave her such unexpected pleasure that she jumped slightly.

Wanting to give herself to him, she was stunned and alarmed by the urgency of her feelings. A moment ago they'd barely made contact, and now she wanted to let him touch her everywhere and go where no man had ever been. In fact her appetite for him made her feel unsettled but also alive in a new way. It was as if she were floating away while still tethered to him. Her mind began to soften and yield to the idea of romance and entanglement.

Yet she recalled her parents' wishes for her, their warnings and threats against an inappropriate match, and the loss of his job. Though tempted by the forbidden, she nevertheless placed a hand on his chest, closed her mouth, and pushed him away. She hadn't expected separation to be painful, but it was. It hurt not to taste him, not to have his mouth on hers.

He complied gracefully, silently, and with warm eyes as she withdrew to her room.

She closed and locked the lovers' door behind her, listened as he did the same, and walked over and lay back on her sofa, exhaling as she looked at the ceiling, wishing she hadn't needed to part from him, wondering at how things might have been if she'd stayed on his side of the door.

This reverie took hold of her with great force and brought color to her face and heat to every other part of her body, causing her to pull open her robe so the air would cool her.

Imagine if he saw me in this state!

The thought led her to consider the unimaginable, turning it over in her mind and predicting how she—how she and Henry—would change if she allowed him satisfaction. Allowed *us* satisfaction, she corrected herself silently. She wasn't going to be one of those women who pretended they had no desires. No, she'd admit to them. She'd always be honest with herself.

And what if she allowed her desires to be met by his? What if she slept with him?

For him, probable ruination.

And for her?

Confusion and regret. And pregnancy, leading to her loss of freedom and the end of her singing.

No, she thought. *The price would be too high.*

19

In the morning, knowing that he was gone, she opened her eyes and sighed. Already she counted in her mind the hours until his return, when she'd have his companionship and his help with David. But there was another reason she wanted him to return—a reason she understood yet didn't admit to herself. She wanted no less than to be kissed, to be touched, to be admired and adored.

Exhaling, she got up off the sofa and called room service for a pot of coffee. While she waited, she opened the blinds and smoked several cigarettes, as if she were in some kind of competition. The sky molted into a faint turquoise and filled the empty place de la Concorde with pale light. She looked at her watch. Six o'clock.

Taking her purse from the coffee table, she absentmindedly glanced at her calendar. Stunned, she realized that her audition with Louis Bellegarde, the owner of La Pomme, would be early that afternoon. Immediately she regretted the cigarettes and called room service for hot water and fresh lemons. While she didn't regret the previous night, she wished that she'd had more sleep and that the dark circles beneath her eyes were less pronounced. Though she worried about Henry's safety in Nice, she focused on her audition. It had been nearly a week since she'd sung anything, and she must practice, but where? Remaining in the suite with David would be impossible. She'd have to find a quiet area near the hotel where she could work on her French and American songs.

An hour later when David ambled into the sitting room, yawning and rubbing sleep from his eyes, he asked where Henry had gone. While he waited for her answer, he hugged her.

"Henry is on a business trip," she explained. "He took the train down to the south, on the Mediterranean."

David appeared to be uncertain and fearful. His eyes darkened.

"He'll return tomorrow," she said cheerfully. "And today I need to go out, just for a little while, and you can remain here in our rooms. If you need anything, you may call Madame Fournier, the concierge downstairs. All right?"

David's forehead grew lined as he swallowed. "How long will you be gone?"

She leaned down and smiled. "A couple of hours, no more. You can play with your sailboat, or you could draw and look at the picture books on the coffee table. Won't you be happy for a couple of hours?"

David's face grew calm. "For only a couple of hours? Yes, Miss Laura. I'm sure I'll be all right. And I won't even leave the room."

Yes, she silently echoed his assurance. *He'll be well for two hours. After surviving the Gestapo, he'll no doubt manage in my suite for two hours. And then I'll return, and we'll go out for ice cream. I just hope to have something to celebrate.*

20

Laura's thoughts ran to the impossibility of war, here in Paris, in the middle of this high bright summer. She walked through the copses of the Tuileries—among gardens filled with geraniums, irises, loosestrife, and asters in bloom under the oak, alder, poplar, and chestnut trees— believing Paris would always be safe.

There were troubles in the East, she knew. Before leaving Saint Paul, she'd read about the Anschluss. And while she'd known the enlargement of Hitler's Reich was an ominous event, the postcard-pretty cities of Vienna and Salzburg had seemed too far from Saint Paul for her to agonize over who ruled over them. Today, when she was several hours by train from Germany, the events of the spring were at least as far away as they'd been from America. And anyone from America or Britain who feared war couldn't know how it felt to be under the trees, her shoes making a pleasant sound when she stepped on the crushed rock.

"Laura," she said aloud. "Pay attention. Pay attention to your voice!" In less than ninety minutes, she'd sing at Louis Bellegarde's café. A tense throat would lead to a terrible audition. She forced her mind to remain here, in the Tuileries, under the sun and the pretty trees.

Beginning softly, she sang a few scales. Despite being in the open air, without a microphone or walls to reflect the melody back to her, she thought she sounded good. Her voice was strong and a bit rough at the edges, exactly as she wanted it. She'd do a few American songs and then a handful of French numbers.

Slowly, in the manner of a dirge, she sang the famous lines of "Begin the Beguine," easily holding the sostenuto of the verses. Her body straightened, and she rose unconsciously to her full height. Her voice deepened and broadened. In the final chorus her lungs filled, and she pushed out the melody and felt great joy in the sensation. When she'd finished, she smiled with pleasure.

Applause came from behind her. When she turned, blushing, there were two old men, both well dressed, who said "bravo!" and *"magnifique!"* She nodded, accepting their praise, and walked away from them to somewhere she wouldn't be heard.

Yet their clapping echoed in her ears, and her heart filled with excitement as her first audition drew near. She smiled to herself as she spread her arms out in the sunshine.

21

After playing with his sailboat by the windows overlooking the place de la Concorde, David grew hungry. For so many months he'd been tamping down his hunger, as if it didn't exist, even when his stomach burned with emptiness. But when Miss Laura and Mr. Henry had invited him into their rooms, he'd allowed himself to eat whenever he could. He smiled this morning, as he did on all mornings with Miss Laura, knowing that he could eat until he was full.

After padding in bare feet to the phone on the small desk in the sitting room, he lifted the receiver and asked for the concierge.

"Bonjour," came the voice on the end of the line. "Concierge."

"Madame Fournier?" David asked.

"*Oui.*"

"This is David . . . um . . . Powell. I'm staying with my aunt, Laura Powell. You recently recommended the Galeries Lafayette."

A hesitation on the other end of the line. "Yes, David? May I be of service?"

"My . . . um . . . aunt has gone out for a while. But I'm hungry. Could you order me breakfast and lemonade?"

"Yes, of course," Madame Fournier replied quickly. "I'll take care of it. I'll bring food and lemonade to your room myself."

"Thank you, Madame Fournier," David said and set the receiver in the cradle.

His stomach churned, but he took up his sailboat and pushed it along the sofa cushions. The boat endured a terrible storm, with loud wind and rain. The storm lasted for a long while, until he heard a brisk knock on the door.

He hurried to the door and opened it.

There stood Madame Fournier, already smiling at him, in her hands a tray heaped with eggs, ham, and fruit alongside a carafe of lemonade. "Your breakfast, Mr. Powell," she said.

He stepped aside as she entered the suite. Once she set the tray on the desk and poured a glass of lemonade, she handed the glass to him.

He smiled at her.

After he took a long drink, she turned to him and gave the common Hebrew greeting: *"Boker Tov."*

Automatically, without considering his reply, he said, *"Boker Or."*

"Mah Shlomcha?"

"B'seder."

Her nostrils flared, and her eyes burned. She threw back her shoulders and pointed at him. *"Juif! Tu es un juif."* You are a Jew. "And Mademoiselle Powell is *not* your aunt."

He set down the glass of lemonade, his hand shaking as he realized his fatal mistake. Ever since he'd watched his parents be burned alive in their apartment building fire, he'd pretended not to be Jewish but to be Lutheran, even though he'd no idea what being Lutheran meant. Because he knew one thing: nobody hated Lutherans. And that was enough to make him yearn to be someone that nobody hated.

His legs twitched, as if they wanted to run away from this woman, but she was blocking the door. And where could he go?

Lowering his eyes, he stared at the rug on the floor, its pattern blurring as tears ran down his cheeks.

22

In her simple black dress and sunglasses and carrying a small black handbag from Chanel, Laura walked into La Pomme, the small nightclub in the boulevard Raspail whose name she knew in English was *apple*. It was larger than she'd expected, with enough tables for a hundred patrons, not including the zinc bar, with its bottle-lined shelves that reached to the ceiling. Though gouged and flecked with imperfections, the floor was tiled in the pattern of a black-and-white checkerboard. The walls were painted a faint apple red. As Louis Bellegarde had promised her aboard the *Île de France*, he was sitting at the bar, bent over his ledger. He wore a black suit, white shirt, and purple tie. Overweight, he nevertheless had a sleek appearance, his thinning black hair combed straight back along his shiny scalp. Three other men were standing nearby, talking in low voices, smoking and sipping at a drink the color of jade, which she guessed was absinthe.

She approached. "Monsieur Bellegarde? Bonjour. We met aboard the *Île de France* last week. We have an appointment. Do you remember me?"

He gave no indication that he'd heard. But the three other men turned to look at her. Their eyes seemed large, and their curiosity made her feel out of place. These men were rough, and she was smooth. *What do you know about singing in cafés in Paris?* they seemed to ask.

At last Bellegarde swiveled around, his large stomach hanging over his belt. He looked silly, sitting on a barstool. And then he did a little jump and was off it, coming toward her. "Of course, mademoiselle," he began. "How is your time in France?"

"Very well," she told him as they exchanged kisses.

"Beautiful here, yes?"

"Yes." She nodded.

"You're here for your audition?"

"If that's acceptable."

"*Oui*," he said without enthusiasm. "Allow me to present the trio that will accompany you. Étienne, on the drums; Lucien, on the bass; and Gilbert, at the piano. *C'est bon?*"

"How do you do?" she said nervously.

"*Enchanté*," they said as one.

"You will play songs of France and America. *Oui?*" asked Monsieur Bellegarde.

"*Mais bien sûr*," she agreed.

The trio set down their absinthe and walked to the low stage, where their instruments waited in shadow. Bellegarde went over to the controls on the wall by the bar and switched on the white stage lights, making her immediately more comfortable. This was what she'd wanted. She could fill the empty room with sound, aided by the single microphone. Volume would be far less important than tone, than the ease of her singing and the singularity of her voice, which she hoped would remain trustworthy. The two old men who'd applauded her in the Tuileries had given her confidence. She'd start with *"Le marins ça fait des voyages."*

In high heels she stepped onto the stage, stood at the microphone, and spoke into it, in order to measure its amplification. It might have been stronger, but other than Bellegarde, there were no people or clothing or conversation to absorb it. She turned to the trio and named the first song. They nodded and began to play. She faced the microphone and realized she couldn't sing those words at such a tempo. She turned and asked them to stop and then asked them to take it faster. It was, she felt, a song filled with more pleasure than most people realized. The trio shrugged and began again. She sang.

Halfway through it, Bellegarde, who'd been standing by his ledger, put down his pen and faced her. He stepped backward, a few times, until he was in the middle of the room. Then he remained motionless, hands on his hips. When she'd finished the first song, which had gone so quickly she barely remembered how she'd sung it, he clapped a few times. "Another," he called.

She began *"Mon cœur est au coin d'une rue."*

When she and the trio had finished that one, he nodded and called for another. She moved to the American songs, the first being Irving Berlin's "What'll I Do," and she thought of separation from Henry and David. Her voice made the words ache.

"One more," called Bellegarde.

A final time she turned and asked the trio for "No Matter What You Say," a recent song by the American Charlie Hawthorne that she'd read was popular in Europe. Slowly, she instructed, patting her thigh with the beat. When they complied, she turned, stood before the microphone, and sang the way she had among the trees and flowers of the Tuileries, this time believing that she'd soon be parted from Henry and would have only a memory of his kisses. Her voice remained hoarse until the final chorus, when she closed her eyes and stretched out her arms and sharpened and brightened her words:

I had a great time,
But I can read the sign.
You don't love me today,
No matter what you say.

I hope to live a long while
And maybe even smile
When I remember our affair
As if I don't care.

But the truth is, I can't get over

Our travels in Roma,
The sun on the Coliseum,
Or holding hands in a museum,
Gray cobbles under our feet,
Deep wobbles in my knees.

We promised never to part,
Never to fight,
Never at night,

Never damage my heart,
Never to part.
Oh, I've lost my heart.

You didn't love me that day,
No matter what you say.

At last she opened her eyes and waited, unmoving, a step behind the microphone. The trio played the final bars and then was quiet.

Bellegarde's face was flushed, and he was shaking his head. She thought he hadn't liked the best she could do. But then he smiled and held a hand to his chest. "That was beautiful, and very sad. The best version of that song I've heard." He looked past her to the trio. "What did you think?"

"Excellent."

"Perfect."

"We want her to sing for us."

"*Mais*, I must ask you to return," said Bellegarde, "tomorrow night at eight o'clock. Your name will be la Perle, after your necklace, your earrings, and your beauty." He grinned.

She wanted to hug him and the trio as well, but she refrained. Her face warmed, and she bowed and said thank you. After stepping down from the stage and approaching Bellegarde, she took his hand. "Merci beaucoup."

"*De rien*," he said. "I know that you will be good here."

As she left, she noticed the door onto the street was made of rusted metal and the wood shutters to the sidewalk had split in a few places, but she ignored these signs of neglect. She was floating in a dream that had come true. She was going to sing at a nightclub in Paris. Tomorrow night would be heaven, especially if Henry and David would be there to watch her.

She stepped off the sidewalk into the street and raised her hand for a taxi. As it swerved from the far lane and stopped in front of her, she climbed in, said the name of her hotel, and wished the day would last a hundred years.

23

In the Crillon's lobby, Madame Fournier placed a call to the gendarmerie.

When an officer entered the hotel lobby a half hour later, she told him of the situation. "The boy has been kidnapped," she surmised aloud. "He's a Jew, a refugee from Germany who is in France illegally and who must be sent to Berlin, where Jews are taught their place."

The gendarme nodded, looked around the ornate lobby and the well-dressed hotel guests. "Yes, the refugee problem is very bad," he said and agreed to speak with Mademoiselle Powell. "When will she return?"

"Soon," Madame Fournier said. Though she knew not to press the officer, her hatred loosened her tongue. "But now you must remove the Jew from her room. He cannot be here any longer."

The gendarme's surprise at this order showed on his face. He colored a little, but his voice remained professional. "Which room is Mademoiselle Powell's?"

When Madame Fournier had given the number, the gendarme gripped his truncheon and proceeded to the lift.

24

David heard a loud knock on the door. He went and stood on the other side of it. The knock and the creak of leather boots reminded him of the Gestapo. Instinct told him to hide, and that is what he did, running into the bedroom and burrowing into the wardrobe that held Laura's dresses, skirts, and blouses.

"Gendarmerie!" came the voice from the hallway, hard and filled with authority. "Open the door."

He stopped breathing and listened. He could hear his heart thumping in his chest. What he experienced wasn't fear but terror—a continuation of what he'd known in Berlin on the terrible day when the Gestapo had barricaded his father, his mother, and his sister in their apartment and had thrown gasoline-soaked rags through the narrow openings.

They're hunting me here, too, he thought, *as if I were a wild boar. Isn't it safe in Miss Laura's rooms?*

More knocking. "Gendarmerie! You must open the door!"

He didn't move. He remembered Laura's telling him not to open the door for anyone except her. Oh, why had he let in Madame Fournier? At the rear of the stuffy wardrobe he began to tremble uncontrollably.

What if the gendarme takes me away? he thought. *What if I never see Miss Laura and Mr. Henry again? What if I'm sent back to Germany?* He imagined the Gestapo shoving him into another apartment and burning him alive. As his skin grew hot at this image, he jerked his arms around, trying to cool them.

The knocking ceased. Did he hear Miss Laura's voice?

He crept to the front of the wardrobe and listened.

Yes, he thought. *Miss Laura.*

Slowly, he pushed open the door and crept across the bedroom to the threshold of the sitting room. He tiptoed to the hallway door and pressed his ear against the enameled wood.

Her voice was angry, loud, and hoarse. She told the gendarme, in a mixture of English and French, that of course the boy was her nephew and of course he wasn't Jewish—she would know. Yes, she had his passport. Or no, her chaperone had it. Her chaperone, Henry Salter, had gone to Nice on business but would return tomorrow. Monsieur le Gendarme could speak with Monsieur Salter when he returned. Perhaps the day after next, at two o'clock in the afternoon, in the hotel lobby. *C'est bien?*

The creaking of the gendarme's boots faded down the hallway outside the room. When the key turned the lock, David removed the chain between the door and jamb, and she walked into the room. His arms relaxed, and his heart slowed. His panic receded, but wouldn't disappear.

She held him so tightly he almost couldn't breathe. He buried his face into her dress, embraced her, and wouldn't let go.

25

When Henry arrived in Nice that evening, he saw that l'Hôtel Negresco was a grand white structure looking out over the Mediterranean, its flanks topped by voluptuous salmon-colored cupolas. He paid the driver and walked into the hotel, silently admiring the enormous solarium with its ceiling made of glass in the shape of flower petals. Visible from the lobby was the dining room, which had rich wood paneling, white columns accented with gold leaf, and a ceiling with fluted inlays of mahogany. How quickly he'd gotten used to such things. After registering under the name Robert de Saint-Loup and giving his occupation as manager at *La Gazette*, he was shown into a well-appointed room with a view of the sea.

After a leisurely bath, he put on a suit before going downstairs for a drink at the hotel bar. While sitting at a table overlooking the promenade and the darkening surf that spread and receded over the rocky shingle, his sleepiness left him. It was pretty here, yes, but he wished that he wasn't alone and that Laura were here so that he could kiss her again, just once, before going to sleep. Those brief moments of contact had become the part of a daydream that had such fantastic detail it nearly came to life.

A waiter approached, and he ordered Pernod and began to worry that he'd be noticed and his Quebecois accent remembered. But there were only three others in the bar.

An older couple smiled at him from a nearby table. The woman had gray hair to her shoulders and large rings on her arthritic hands. The man wore gold-rimmed eyeglasses, a white shirt, and a royal-blue-and-cream-colored polka-dot cravat. Their conversation, about their grandchildren, was barely audible.

In the terrace's far corner sat a man in his forties. Despite the heat, he wore a black fisherman's cap, and his clothing wasn't fine. With a high forehead, small eyes and nose, and a jutting chin, Henry thought he resembled the American movie actor James Cagney, in *The Public Enemy*. This man sipped an espresso and kept to himself, and for an instant Henry wondered if the man was in fact the movie star, visiting for a week or two the resort town on the Mediterranean. But then the man looked over at him and nodded briefly, before continuing to gaze out at the sea, and Henry knew the face didn't belong to the famous actor.

Later, after a dinner of oysters and coffee taken in his room, he dressed in black: trousers, long-sleeved shirt, shoes. He left his wristwatch in his valise and carried no identification as he went out for the night. His single notion, other than that he must remain undiscovered, was that he'd no idea what he was doing. Laura had been right to suggest that he was naive.

As he walked along the promenade, the streetlamps and the lights of the hotels and shops made the pavement gleam. Cars passed him, going both directions—large sedans and convertibles with the tops down carrying well-dressed men and women who were smoking, singing, laughing. But merrymaking was far from his mind. With relief he turned north along the Quai Lunel that led in the direction of the port.

Fewer lights, more shadows. To his right, trawlers, sailboats, and motor cruisers swayed in the calm black water like pale ghosts. Metal halyards clanged rhythmically against mast hoops. In the near distance a large engine started and rumbled as it powered an unseen boat out to sea. He felt better here, away from the parade along the strand, though he knew it was more dangerous. Here, a gang might beat or kill him, and nobody would hear or see a thing. His pulse quickened. He smelled the briny air.

From behind him came the sound of boots—hard leather striking asphalt. Slowing his pace, he moved to the left, into the street. The boots kept their pace, drew alongside, and passed him. At first he kept his head down, but then he looked up and, even in the darkness, saw that it was James Cagney, the man with the knit cap who'd been sitting on the terrace of the Negresco bar.

Coincidence, he told himself as he stopped and listened. Cagney's steps faded until he couldn't hear them.

He looked left and right. He turned and behind himself saw the lights of cars on the promenade.

Nothing threatening.

He breathed deeply and began walking.

Soon he reached the Quai Cassini, at the north end of Port Lympia. A café served a handful of patrons drinks or a late dinner outside. Trying to avoid the streetlamps, he approached the quay and walked along the seawall. Below him to the right was black water that lapped against the concrete. Even in the darkness he thought he could see faint multicolored patches of motor oil. A few dead fish, their white bellies upward, added their pungent scent to the humid night air.

He came to a pair of fuel tanks that had been placed side by side, waiting to be installed in a freighter or other large craft. Silvery metal in appearance, they reached half a meter above him and were more than four meters in length. He kept his head down, as if he had somewhere important to go, and stepped behind them. He hoped nobody had seen him.

26

At three o'clock in the morning several men gathered on the Quai Cassini.

In a southern patois mixed with Parisian French, they discussed a waitress and whether she had a better figure than her sister, who worked at a patisserie in the rue Guiglia and was rumored to be a whore each Lent. Peeking around the steel tanks, he saw the café lights were off, but the three- and four-story buildings along the quay had exterior lights that weakly illuminated the area around the seawall. The men were smoking cigarettes in the gloom, talking over each other in loud voices. They appeared to be unafraid and at ease.

Henry filled his mouth with air and silently blew it out. *Would this be the job Levy gave me?* he wondered. *Standing on filthy concrete in the cold, watching a group of crude men unload cargo, before returning to the hotel and collapsing into bed, more from boredom than exhaustion?*

His annoyance faded with the harsh noise of a diesel engine. He went to the ends of the tanks and peeked out.

A truck with a covered bed pulled near the men and then reversed until it was perpendicular to the quay and its rear door faced the water. The engine was shut off, and two men climbed out. One of these was Cagney. The other was taller and heavy, his face nearly invisible under a hat with a brim, and he appeared to be looking at Henry. This unnerved him, but he knew that he was well hidden behind the tanks.

Cagney directed the others, who tossed aside their cigarettes and walked to the seawall. A barge glided in, moving through the water without engine power. Perhaps it was pushed somehow—Henry couldn't see. The men fended off the barge, keeping it from scraping against the wall, and lifted a wide steel plank that stretched across the narrow band of water to the stern. Then they boarded.

Onto dollies they loaded two large crates that were apparently quite heavy. They strained as they pushed and pulled. *Un, deux, trois,* they called, and the dollies went up onto the inclined metal plank, before settling smoothly onto the concrete seawall.

Moving around the tanks, Henry peeked out at the truck. About six meters in length, it had a covered bed that would easily hold the crates. Cagney raised a hand. "*Arrêter!*" he called quietly, then switched on a flashlight and moved toward the first crate. "*L'ouvres.*"

A crowbar was brought and used to pull apart the wooden slats. As Cagney aimed the flashlight, Henry strained into the darkness to see. Cagney reached into a mass of straw and withdrew a metallic object. Squinting, Henry could tell this was the new MP 38 submachine gun that was manufactured by ERMA in Germany. He knew the magazines held thirty-two rounds, enough to kill over two dozen men in half a minute.

Placing his hands on the cool silver tanks, he pushed until his fingers grew sore. His leg muscles grew sore from standing for so many hours.

Why are these men importing weapons that will be used against their families? he thought. *Is it money? Are things so bad for fishermen and stevedores that they'll betray their country?*

But he tamped down his anger. He could do nothing, not tonight. Tomorrow he could write a newspaper article that would expose these traitors. For the first time in his life, he could do something that mattered.

Cagney nodded to the group of men. They lifted the metal ramp off the barge, which floated seaward, and attached it to the truck's rear bumper. Then they pushed and pulled the crates up the ramp and used ropes to secure them to the metal stays of the truck bed. While Cagney supervised, another man, tall and emaciated in appearance, surveyed the port and the quay. For a long while this man stared in his direction. But Henry didn't pull his head behind the tanks. That would have been movement, and he wouldn't move. He drew his breath as shallowly as he could. But the heavy man continued to stare at the tanks as the others stowed the ramp on the side of the truck.

This man began walking toward the tanks, toward him. The man reached into a pocket, then extended his right arm.

A pistol, Henry thought.

Energized by terror, he ran out from the far side of the tanks, away from the quay, the water, and the man with the gun. He kept his head down, expecting the rough impact of a bullet to the head or shoulder.

But there was only quiet. As he sprinted, he heard no shot behind him, no sound of shoes or boots or even shouts. Yet he ran onward, hard as he could, until his breath came so fast he felt dizzy. Leaning up against the wall of an apartment building along the promenade des Anglais, he rested for a moment. He'd been recognized. Cagney knew he was staying at the Negresco, and the hotel clerk would be bribed or forced to give up his name and room number.

He began running again, fast as he could manage, along the promenade. When he reached the hotel, he went into the lobby, retrieved his key, and went upstairs to his suite. There, almost in one motion, he threw his things into his valise and left the rooms. Instead of returning to the elevator, he bolted the opposite way, down the long hallway and through the door to the fire stairs. He waited, the door slightly ajar. Not a minute later the skeletal man entered the hallway from the elevator, striding rapidly, his back to Henry, in the direction of the suite.

Henry let the door close and went noiselessly down the stairs. At the ground floor he pushed open the exit door and went outside.

The alley was dark, and for a minute he was blind as his eyes adjusted. But he quickly saw that he was alone. He ran behind the hotel, into a narrow street that wound north and east, toward the old town.

He wouldn't choose another hotel. The men would find him, would murder him in his bed.

In the old town he found another alley. It was so dark he had to walk from one end of it to the other to confirm it was unoccupied. If Cagney or the larger man came for him here, they wouldn't see him. But he'd hear them. In the darkness he paced and paced until he grew so tired he sat down on the cobbles and leaned against a building's cool stucco. He listened as closely as he could to the sound of night: distant cars and motorbikes, a siren, the drunken laughter of young people coming out of a bar, a dog barking in an apartment above the alley. Nothing seemed dangerous or extraordinary.

But that was the problem.

He'd entered a world that appeared safe but wasn't. An additional minute in his hotel room, and he'd have been killed.

"Jesus," he said aloud, his hands trembling. "Jesus."

27

Heat blew into the alley and woke him. Henry stood with great difficulty, his muscles aching. In the morning light he could see where he'd
been sitting. The cobbles were filthy, the gaps between them filled with
paper and rubbish. Nearby a dog had urinated against the wall of the
building, which he could see held the offices of an architectural firm. He
leaned over, opened his valise, and found his wristwatch. As he fastened
it to his arm, he saw that it was after six.

Walking in the direction of the Gare de Nice-Ville, he passed by a
boulangerie, where he bought a croissant. He wanted to avoid public
transport, fearing Cagney's men would watch it. But the train was the
only practical way back to Paris. Eventually he went outside and walked
to the station. With relief, he saw no one who'd been at the port the
night before. He purchased his ticket and stepped into a telephone
booth. Laura might be asleep, but he found that he wanted to hear
her voice and let her know that he looked forward to seeing her that
evening.

"Are you all right?" she asked, her voice filled with worry.

"Yes, everything's okay here. Maybe next time it will be more
interesting."

"I should think you'd avoid a next time, when you hear what
happened."

His chest tightened. "Are you all right?"

"Yes, I think so."

"David?"

"Until tomorrow, yes."

"What happens tomorrow?"

As she told him, he realized they'd have to leave the Crillon, for even if they could make excuses to the gendarme who'd nearly taken custody of David, there would be other malicious concierges and other gendarmes. Worse, he recalled that he'd registered at the Negresco as a manager of *La Gazette* and used the newspaper's address rather than his own; Cagney and his men would attempt to track him via *La Gazette*. Leasing a private house was the only solution, together with finding the boy a passport.

"I'll call Émile Levy," he told her and rang off.

A few moments later he'd spoken with the editor, not about arms smuggling—he refused to discuss it until his housing was resolved—but about a friend of Levy's, a Madame Bernard, who owned a residential leasing company. He dialed Madame Bernard, waking her. Her acidic manner became gentle when he explained that he wanted, beginning that afternoon, a house in Paris. He required, he told her, spacious furnished rooms where he and his wife (inwardly he thrilled at his use of this word) and son could live for at least six months. Could she find such a property?

Indeed she could, her voice becoming clear as sleep left her. "There are several of that description. Would you like to visit them this afternoon?"

"No, I need to make a decision now."

She couldn't hide her joy. "Now, monsieur?"

"Yes."

"Please, let me take up my papers and check the specifications. One moment, *oui*?"

"All right," he said, amused by her excitement.

There was a great deal of noise on her end of the line and then, "Hello? Monsieur?"

"Yes."

"There are many beautiful neighborhoods in Paris. Perhaps . . ."

"No, madame," he interrupted. "We must be close to everything, including the Métro. You understand?"

"Oh, yes, monsieur. Why don't we consider the *seizième* arrondissement? It extends south from the avenue de la Grande Armée, near the Arc de Triomphe, past the area to the west of la Tour Eiffel and down to the Seine. Unfortunately, there is nothing in Passy or in the avenue Foch, but I have other properties in the *seizième*. Would that area meet with your satisfaction?"

I don't have any idea, he thought, but said, "Yes, somewhere in the sixteenth arrondissement would be acceptable."

"Tell me, monsieur, do you prefer a quiet street or a street with activity?"

"Very quiet, please. Inconspicuous and away from all busy roads," he said, thinking he was going to hide David in a deceptively large house. If war came suddenly, ostentation might be fatal.

"*Oui*, monsieur. Then what I'd recommend is a three-story property in the rue Dosne, a private street with pretty houses, although this *maison* isn't near the retirement home for women that is also here. You'll find the rue Dosne is near the avenue Bugeaud and a fifteen-minute walk from l'Étoile."

"How many bedrooms?" he asked.

"Ahm. *Un, deux, trois. Trois.*"

"And bathrooms?"

"*Quatre.*"

"Servants' quarters?"

"*Oui*. A separate apartment in the attic for a maid and a very small adjoining room for a valet. Those rooms have a terrace overlooking the street. Warm in summer, monsieur, but pretty in winter when the light is weak. And the first floor has an especially beautiful sitting room that looks onto a small *jardin*. You would like this property, monsieur."

"Is the house available this afternoon?"

"Yes, yes. It is available now."

"Then we agree to lease it."

"But the rent, monsieur! You must know the rent."

"Certainly," he said, having forgotten to ask.

When she related the figure, he converted it to American dollars and realized the house would be far less than their rooms at the Crillon. "*Oui*, that is acceptable. At what time shall my family arrive?"

"*À la mi-journée*, monsieur. I will have the maid clean before you arrive. The house will be perfect, and there will be freshly cut flowers."

"Excellent, madame. My wife will give you the first month's rent."

After ringing off, he telephoned Laura at the Crillon and told her that Madame Bernard would be waiting at the house in the rue Dosne at noon and that madame was expecting Laura Salter. His throat swelled as he used his last name after her first.

For a moment she was quiet, her breath nearly inaudible. Then she said, "Isn't that impossible?"

"Yes, I know it is," he replied. "It was just something I told Madame Bernard, to keep her from asking questions. I'm sorry if it upsets you."

Another pause on her end of the line. "I don't . . . dislike you anymore," she said softly.

He thought of the night just ended that he'd barely survived and how he yearned to see her tonight. Yet he knew to remain cautious around her, to be sure the end of her dislike would endure. The idea of living with her in a house where there were no concierges, stewards, or anyone else to watch them together, to note when they came and went and where they slept, made his stomach turn over. It made him sick with desire, with possibility, with danger, but it also thrilled him. Though he kept his voice serene, he spoke slowly and tried to express his emotions in each word. "I look forward to seeing you tonight."

She seemed to weigh his words and didn't reply immediately. At last, she said, "When will you arrive at the house?"

He checked his wristwatch. "Late. Nine or ten this evening."

She sighed. "Who will take care of David?"

"Why not you?"

"I have to go to La Pomme."

"Your audition?"

"The audition was yesterday. And Monsieur Bellegarde must have liked what he heard. He's asked me to sing at his club tonight. He has a trio that will accompany me and . . ."

"Congratulations," he broke in, smiling into the telephone. "This is absolutely the best news." He laughed and, hearing him, she did as well. The weight of last night's experience began to lift from him. Suddenly, he believed things would turn out all right. He wouldn't be caught—the Negresco had the name of the newspaper *La Gazette*, but nothing more.

28

Before stepping onto the low stage at La Pomme, Laura glanced around the large room. Half the tables were filled, no more.

Monsieur Bellegarde visited with his regular customers—bowing, inquiring, encouraging, laughing. He seemed to share none of her trepidation.

The usual fear before a performance made her jittery. She sipped at a whiskey and soda and practiced the breathing exercises she'd learned in the choir at Smith College. Her throat wasn't as relaxed as she wanted it to be, and she tried to focus on her complete anonymity. There was nothing to lose, was there? Unknown faces made up the audience. Henry hadn't arrived, and she'd left David at the unfamiliar but pretty house in the rue Dosne. She could sing without fear of consequences. A month ago this situation might have been liberating. Tonight she could think only of how nice it would be if Henry and David could be present for her Paris debut.

But her being alone was a minor disappointment compared with the summons she'd received late that morning from her father. A messenger from the Crillon had delivered a telegram that read:

> War coming, you must leave Paris.
> My mistake to let you travel.
> You and H must leave for USA within a fortnight.
> No argument permitted.
> Barton Powell

She'd wanted to scream, to cry out that she wouldn't and couldn't leave, but with David standing near her, she'd simply explained to him that her father had written with concern about a possible war. Her father, she'd noted silently, might be correct. Yet he was far away, on the other side of the Atlantic, and did he really know the truth about peace in France? She'd folded the note and pushed it into her pocket, continuing to visit with David as if nothing had changed, as if she could remain in Europe for the several months that she and Henry had planned.

Now, at La Pomme, Bellegarde caught her eye and nodded. It was time.

She took a final sip of her whiskey and stood. Straightening her dress, she stepped onto the stage and smiled at the trio—Étienne, Lucien, and Gilbert—each in turn. Then she breathed deeply, in and out, very slowly and then turned to the half-filled room, where a few of the patrons watched her with interest and a few others with skepticism. Not smiling at the small crowd, projecting a confidence she didn't feel, she moved close to the microphone and bowed her head—the signal for the trio to begin.

Her first set would be the songs she'd done at her audition, including *"Le marins ça fait des voyages"* and *"Mon cœur est au coin d'une rue."* From there she'd move on to "Never Let Go," another Charlie Hawthorne number she liked. After a short rest, she'd return for a second set that would be filled with lighter songs that relied on humor and wit. She'd end with Hammer Smith's popular number "New Life."

Halfway through *"Mon cœur est au coin d'une rue,"* her legs stopped shaking, her lungs relaxed and gained a nice rhythm, and she projected her voice out over the room at the volume and in the timbre she chose. Once again, she found that she could control this part of her life and derive success from it. Her voice and her ability and desire to stand in front of a room of strangers and sing to them, perform for them, hadn't failed her before tonight, and they weren't failing her now. Her feigned confidence became genuine. Her movements loosened. All at once she began to enjoy herself more thoroughly than she did anywhere else.

The people at the tables clapped politely, some enthusiastically, after the first song. She said, "*Merci, merci,*" and began the second. Over time, more patrons came in through the door to her left, and she ignored them to focus on the back of the room and the first notes of "They Can't Take That Away from Me," a Fred Astaire song that had been big in America the previous year. And then she saw Henry and David take an empty table to the right of the stage.

Her voice didn't crack. It held the higher notes toward the end of the second verse. Yet she felt herself warm, sensed that her neck had turned slightly pink. Her confidence was replaced by elation. As unobtrusively as possible, she raised an eyebrow and smiled at them.

They waved openly and excitedly. Henry was haggard and unshaven but cheerful; David looked adorable with short hair, tanned face, bright eyes, and a wide grin, but he was still too thin.

When she'd sung aboard the *Île de France*, Henry's presence had irked her. Now she was glad for it. His calm demeanor eased her nerves. He supported her singing—he was the only man who did. And in that moment, having him in her corner meant the world.

Patrons across the room—and not only the two who knew her at the table to the right of the stage—applauded with enthusiasm the moment she'd completed the song. She gave a slight bow and thanked the group. As she prepared to begin another, she noticed with some satisfaction that even as new people were arriving at the nightclub, none had left. Perhaps she could hold their attention after all. Perhaps it wasn't just her blond hair and skimpy black dress. Perhaps they wanted to hear her voice. God, she hoped so.

She turned to the trio and smiled, and they began the opening bars of Hammer Smith's up-tempo number. When she and the trio charged into the first verse, some members of the audience stood and clapped to the beat. She hiked up her already-short dress and belted out:

It's a strange thing,
We no longer have a king.

But why all the hurt
About the length of a skirt?

I've had enough control.
Now it's time to be bold.
We aren't going back there,
When we can live without a care.

The crowd at La Pomme laughed and clapped loudly. David had jumped up from the table and was dancing in front of the stage, gyrating crazily, eyes wide as he spun like a drunken top. She spread her arms, flicked her wrists, and sang the chorus:

Let's hear it for expression,
Not just an impression.
Let's leave behind the knife
And discover a new life!
A new life!
A new life!

As she finished, most of the crowd was singing along with her. She bowed and thanked them, their cries of approbation loud in her ears, their standing ovation giving her the sense that she'd climbed Mount Everest and was standing on top of the world.

"La Perle!" Monsieur Bellegarde shouted.

"La Perle!" his patrons called to her.

Waving to them, blowing a kiss to the audience, she bowed a second time and glanced at Henry.

He was standing along with everyone else, clapping and smiling at her. As she beamed at him, she accepted her desire and decided that the next time he drew close and kissed her while his warm hands gently touched her skin, she wouldn't push him away.

Later, as the taxi crossed over the Seine via the pont du Carrousel, the lights of the bridges and the buildings reflected like luminous confetti in the river down to Notre Dame, standing regally on the Île de la Cité, and to their left, up to the area of le Grand Palais. As David slept between them, she turned to look at Henry and found him already watching her.

His eyes held hers. She could hear his breath. She could hear her own breath.

29

Darkness surrounded them in the large bedroom. His hand touched her side. Its warmth and firmness made her yearn for it to move all over her.

Will he kiss me again? she asked herself in the moment before he did.

Desirous of him in a way she'd never felt with anyone, she met his lips and put her arms around him. His hands pressed against the small of her back, making her spine tingle all the way up to her head, and pulled her close. Through her summer dress she could feel him harden, a warning but also a dare.

She couldn't see him clearly, and she wanted to admire him when he removed his shirt, but she wouldn't switch on the light in case he became disappointed with her figure. Perhaps her modest breasts would bore him. Would he want a taller, fuller, more dramatically shaped woman?

Yet he kissed her again and made no movement away from her.

"*Oh . . .*" She shivered involuntarily as goose bumps appeared on her arms. She made to turn around, to seek in the bed a shelter from her excitement, but when she faced away from him, he held her hips, and then, when she was still, he reached up for the five buttons at the back of her dress. Nervously lifting her hair with her hands, she looked down, exposing her neck to him. His lips touched her there, and she tried not to sigh but couldn't help the sound that came from her.

One button, two, three.

He parted the linen and touched her shoulder blades, causing her to jump—and then laugh to hide her pleasure.

Four and five.

Her back was exposed down to her waist, her panties within reach of his hands. Quietly, without hurry, she slipped the straps of the dress from her shoulders, let down the fabric, and stepped aside. After laying the dress over the chair to her right, she faced him, wearing only panties and heels. Unable to speak, she stood with her arms tensely at her sides, hoping that he'd act again, that his desire equaled hers. His reaching for her would be the only way to know for certain. He let her wait for what seemed like an hour but was closer to fifteen seconds.

Silence surrounded them. She could hear her breaths as she trembled once, and then she was still.

His hands began touching her everywhere. Her hair and her shoulders, her stomach and her breasts, which began to ache delightfully. It was then she pulled back the duvet, sat on the bed, removed her shoes, and waited for him to undress, which he did with such haste that his shirt ripped.

They laughed, and that laugh diminished their seriousness and gave them permission to enjoy themselves, though she wouldn't allow him the ultimate privilege. To his—and her—disappointment.

Later, she lay with him curled round her, their heat mixing pleasantly. It was then that she remembered her father's telegram, and the idyll of romance faded, if only slightly.

"I've heard from my father," she said.

"What did he say?"

"He said it was a mistake to allow us to visit Europe. He said war is coming and we can't be here when it does. We have to leave Paris within two weeks."

"How can he make that decision?" Henry complained in a soft voice. "He isn't here. He doesn't know that we're safe in Paris. Whatever I saw down in Nice, it wasn't enough to start a war."

She shook her head into the pillow. "He doesn't know, but he can still make the decision for us. What matters is whether we obey him."

Henry caressed the skin at the small of her back, giving her pleasurable goose bumps. "What will we do?" he asked.

"Oh, Henry. I don't know. What can we do? His telegram said 'No argument permitted,' as if we're children and God forbid we disagree with him."

Henry kissed the back of her head. "Wouldn't you like to stay?"

"Of course I'd like to stay, you idiot." She patted his arm to show she wasn't upset with him. "At least for now, I'm a success at La Pomme. I'm in Paris, and it's beautiful. And I'm with you and David. Do you think I want to give up singing and go home and marry some dullard from Saint Paul?"

"I'm from Saint Paul."

"You're different. I thought you were like the others, but you're not. I've never known a spy before. Or a journalist."

He laughed. "My career at both will be short."

"It doesn't matter. You want to try new things, to do something other than what everyone else does. I do too. And that wanting has gotten us this far, but to have my father pull the rug out from under us isn't fair."

She heard Henry sigh. "But your father pays for everything, doesn't he?"

"You're right about that. If we don't obey, you'll lose your job and he won't give us the money we need to live. Not enough for me or you or David. We'd be broke in Paris, and my singing won't earn much."

He considered what she'd told him. "Do you think," he asked, "that your father knows more than we do, about a war?"

"Maybe. Or he senses it. Maybe his company has received more orders for weapons."

"It has. I got a large one from the British, but I don't see Britain attacking Germany, not unless Germany attacks first. Hitler talks about uniting the German-speaking peoples of Europe, not about making

France part of Germany. So I think we're safe here, at least for now, if your father would let us stay."

She rubbed his shoulder, hoping he was right and that they could find a way to remain. *Not now,* she thought. *I can't go now, not after being naked with Henry, not after my night at La Pomme. I'd have to give up far too much if we left now.* "There doesn't seem to be a way out," she said, "but we'll think of something."

Henry's voice rose in volume. "I'd like to stay for the several months we planned. If we go back to America, I'm not sure what would happen."

She kissed his chest. "Happen between us, you mean?"

"Yes."

"We couldn't continue—my parents wouldn't permit it."

"We'd be acquaintances."

"Not even that, I'm afraid. Everything is different at home. I'm different. You're different."

"No," he said. "Our worlds are different, that's all."

"Well, that's enough. Enough to keep us apart."

She hadn't meant this last comment to sound so final, but it did, and she didn't amend it. The word *apart* hung between them, and she feared it and knew it was true and powerful. She knew it was real.

30

This won't last, Henry told himself. *This house is leased, and so is this life with Laura.*

He walked through the rooms, not quite believing his good luck. The house had a blinding-white exterior and a small balcony on the third story, with a wrought iron railing and blue-glazed ceramic pots filled with *jasmin de virginie, circée,* and *jacinthe d'orient.* In the maid's room was a bed in which nobody slept, but they'd soon find someone who could help with the housework. The second floor had three bedrooms, and they used the spare to store their trunks and other luggage. The now-familiar master bedroom contained a large bed with a walnut headboard and a white duvet, an armoire, and a single overstuffed chair in ivory silk with a pattern of light-blue fleurs-de-lis. On the wall near the armoire was a painting of Mont Sainte-Victoire that resembled, and might be, a Cézanne. Henry had never imagined living in such a place, and yet here he was.

He stood in the small backyard, which was bordered by the high walls of the neighboring buildings. A brick patio with a teak table and chairs looked out over a small lawn with beds of ferns and small evergreens trimmed into perfect cones. In the morning sun David was playing on the patio with toy soldiers left by a previous occupant. Henry touched his head and went inside, along the center hallway. The ground floor had twelve-foot ceilings and herringbone parquet floors except in the foyer, which had been finished with tiles of gray-and-white marble.

The living room had a molded ceiling, an ornate crystal chandelier, and a large fireplace surrounded by a mantel of carved marble. Its furniture, in ivory silk, was delicate, hand-carved, and very old. Already he pictured himself reading and working in the main-floor library, which was stocked with the novels of Stendhal and Balzac as well as modern fare by Waugh, Isherwood, and Maugham. To the side of the low hearth were a heavy oak desk and a comfortable leather chair, and it was here that he'd presently set down the events at Port Lympia in Nice.

Sitting on the edge of the desk, looking out the casement windows at the quiet street, he realized he was happy. Everything had changed. The sun was warmer, the sky bluer, and the tree limbs in the small backyard danced in the breeze. His skin burned pleasantly wherever Laura touched it. Affection for Laura and David infused his being. Anything was possible.

And yet it wasn't. This time and place and makeshift little family would soon vanish. *Perish* was the word in his mind. Every third thought the grave—and the grave was his departure from Paris, his abandonment of David, his separation from Laura upon landing in New York. A return to the New World meant living in the old way, and the old way made him feel dead. It was his new life in the Old World that made his heart beat faster.

He bent over his desk and wrote a story—that's really all it was, containing facts but no opinions—and telephoned a courier to deliver it to Levy at *La Gazette*.

31

At the Café des Patriotes that afternoon, Levy greeted him with enthusiasm, though Henry noticed the fatigue in the older man's face. Yet even with dark semicircles hanging below his hooded but visibly bloodshot eyes, Levy smiled broadly, lit a Gauloise after offering one to Henry (who took it and this time didn't cough after lighting it), and sat down with a jaunty air.

"Your article was *spéciale*," he pronounced, having received it by courier a few hours before. "You captured the atmosphere: the filthy docks, the smell of salt and dead fish, the rough-looking men who handled the guns. Too bad you didn't get a better look them."

Henry shrugged. His article hadn't included a description of James Cagney or of his flight from the hotel.

"You're a better journalist than you led me to believe," Levy continued. "So good and at such bargain wages that I'll offer you a second assignment, yes? You'd go to Metz. An informant has told us the guns arrived early this morning."

"Then you have everything you need."

Levy shook his head and exhaled up into the awning. "Our informant is too young."

"How young?"

"Fifteen or sixteen."

Henry felt his brow rising in disbelief. "You don't trust him?"

Levy shook his head. "The informant is a girl, and I don't trust her enough to publish a report, though we believe she's honest."

"Tell me," Henry said, leaning forward, "how a girl came into contact with crates of submachine guns."

Levy grimaced. "A bad story."

"If I'm to trust and work with her, I must know."

"She's of German descent," Levy began, his voice lowered. "The German language is spoken in her house, and her father and brothers have affinity for all things east of the Moselle, especially the policies of Herr Hitler."

Henry leaned forward, until his face was inches from Levy's. "She's informing on her family?"

"Yes."

"How did she communicate with you?"

Levy shook his head. "Not with me. Through her schoolteacher, whose sister works with those of us who oppose the Germans. More than that I cannot say, except her name is Mademoiselle Koeppel and I will have her meet you in Metz, if you choose to help us."

Henry raised a hand and ordered an espresso. He wondered about this girl who was willing to betray her own blood. Might she be playing a double game? How could he know? But the overwhelming question for which he hadn't received an answer was *Why him?* He narrowed his eyes, hoping to appear mildly threatening, and asked, "If you and Richard Crescent knew the guns would be unloaded at Nice and you know the crates have arrived in Metz, why not call the gendarmerie? Why not send a staff reporter to observe the smuggling?"

Levy sipped his espresso. "This is a complicated matter."

"Why not use the man who got you the information in the first place?"

"That man is dead."

Henry was quiet.

"Yes, Monsieur Salter. He gave us the information, and then he was shot a hundred meters from his house. The gendarmerie explained it as street crime, as robbery, because our man's wallet had been taken. But it was not street crime."

"I'm very sorry. But all the more reason the gendarmerie should watch the docks and make arrests."

Levy crushed his Gauloise in the ashtray between them. "We want to know who is commanding these operations. The gendarmerie cannot observe, for they are observed. But you can slip between the nets. You're invisible. So now we ask you to visit Metz and find the guns."

As Levy had described the job in Metz, a feeling akin to static electricity had raced over his skin, worrisome but enticing. "I'll consider going to Metz," he said at last, smoking in silence while Levy lit another cigarette and made no response. "Have you found me a pseudonym?"

Levy flashed his espresso-stained teeth. "We published your first story without a byline. But if you write about Metz, you'll be the Scarlet Pimpernel. And because he was English, our enemies won't suspect you. You will be my most famous correspondent."

He sat up, unexpectedly proud of this accomplishment. "Famously invisible, I hope." As he drank his espresso, he waited for Levy to respond to his unasked questions about a passport for David. When the editor said nothing, he spoke calmly but firmly. "Perhaps you've read the recent news from America in the *Herald Tribune*. No? Well. A priest, Father Coughlin, rails against communists and Jews. And you must know of next month's conference in Évian-les-Bains, where France, Britain, the United States, and other countries will decide if they'll take Jewish refugees from what is becoming Hitler's Europe. The British don't like the Jews. Neither do Roosevelt and the Americans. In this unhappy world my Jewish son has no passport. So, I will go to Metz in the next few days. I'll investigate the crates of submachine guns, and the Scarlet Pimpernel will write his article. But he won't give it to you until my son has an American passport—and I need the passport within two weeks. *Est-ce que vous comprenez?*"

Levy groaned. "I'll contact Mr. Crescent—again—and discuss the matter of the passport. I know the situation with refugees is difficult, but

I help where I can, you must believe me. Please, let me know when you intend to be in Metz, and I will get word to Mademoiselle Koeppel." He placed a few coins on the table and meant to leave.

"One moment," Henry said. "Let me give you the information for Crescent." He took out a pen and, on Levy's copy of the morning's *La Gazette*, wrote his full name, Laura's as Laura Powell Salter, and the boy's as David Powell Salter. After adding his new address in the rue Dosne, he returned the newspaper to Levy and left the café.

He watched Levy waddle across the street in his rumpled suit, gray smoke rushing upward from the cigarette in his mouth, hands in his pockets, newspaper tucked under one arm, head angled upward as if he were searching the sky for the Luftwaffe.

Neither of them had noticed a tall barrel-chested man standing to the side of the café, pretending to look into a shop window as he watched them. When they parted, the large man turned and followed Henry.

32

Near the end of their first full week in Paris, Laura walked over to the rue Scribe, where she sent her father the following telegram:

> Father. Will book passage after purchase wedding gown.
>> Home in one month.
>> Laura

Would her telegram convince her father to let her stay in Paris awhile longer? No. No, she didn't think so. Perhaps it would give her more time in the city, perhaps not. Silently, she braced herself for his inevitable response. Barton Powell, wealthy arms manufacturer, sought to destroy any opposition to his wishes, especially, she knew from experience, when that opposition came from her.

That evening, a Sunday, was the only night when la Perle didn't perform. But the other six nights she worked, though didn't consider her singing work. It was too new, and it made her feel too good, for it to resemble an obligation.

I'm alive, she often thought as she took the stage. *I can be the singer I've wanted to be, the woman I've yearned to be.*

And the men who came to La Pomme to hear her sing, the men who bought her drinks and offered her dinner and tried to take her home—these she deflected with a now-practiced grace and firm refusal.

Yet they continued to appear, Frenchmen and also a German named Frederick Abendroth, forming the core of a worshipful audience that made the name la Perle echo through the sixth arrondissement.

But now, as they walked home from dinner at a bistro on the place Victor Hugo, she wondered for how long. The month her father had demanded? The three months she'd wanted?

Yet even these questions couldn't stem a growing excitement in her chest, a quickening heartbeat that told her soon, soon, she'd be lying in Henry's arms, as she did each night. Not once had she asked him to sleep in a separate bedroom. She wanted him with her, kissing her, lying against her, touching her—and was that so wrong?

Yes, she was certain it was, in many ways. But perhaps in other ways she deserved his affection, having lived for years without any. Her reverie on this quiet night ended quickly, though, and shockingly.

In the darkness between two streetlamps, an older man and woman were crawling on the ground, being helped up by a group of two young men and a young woman. No, she realized, that wasn't right. Henry gripped her arm as she faltered, unable to comprehend the scene before her.

The group wasn't helping the older couple. They were beating them. Kicking them and laughing. The young woman cracked an empty wine bottle against the old man's head. He fell prostrate onto the flagstones, but the bottle didn't break. She raised it, threateningly, sneering as the old woman cowered.

The beating remained in shadows. The young men might have knives or guns, Laura knew. She took David's hand and pulled him to her, away from the group and its prey.

◆ ◆ ◆

Henry stood where he was, silently watching the young men and comparing his physique with theirs.

A step forward, two steps. Now he could see they were younger than twenty, wiry and thin. Realizing he was no match for both men, he made a calculation and moved forward. Calmly as he could, he took a Gauloise from his platinum cigarette case and lit it. He buttoned his double-breasted gray suit and made sure his shoes' hard leather soles made a firm sound on the pavement. As he drew near, they looked up at him. With the nearest streetlight behind him, he knew he was in shadow, his face made slightly red by the burning cigarette. He kept going, closer toward them. The woman let the empty wine bottle dangle from her left hand and moved away from the old man and woman, away from Henry.

In French, he said, very softly, "What are you doing?"

The young men looked at him, their confidence waning before this authority figure. "This Jew and his wife have been robbing my family for years," answered one of them.

"Who are they?"

"The Tschelikovs. They have the butcher shop halfway down the avenue Bugeaud. They've cheated our mothers and fathers. They're merde."

Henry was quiet a moment, as if taking their allegations seriously. At last he said, "If this old man and his wife have cheated your families for years, why haven't you gone to a different butcher? There are many in the *seizième*. Why would you allow yourselves to be cheated over and over?"

To this the young men had no answer.

He took another step. "Leave these old people. I'll take care of them."

The men moved backward a few meters. At last they turned and walked away, the woman following them. One of the men yelled at Henry, *"Défenseur des juifs!"*—Jew lover!—and then all three were gone.

Relieved he hadn't had to fight, he knelt by the old man and eased him into a sitting position. The face was bloody, yet the man was conscious. "How bad is the pain?" he asked.

"*De rien, de rien,*" said the man, proud but straining to catch his breath.

With his wife's help the man stood and began limping in the direction of his apartment. He paused, one hand on the back of his head, and looked back at Henry. "*Merci.* God has sent you."

"*Non, monsieur. De rien,*" Henry told him.

He heard soft footfalls behind him and felt David's soft hand grasping his. He squeezed it and looked at Laura. She was elegant and beautiful in the dim light, her face tilted downward to where the man had fallen. When she realized the black spot in which she was standing was the old man's blood, she stepped to the side.

Sweat dripped from Henry's forehead, and he gritted his teeth in anger. He'd just saved the lives of an older couple, in this small way changing history. He found himself wanting to do more. Without considering what the consequences might be, he announced in a harsh tone, "I'm going to Metz tomorrow. A journalism assignment for *La Gazette.*"

She must have known what his resolution meant, but she didn't try to prevent him from leaving. This would be another trip of his that she'd have to endure. She turned to him and to David. "Let's go home. It will be safe there."

They walked in silence, David between them, each holding one of his hands. Passing under the streetlamp, they were briefly illuminated in a golden haze, and then the dark closed around them.

33

In the morning Laura heard David pad into her bedroom. He was rumpled, his hair askew, his pajama top half-buttoned, revealing his slender chest. She slid over, and he sprawled over the duvet. In a rush of solicitude for him, she decided that she'd never send him to an institution. For there, his goodness and innocence wouldn't survive. No, she must find someone to take care of him—someone who'd develop as much affection for him as she had in just a short while. She leaned down to kiss him good morning. For a moment, she recognized that her idea of sending him to the Red Cross was recurring less and less frequently in her mind.

He moved his head and rested it on her upper arm. "What will we do today?"

"What would you like to do?"

He lay quietly for a moment and then said, "I'd like to have lots of ice cream."

"All right." *Why not spoil him?* she thought, fatalistically. *We have only a month together.* This fact made her chest cold, and she had to breathe in with care. No, she wouldn't hint at what was to come. Brightly, she asked, "How about *une glace?*" An ice cream.

"I would like that."

Running her hands through his newly short hair, she decided to bring up a difficult subject. "Soon it will be September," she said, "and the beginning of school."

"I don't want to go."

She laughed. "I realize that. But you'll find you enjoy some of it, just like everyone else. But first we must have a passport for you."

"Then I hope we don't get a passport."

"No, David. A passport is important. It will keep you safe from the Germans and even from the French. It will prove that you belong, and they won't be able to . . . to . . ." Her voice trailed off. Why describe the horrors he'd already experienced?

He was quiet.

She decided to skip to a concern she hadn't shared even with Henry. "You've missed so much school," she said. "Why don't we hire a tutor for you?"

"No. A tutor will call the police, and they'll take me away."

"A friendly tutor who won't hurt you."

"I don't want a tutor."

"Yes, I know you don't." She touched his shoulder to reassure him— the question of a tutor would wait for another day—and to introduce an important change that she'd decided to make. "David, I need your help today. I need to buy an engagement ring so people believe Henry and I are married. Not because we're married or we're going to be married—we're not. You see, there are men who come to La Pomme who are bothering me because they think I'm unmarried, and I need them to go away. Do you think you could help me find something suitable?"

He turned on his side and looked up at her. His expression had grown serious. "I know about rings."

She nodded. "Yes, that's why I'm asking for your advice."

"What kind of ring do you want?"

"I'm not sure. You'll need to help me choose."

"Would you like a diamond?"

"Possibly."

"I will help you," he announced, sitting up. "I will help."

34

Later, walking along the rue Saint-Honoré, they passed the distinctive green cross of a *pharmacie*. Laura asked David to wait on the sidewalk while she quickly bought something. Inside, she browsed the cramped space but couldn't find what she needed. Embarrassed, she persevered nonetheless by asking the pharmacist for help.

As soon as she began her description, he laid a hand on her arm, nodded, and said, *"Oui, oui, ici."*

He led her to a narrow section by the back counter. A small round sponge and vinegar.

She paid and thanked him, and he put them into a bag.

It might take practice, but she knew how the procedure worked. She'd soak the sponge in vinegar and, while sitting on the edge of the bathtub, place it inside her and up against her cervix. The vinegar would burn a little, but this was the method her mother, furtively but urgently, had described to her some years ago. Her mother who'd told her she mustn't sleep with a man until marriage (meaning, she assumed, until an engagement). But after spending night after night with Henry—both of them naked and desirous and hungry for each other and the single thing they both wanted to do—she'd begun to consider that single thing.

"What's in the bag?" David asked when she'd rejoined him out on the sidewalk.

She hesitated, wondering how to respond. "Just something for the kitchen," she said.

He gave no response, only walking quickly along, glancing in the shop windows. She was relieved that the mysteries of the kitchen held no interest for him.

Farther along the rue Saint-Honoré, near the Cour des comptes, they found a jeweler. It was an old shop with a stone floor and walls papered in silk the color of eggplant. The glass cases had been polished until the jewelry glittered under the lights. A small man, dressed in a blue-and-white plaid waistcoat with a blue iris in his buttonhole, introduced himself as Joel Frisch. He asked if they cared for an espresso, and when both of them nodded (David uncertainly), he glanced at his assistant, a plain younger man, who disappeared into the back room.

Laura had intentionally dressed well for this outing. She wanted whichever jeweler they visited to pay her attention and not believe that she was only looking until her husband would arrive with a checkbook. For this occasion she wore a chocolate-colored Chanel suit and her ever-present string of pearls and matching earrings, and she carried a small aquamarine clutch she'd found at Bergdorf's in New York and the small bag from the pharmacy. For only the second time she wore the dragonfly pin that David had stolen from the busybody on the *Île de France*.

"A beautiful pin," Monsieur Frisch cooed as he leaned closer to examine it, his skin smelling of coriander. "Is it Lalique, perhaps from the 1920s?"

She smiled at him. "Yes, I think so."

"Late 1920s," David said.

Monsieur Frisch looked down at David with astonishment. "Are you a jeweler, young man?"

"No, monsieur. My father was a jeweler." He'd followed Laura's lead and was dressed handsomely in a charcoal gray suit, polished black lace-up shoes, a light-red shirt with cuffs fastened with Henry's golden apple links, and no tie. He'd bathed, and his skin was lightly tanned from playing in the backyard and taking walks with Henry. His eyes brightened as he showed off his expertise. "I'd guess the pin is from 1929, before the work became thinner and smaller."

Monsieur Frisch smiled at David and must have been uncertain how to deal with a boy who, at least in the matter of the pin, knew more than he did. Then he fastened his eyes upon Laura. "How may I be of service?"

"I'm looking for a ring," she said.

"*Très bien*, mademoiselle. What kind of ring?"

"A ring such as a young man might buy for me." She blushed. "An engagement ring. *Une bague de fiançailles.*"

Ever so briefly, the man's face clouded. But he recovered and smiled at her. "We have many such rings. May I direct you this way?" he said, leading them to a large case, in which lay three or four dozen rings on a field of black velvet.

David peered through the glass. "My father," he said to Laura, "told me that settings that are too bright or have too much metal are bad. He always said that simpler is better."

She smiled inwardly at this transfer of knowledge from a man she'd never met, a man whose son she now cared for. "Which would be best for me?" she asked.

"Hmm," he said, glowing with pride at her request for his help. He pointed. "These, over here."

She followed his hand to a corner of the case in which the stones and settings were modest. "You're sure?"

He shook his head. "No. But you have slender fingers and small hands. A large diamond would look too big."

She nodded, thinking about this. Her mother had a two-carat diamond, but her mother's hands were thicker than hers. While she didn't want to be ostentatious, she felt it necessary to let the male patrons of La Pomme know that she was unavailable. They'd become a flattering but growing problem for her, especially since Frederick Abendroth, a German businessman with striking blond hair, had begun showing her gracious but unrelenting attention. Although she'd told him that she was engaged, he didn't seem to believe her. Perhaps having a ring on her finger would convince him. She looked up at Monsieur Frisch. "May we see several of the rings my nephew has pointed out?"

"*Oui,* mademoiselle," he replied. *"Mais bien sûr."* He took a key from his pocket and unlocked and opened the glass door. Once he removed the tray, he set several of the rings on a black velvet cloth he'd spread across the top of the case. Then he crossed his hands in front of him and watched in silence.

She decided that she preferred the four- to the six-pronged setting. *Less metal,* she thought. A few stones were sapphires, like her dragonfly pin, but most were diamonds. She knew the sapphires were pretty but might not complement certain colors that she liked to wear—black, for example—when she was singing. Yes, she'd choose a diamond, or diamonds. "I don't think the sapphires are right for me," she said. David nodded sagely, leading her to smile at him. *He is,* she thought, *my little wise man.* "Should I try on a solitaire?"

"Yes," he nodded, pointing to a square-cut diamond of not inconsiderable size.

As she slid it onto the third finger of her left hand, this errand became more than a purchase of jewelry necessary to keep away Abendroth and other men. It became monumentally important. One of these rings, she knew, would mark her fantasy engagement to Henry, though she knew it could never be consummated. While she was on this important errand, his absence filled her with a presentiment of the loss she'd feel when they parted upon their return to America. Suddenly she wished he weren't on a train to Metz but here, with her, helping to choose a ring. Imagining him slipping it on her finger, she quavered with pleasure. How exciting this moment would have been, and what a surprise, as they'd never considered the possibility of such a thing. Yet because of David's presence, her mood remained buoyant. She turned to him with a questioning glance.

"It isn't right," he said of the square-cut diamond.

"True enough." She removed it and tried a solitaire in a brilliant cut. It was better than the first and seemed the appropriate size for her hand. She estimated it to be one carat. But she wasn't convinced and took it off.

She leaned over the case and looked where David was pointing.

"Try this one," he said.

As Monsieur Frisch withdrew it, he murmured, "Very beautiful, for an engagement or a gift or perhaps as an *objet magnifique*."

Surprising her, the platinum band with channel-set diamonds fit her slender finger. Though the ring's meaning was ambiguous as to engagement and marriage, it was without question a ring that a man would give. "Do you like it?" she asked David.

"Very much," he said, his fingers running over the diamonds in the channel and then tracing the platinum band.

She smiled at Monsieur Frisch, who was looking at her expectantly. "I'd like this one."

He grinned. "Excellent choice, mademoiselle. I have a handsome box. Would you like me to wrap it?"

She shook her head. "No, I'll wear it, please. But I'd like the box as well."

"Mais bien sûr." After turning to his assistant, who went to the back room for the box, he indicated the espresso the assistant had brought.

"Thank you," she said, taking the demitasse. The caffeine raised her spirits further, and she decided that even though she, and not Henry, had bought the ring, she liked wearing it and enjoyed the added warmth she felt for him when it was around her finger. While she'd have to explain to him that the ring was meant to deter Abendroth and the other men who'd invited her to share a drink or more, she hoped he'd appreciate the symbolism of her decision.

She signed her name to American Express traveler's checks sufficient to cover the purchase; Monsieur Frisch handed David a small bag containing the pretty green box where she could store the ring; and she and David walked out into the bright sunshine and the July heat. She

turned onto the rue Saint-Florentin and began heading in the direction
of their new house.

David pulled on her hand. "Miss Laura?"

"Yes?"

"Aren't you forgetting something?"

She checked her finger. The ring was there, and very beautiful in
daylight. The strap of her handbag was looped around her shoulder. "I
don't think so," she said. "Am I?"

He nodded vigorously and said, *"Une glace."*

She laughed and leaned over and kissed his cheek, and they turned
and walked east in the rue de Rivoli, until they found an ice cream shop.
As they went, her delight faded as she considered the danger in which
Henry must certainly be.

Oh God, she thought, dizziness coming over her. *If he's hurt or . . .*

She dropped David's hand, halted, and pretended to look into a
shop window as she caught her breath. In the clear reflection she saw
her pretty face and her long neck. But her eyes showed fear that was
almost terror.

35

Metz was east of Paris and near the German border. This was all Henry knew about it.

He arrived in the early afternoon and walked into the center of town and along the rue d'Estrées, where he found the sidewalk café Le Corbeau Nid. After choosing a table off to the side, he ordered a ham sandwich, fried potatoes, and a Pilsner from across the German border. He took off his solid navy blue suit coat and let the sun flash off his blue-and-white checked shirt. A wind coming up from the south soothed him on the hot day. As he drank the Pilsner, he looked over at Saint-Étienne Cathedral and its Gothic tower, flying buttresses, and nave that reached far up into the sky, and the city's limestone buildings, which had a golden tone.

While his head was turned as he watched people stroll through the square, the chair opposite his was pulled back. He looked up and saw a young woman in a rose-colored sundress. Her black hair was tied with rose-colored ribbon into a ponytail, and her face and eyes were dark.

"Are you Monsieur Salter?" she asked.

He stood. "Mademoiselle Koeppel?"

"Alisha," she said, drawing out her name slowly.

"Good." He waved toward the empty chair.

As they sat down, he could see that beneath the loose-fitting dress, her ample breasts, not constrained by a brassiere, pushed against the fabric. Her face reddened as she looked at him, and she lowered her eyes and stared at his cigarette case.

"Would you like one?" He took up the case, opened it, and held it toward her.

She looked around the café and the square and then smiled. "Yes, please." She reached for a cigarette, and he held out and flicked his lighter. She inhaled gratefully. "Thank you." The cigarette, or perhaps the act of smoking itself, helped her confidence. She sat up straight and watched him, possibly assessing his goodwill. "I don't want my family hurt."

"I don't intend to hurt anyone. I won't even mention a name."

She glanced at the square and the sidewalks. Apparently satisfied, she looked at him. "I will show you the barn where they keep the crates."

He leaned forward. "Do crates often arrive at your farm?"

"Yes."

"Where do they go?"

She proudly raised her face. "My father and brothers don't tell me, except I overhear them. They've formed a secret army that will join the Germans during the invasion. A stupid game, with fake German uniforms. My God, they're like boys playing soldier. But I act innocent and come here, to the city. I go to the *cinéma* with my school friends." She aggressively inhaled her cigarette, held the smoke in her lungs for quite a long time, and exhaled through lips in the shape of an O. "My family says nothing. And I ask nothing and pretend to be dumb."

"Smart girl," he said, concluding that perhaps she was honest.

She squinted at him and pushed out her chest. Despite his typically good manners, he allowed his eyes to delve for a moment into her décolletage. He saw the faint redness of her hardened nipples. When he raised his eyes, she lifted her chin and looked at him defiantly. "I am not a girl."

His face warmed. He looked down at his platinum case and removed and lit a cigarette, all the while avoiding her eyes and especially her chest. At last he felt sufficiently composed to ask, "Where is your family's land?"

"Southeast of the city, by Ars-Laquenexy."

"Will you take me there?"

She shrugged. "I have no car."

"How did you get here?"

"My oldest brother drove me to my friend's house at the edge of the city."

"Is your brother in Metz?"

She angled her head. "I do not care."

"But how would you explain your talking with me, an American?"

"By now," she said, sighing, "they expect me to talk to all men."

He'd been smiling, but his smile vanished. "Do they expect betrayal?"

She laughed. "No, they expect me to behave like a *putain*, but not to tell of the crates."

He stared at her and then looked away, along the street. As he considered how to get to her family's farm, a green Renault drove by, followed by a motorcycle. Then he made his decision.

36

In the late afternoon Laura left David alone at the house in the rue Dosne and took a taxi to Vionnet, the fashion house at fifty avenue Montaigne. She'd promised her mother that she'd find a bridal gown designed by a celebrated couturier for her eventual wedding—a wedding for which her mother hoped and schemed daily. Laura believed that if she were engaged to marry Henry, she'd be excited to be measured for a gown. But imagining herself making a vow to anyone else, thereby losing her independence forever, made her cringe. Yet she was dutiful, and her mother had told her that she must buy a gown.

Smiling at the salesclerk, she walked around the all-white store, with gowns on hangers along the walls. The clerk asked when her wedding would be, which led her to laugh and explain that she was American and would buy a dress before she returned to Saint Paul, that she had no fiancé, not even a boyfriend. The clerk nodded and said she understood and then brought out drawings of the style of gowns that Madame Vionnet had designed and that could be made, with variations, for her.

Upset by her father's insistence that she return to Saint Paul, she asked, "Which are the most expensive?"

"This style," said the clerk, indicating several drawings, "with lace from Flanders. And the dress may be made more beautiful, and more costly, by adding silver, gold, or stones to it."

"Could you add pearls?"

The clerk nodded. "*Oui*, mademoiselle."

She pointed at a simple dress that would make her look taller than she was. "This would be nice, with pearls here, around the neck." She relished the gown's expense. It would at the same time anger her father and satisfy her mother, a perfect result.

Even as the clerk measured her, the notion of marriage had no reality for her. If she couldn't marry Henry, she wasn't sure who else would be right for her. But the practical side of her realized that life might lead anywhere, even to forbidden places.

37

They walked through Metz as he searched for a particular store, and in the rue Mazelle he found it. From a motorcycle dealer he purchased a small black BMW with saddlebags. It appeared to be unsafe but started easily and cost little. Alisha got on behind him and tucked her dress under her legs.

He turned back to her and said, "Where?"

She directed him along the avenue de Plantières and then southwest in the avenue de Strasbourg until they turned east into the countryside, on the route d'Ars-Laquenexy, in the direction of Germany.

Amid the handsome fields they passed stone and stucco farmhouses with roofs of blackened clay shingles, some barns made of concrete and metal but most of wood and stone. The setting was pastoral and pleasant, despite the overcast sky and the wind. Cows and horses grazed in pastures. He saw fields of corn, wheat, and oats and the occasional village with a handful of houses bordering a main street of less than thirty meters. Beginning to relax, he warmed to this adventure. But then Alisha reached her hands under his suit coat and around his stomach more tightly than was necessary. Her head, too, was angled forward so that her chin rested on his shoulder. Someone on the road would think they were lovers. Perhaps she wished for such a thing.

The head on his shoulder lifted. One of her hands moved from around his stomach and pointed. "We go left, along that dirt road," she said loudly, over the whine of the engine.

He slowed the motorcycle and turned left onto heavily rutted soil mixed with rock. They passed a number of farms and soon came to several in a row. Another, perhaps a hundred meters distant, flew the German flag with its swastika and bands of red, white, and black.

"My house," she told him, "but please turn around. I don't want them to see us."

He stopped, put down his feet, and held the bike steady. This would be different from the work he'd done in Nice. There he'd been passive until he'd run back to the Negresco. Here he'd trespass on another's property by crossing a pasture and entering a barn, exposing himself to discovery and probably violence. Another decision that surprised him: he'd gladly do this job. A cold and thrilling dread surged through his arms and legs. His heart began a staccato beat. He briefly wondered if he was the same man who'd boarded the *Île de France* weeks earlier. At the very least he was discovering elements of his character that would have remained hidden if he hadn't left Saint Paul. *My God,* he thought silently as an image of home came to him. *It's as if that were the old world and this the new.*

"Please," Alisha urged him. "Let's *go*."

He did as she asked, the front tire almost catching in one of the ruts of clay and dirt made by tractors and heavy farm equipment, nearly causing them to spill onto the ground. In a moment they sped west, away from the Koeppel farm, and he tried to remember the route so he could find his way in the night.

He drove several kilometers northwest, to one of the miniature main streets they'd passed. At a nearly empty café they took a table outside, and he ordered a carafe of the red wine kept in a cask behind the counter. The wine, cool and tasting of oak, helped him relax and think how to handle Alisha. She drank a large glass of the wine very quickly and poured another. Without asking, she reached for his cigarette case and lighter, which he'd left on the table, and began smoking. It was warm, and she watched him as she unfastened another button of her dress.

He didn't care to spar with a fifteen-year-old temptress when he should be thinking about his work. It wasn't long before they ordered dinner, and he found a way to make Alisha stop speaking. When he asked about her classes at school, she said nothing. Their pot-au-feu arrived, and she ignored him in favor of her dinner.

Night came to the farms outside Metz. There had been a long overcast dusk, and then, in the blink of an eye, darkness infused the countryside. He and Alisha smoked the last of his cigarettes, he settled with the café's proprietress, and they left.

No vehicles passed them on their return to the Koeppel property. Stars gave the only light in the area, yet there was a ferrous glow in the sky a few kilometers away, above Metz. At the unpaved road, he shut off the headlight and proceeded in darkness. Several hundred yards from her parents' house, he pulled the motorcycle to the side of the dirt road and switched off the engine.

She loosened her arms and climbed off. He turned to look at her but kept his hands on the bike's handlebars. They were alone between two large fields that spread outward and invisibly into the night. Around them everything was quiet except for the wind. Shifting her weight to one foot, she watched him. Though he couldn't see her eyes, he sensed the warmth of her body. She reached for his hand, and he allowed her to take it, thinking she wanted to grasp it in farewell. But she moved it against her sheer dress and pressed his palm to her half-exposed breast.

Immediately he drew back, though her boldness and supple skin aroused him slightly.

"If you want me in Paris," she said and then turned and walked toward the farmhouse.

After she disappeared in the darkness, he pushed the bike into the shallow ditch by the road and up the other side, into the tall grass between the road and the posts to which the farm's wire fencing was attached. There he stood and waited, hoping that since farmers rose early, they'd retire early. He'd avoid waiting too long before approaching the Koeppel barn. But he needed to be sure Alisha didn't confess to her family that she'd informed on them and that a newspaper reporter stood at the edge of their property. For a long time he paced by the fence line, wondering at the Koeppels' duplicity. He suspected the story Alisha's parents and brothers told themselves explained and justified all they did. But that story would have elevated politics over life. His stride accelerating back and forth along the fence, he knew it was right for him to tell what he found here, if he found anything. Hot with anticipation, he was excited and worried to be at the edge of a strange field in the night.

An hour later he chose to trust the girl and approach the stone barn. His dark suit made him invisible, but he knew a dog could smell him, and a farmer wouldn't ignore a hysterical dog in the night. The wind continued to blow from south to north, so his scent wasn't taken in the direction of the house. He fastened the top button of his coat and raised its collar and lapels in order to hide, as best he could, his dress shirt.

As he approached the stone building, he saw that he'd have to cross a pasture containing cows, most of which were quietly munching grass. He threaded himself through the fence and walked in the mud and grass to the barn. The cows looked at him without interest, though a few lowed in his direction. Too many things might alert the farmer to his presence; there wasn't time to search for a window. He walked up to the door and opened it just wide enough to enter and pulled it closed behind him.

In the starlight he saw animals moving about in pens. As he stepped forward, a group of hogs began to squeal and thrash at each other. He froze, feeling his heartbeat in his throat. *The blasted noise,* he thought about the hogs and figured he had at most thirty seconds before Alisha's father or brothers came to investigate. Forcing himself to move, he knew he was about to panic.

In the far corner he discerned two large rectangular shapes, both about two meters high. Covering each was a canvas. He ran to one of them and pulled, but it wouldn't come free.

Goddamnit!

By touch alone he unraveled the knotted rope and drew aside the canvas, exposing the base of a wooden crate. He kicked at one of the slats until it snapped, and then he reached inside, pushing into the straw packaging. His hand found metal. He traced it to be sure but knew it could only be an MP 38 submachine gun.

Then he pulled it out of the straw and stopped breathing. Someone had come into the barn.

38

Standing at the microphone on the small stage at La Pomme, Laura tried to move smoothly and happily, as she usually did. But her efforts only made her more awkward. Failing to anticipate how much breath she needed for the next line, she drew in too little and had to hop roughly over the line, syncopating the words in order to inhale in a single gulp. A beginner's mistake. To prevent her hands from betraying her anxiety, she grasped the microphone tightly.

Her peripheral vision revealed, at the edge of the lights, the presence of Frederick Abendroth. He wore his blond hair straight back and with so much pomade that it looked wet. His skin was fair and his eyes blue. She found him vaguely attractive but also repulsive, and she didn't care for his continued attentions. Before going onstage, she'd reminded him that she was engaged, and she'd made sure that he saw her new ring. Yet he'd only smiled and asked her to travel with him. Berlin was sophisticated, he'd told her. It had great music, though some of it had become degenerate.

Tonight he wore a charcoal gray suit and a white shirt with a narrow black tie. He crossed his long legs and leaned back in his chair. He smoked and watched her. Each time she and the trio ended a song, he set his cigarette in his full lips and clapped with his enormous hands. Never once did he cheer, whistle, or do anything impolite. After her sets he'd order her a kir, and they'd visit. There wasn't a graceful way to avoid him.

Her drink was waiting when she finished "Lover Man." She curt-seyed and then bowed to the large room, which hadn't been full when she'd begun singing a week ago but now had nearly all its tables occu-pied. *A promising start,* she thought. "*Merci,*" she said into the micro-phone. "*Merci.*" She turned and clapped for the trio, blew the room a kiss, and stepped off the low stage.

"You were excellent tonight, la Perle," Abendroth told her, standing and offering her a chair.

"Thank you." She sat and drank deeply, immediately feeling herself grow cooler and calm. A moment ago she'd been alive with energy. Now she was tired. She thought of David, alone at the house, and knew she must leave as soon as she finished her drink. "But my voice wasn't as clear as I wanted it to be." She watched the corners of his lips turn up into a grin and decided he was too pretty to be a man. He was more like a boy, but with a man's appetites.

"You were excellent, excellent," he said. "Why not allow yourself to enjoy how good you are? You are a marvelous singer, and you will be famous, Mademoiselle Powell. Very famous here and in Berlin. You must speak with Pathé. They will make records of your songs."

She laughed, hiding her interest in making recordings. "Thank you, Herr Abendroth. Perhaps I will."

"Don't wait too long, la Perle. And please call me Frederick. You must know that if there is war, the record company may stop work."

She hadn't thought of this. "Won't people listen to music?"

"Yes, they will listen. They will listen to records they have. But new records?" He shrugged. "Men who work at the studios will be forced into the army, and there won't be new recordings. And if Paris is bombed, the record companies will be destroyed."

"Paris, bombed?" she asked. This seemed incredible. War happened in forests or fields, where men dug trenches and set down barbed wire and shot at each other. It wasn't as if there would be warfare in the boulevard Saint-Michel. Or was she wrong? Would Paris be destroyed like Carthage?

"Yes, Mademoiselle Powell. It might be bombed, if the British or French attempt to destroy Berlin. Of course, they will be unsuccessful."

She drank the last of her scarlet-colored cocktail. "I think we must prevent war."

He smiled and nodded his dome-like forehead. "I will do what I can."

"But what can you do? Aren't you only a businessman?"

"Yes, a businessman. For a company that makes kitchen and bathroom fixtures. We are well known in Berlin."

She remembered the leaking faucet on the ground floor bathroom at the house in the rue Dosne. She thought perhaps he could sell her a new one, though she wouldn't tell him her address. "Do you have a showroom?" she asked. "I have a faucet that should be replaced."

His expression was one of great sadness. "No, mademoiselle. Not here, not tonight. We will speak of business another time, yes?"

"Yes. Another time." She stood and nodded at him. "Well, then. Good night. I must go home."

He got up quickly. He was tall and filled her vision. In his presence she felt like a tiny creature. This sensation wasn't always unpleasant, but tonight it was.

"May I walk you home?" he asked.

"Thank you, but no. My fiancé is waiting for me."

"As you wish. Until tomorrow."

She stepped outside, into the lights of the boulevard Raspail, and walked quickly up to the boulevard Saint-Germain. At the corner she found a taxi, climbed into it, and gave directions to her house. As she looked out the window, she saw Abendroth outside La Pomme. He was smoking a cigarette and speaking intently to a thickset man whose hairless scalp was partially covered by a black cap. This short man wasn't looking at Frederick but at the taxi, at her.

39

As quietly as he could, Henry moved around the crate so it was between him and the person who'd entered the barn. In the darkness he hoped he might remain undetected and then remembered how he'd pulled back the canvas that had covered the crate.

A light was switched on. It was overhead, in the middle of the barn, and cast a dim glow over the corner where he stood. Footsteps on the soft dirt and straw rushed toward him.

In that instant he decided that he must survive. He'd run out of choices. It would be the other man or himself. He lifted the MP 38 and hoped the farmer wasn't armed.

Listening to the man's breathing, he saw a hand—of a young rather than an old man—reach for the corner of the canvas and touch the rope. He could tell the man was crouching and below him. "Merde," came the voice.

In one motion he stepped from behind the crate and hammered the stock of the submachine gun into the farmer, catching the stout man in the chest. The man wheezed and doubled over, though not for long. Recovering rapidly, he began to raise a pistol at Henry. Already Henry had drawn back the submachine gun. The man now visible to him, Henry swung hard at his head. There was the thunk of metal on human flesh and bone, and the man crumpled and lay still.

Henry dropped the gun as if it were possessed, swallowing against the nausea that rose from his stomach, and ran through the barn and out the door. He turned and headed west, toward the ditch where he'd left the motorcycle. Already there was commotion in the farmhouse. A gun was fired, but the shot went far over his head. In the darkness he was invisible. But Alisha's father and second brother would catch him if he were delayed in reaching the bike. After what he'd done in the barn, his fate would be certain.

Running through the pasture amid the cattle, he slipped on a clump of manure. He got up and ran in the direction of the wire fence but had to slow himself. If he hit the fence at full sprint, the top wire would decapitate him. At last he came to it and stepped through. Now running along the ditch, panting, falling twice more but this time only in damp grass, he came to where he'd hidden the motorcycle. He climbed up into the high grass, took hold of the handlebars, checked the throttle, and jumped on the starter. *Thank God,* he thought as the machine buzzed to life.

As he rode down into the ditch and up the other side to the dirt road, he saw the lights of a car speeding from the farmhouse toward him. He opened the throttle, switched on the bike's small headlight, and drove as fast as he could out to the paved road, where he turned north toward Metz. The lights of the pursuing car faded and disappeared as he entered the city.

He'd planned to take an evening train, to sit quietly in the dining car with a bordeaux, and then to sleep until the train reached Paris. But he couldn't wait on a train platform and enter the first-class compartment wearing shoes and a suit caked with mud and manure. His appearance wouldn't go unnoticed in a town that wasn't large. And when *La Gazette* published the story he'd write, people, not all of them friendly, would recall his presence on the train that night. Eventually he'd be found, together with Laura and David.

His luck would end, and so would his life. He thought of Laura and David, and concluded that he didn't want to die.

Not tonight, he thought. Not ever.

He swerved onto the *route nationale* that would take him west to Paris, avoiding train stations and trains. Leaning forward over the handlebars, he rolled open the throttle. As he squinted into the darkness and at the rush of cars driving east, the high-pitched engine deafened him. The wind cooled the sweat on his face and chest, chilling him. The cold penetrated every part of him, making him shiver, and he knew that dawn was a long way off.

40

In the early morning Henry sat in a hot bath, scrubbing the dirt, cow dung, and grass stains from his arms and hands. His neck was tender and his shoulders hurt from bending over the motorcycle on the nearly four-hour ride to Paris. He lay back in the tub, resting his head on the cast iron, and reached over to the cool radiator, where he'd balanced a fresh pack of Gauloises and matches. After lighting a cigarette, he thought about the way he'd left the BMW, key in the ignition, near the Gare de l'Est. A shame he couldn't keep it, but his enemies might be looking for such a bike. And who were his enemies? He wished he knew.

The door of the bathroom opened, and Laura walked inside, closing it quietly behind her. She wore her pearl necklace and a summer nightgown that was so thin he could see her nipples, the curves of her breasts, her slight hips. Cotton panties hid her sex. Reaching up and rubbing her eyes, which had gray circles under them, she said, "I heard you come in."

"I'm sorry."

She shrugged. "I couldn't sleep."

He took a drag on the cigarette. "This was my last assignment for *La Gazette*."

"What happened?"

"I ruined a suit."

"That's all?"

"I might have died."

"Oh, Henry." She crossed her arms over her chest. "I was so worried."

"Yes? I was worried too. Not that it helped."

"What do you mean?"

He shrugged. "There's too much risk. I didn't tell you before, but the last person who worked on these assignments for *La Gazette* was killed on the street near his house."

"My God!" she said, eyes wide. "Did anyone see you? Do they know who you are?"

"Not exactly," he replied with studied nonchalance. "Nobody saw my face last night. We're safe, and I won't be stabbed in the rue Dosne. But I won't accept more of this work. After I write the article and give it to Levy, I'm finished."

"You promise me you'll stop?"

"Yes. You can pour us champagne and ring a bell when I courier the article to Levy. I'm returning to private life."

The word *ring* led her to pause. Her face lost its color, and her hands moved nervously to her thighs. "There's a German at the club. He comes every night when he's not in Berlin. If you're there, he sits in the back and leaves early. If you're away, he buys me a drink sometimes. I say hello and then goodbye."

Henry smoked. "Did you tell him you're engaged?"

"Yes, I've told him I'm engaged and have a son. He doesn't care. Tonight when I left La Pomme, he and another man I've never seen were standing on the sidewalk. The other man watched my taxi drive away."

"Perhaps the beautiful la Perle fascinated him."

The hint of a smile appeared at the corners of her mouth, before she shook her head. "It didn't feel that way. The man with Frederick Abendroth—Frederick is the bourgeois from Berlin—must be a gangster. Squat, with a large head and a fisherman's cap. He was frightening."

Henry sat upright in the tub and set his cigarette on the radiator. "Did he look like James Cagney?"

"You've seen him?"

"I think so. He was smuggling weapons in Nice."

"Is he dangerous?"

"He might be," Henry admitted, leaning back against the tub. But then he stated aloud the connection he'd just made: "My God. Frederick Abendroth must be an agent of the German government."

"You think he's a spy?" she asked, her eyes widening.

Henry stubbed out the cigarette, wondering why and how Frederick Abendroth had become a habitual patron of La Pomme. *They couldn't have discovered my work for Levy until after Abendroth began watching Laura. Why is Abendroth at the club? Is he in love with Laura?* Perhaps, but the coincidence seemed impossible to him. *There's something I'm not seeing,* he thought, *but what is it?*

He'd tell Laura what he knew, without speculating about Abendroth's patronage of La Pomme. He nodded to her. "Maybe he's a spy or some kind of intelligence officer or propagandist. What's important to our safety is that we show him and Cagney that, after my second article is published, I'm back in private life and you're la Perle, a renowned singer who has nothing to do with politics. And if we decide that we're in danger, we'll leave for New York, either with David or after giving him a safe way to live."

She nodded. "All right. I trust you." Sitting on the edge of the tub, she leaned over and kissed the top of his head. "You're wrong to call me *renowned*. I doubt that more than a hundred people have heard of me."

Then he saw her new ring, took her hand, and held it close. "Where did you get this?"

When she made to pull away, he looked up at her. He searched her eyes for deception—could she have been seeing another man?—but found none. His heart assured him that she belonged to him, at least for their time in Europe.

"I bought it," she explained in a soft voice. "David and I bought it while you were gone. I wanted people at the club and everywhere else to know I was with you."

His grip eased. "Why didn't you ask me for a ring?"

She withdrew her hand and gazed at him proudly. "I shouldn't have to ask—and we can't be engaged, as you know. But I've had too much interest from the men at La Pomme. So David and I went to a jeweler on the place Vendôme. It really was David who chose." She once again extended her hand. "Do you like it?"

He gently touched her fingers and peered at the ring. He turned it around and saw that the channel-set diamonds ran the circumference of the band. "It's very beautiful. Sometimes, I wish that I could give you a ring, even though I know it's impossible and, even if it *were* possible, you wouldn't accept it."

Smiling, she removed her ring and handed it to him. "You could give it to me—if you wanted—you could do it now. But you don't have to. I won't force you, or even ask you to do it. It wouldn't mean anything, I suppose. But I wouldn't mind if you . . ."

Compelled not by obligation but by a desire and a need to show his affection for her, he awkwardly knelt in the tub. The cast iron hurt him, though he forced himself not to wince. He was performing a sort of penance for not buying the ring himself, for not doing the right thing that was also the wrong thing. But he knew that he deserved little blame for living in the world as it was rather than the way he wished it to be. What she'd invited him to do was to imagine an artificial world where their pursuit of happiness was the only law. Well, why not live in that world, at least for a while?

His chest and shoulders dripping with water and hot with the thrill of this forbidden moment, he held the ring aloft and looked up at her. After a long breath he said, "Laura, will you accept this ring and . . . and whatever we decide it will mean?"

"Yes," she murmured. "Yes, I will."

He took her hand and pushed the ring onto her finger, watching it slip along her fair skin, finding this experience both erotic and sacramental. Her hand was so pretty and elegant, and his so much larger and rougher. He wanted the right to touch her hand for the rest of his life, but knew he'd be able to do so for only a few weeks. When he raised his eyes, she looked at him, tears on her cheeks. He leaned forward and she bent over and kissed him, her hands cupped around the back of his head.

41

Laura couldn't have said when she decided to make love to him. There hadn't been a single moment when she consciously chose. After she came to know and admire him, she tried to ignore her fantasy of taking him to bed. But with their constant physical nearness and the nights when she allowed him to touch her between the legs and she, in turn, held him in her hands, the fantasy of having him inside of her, filling her, became something she ardently desired to make real.

When they began to share a bed in this very house not long ago, the idea became a boundless urge that each night she tried to harness, though for days she sensed her resolution faltering—faltering so completely that she'd gone to the pharmacy the previous morning. In the past when she'd considered sleeping with her beaux, she hadn't been afraid of the sexual act, perhaps because in the end she wouldn't have allowed it. But as she sat above Henry in the tub, she decided it would happen. And if she returned to America in two weeks or in four, even if he were with her, this chance would be forever lost. Moralizing seemed irrelevant when compared with how great that loss appeared to her now. Failing to know Henry in this way would be something she thought she'd never get over. Why not seize the day, because so few remained?

But she didn't want her first time to be in a bathtub. Wouldn't his entering her the first time be less painful if she were lying in the soft linens of the master bedroom? For all her purported modernity in bed (as Henry had referred to her rapid loss of inhibitions), she couldn't ignore her fluttering stomach or the shiver at the back of her neck.

How should I move? she wondered. *How intensely will it hurt?*

Quickly, she stood. In one motion, she took hold of her nightgown and lifted it over her head, then draped it over a towel bar. Wearing only white panties, she made no effort to cover her breasts. "The bedroom," she said, angling her head toward the next room. "Not in the bath. Not the first time."

As she turned and went into the bedroom, she smiled to herself at the hurried sounds from the tub. Splashes, the fluff of a towel, followed by rapid footsteps behind her. But she reached the bed first and slipped under the white sheets and white duvet. She thought about putting a towel beneath her, but she wanted comfort, the linens be damned. This would happen only once in her life.

She remembered the sponge and the vinegar she'd hidden in the middle drawer of her night table. She'd have to use them, she knew. Pregnancy would ruin her, would close all the doors that had recently opened, and la Perle would die.

She looked up and saw him walk into the bedroom and close and lock the door behind him. He'd haphazardly dried himself—drops of water clung to his shoulders and chest. He was fully aroused, and his size and strength made her hot.

As he pulled back the covers on his side of the bed, she burned with excitement. There would be no excuse this morning. She wanted his passion, and she wanted him inside her, but desire didn't remove anxiety. Pushing herself up onto her pillow, a single sheet reaching only to her waist, she took the half-empty tumbler of whiskey from her nightstand and drank. It soothed her even as it stirred her stomach. He got into bed and lay beside her but didn't reach for her.

For a second or two she wondered if he'd misunderstood. But of course he hadn't.

She sipped the whiskey until it was gone and set the empty glass on the night table. Turning toward him, she stared into his hazel eyes and waited. And waited. "Well, come on," she said with exasperation. "Let's get on with it."

His face reddened against the white pillowcase. "Are you sure?"

Playfully hitting his arm, she said, "What do I have to do? Beg?"

"You . . . you've always said no, before."

"I'm through saying no. Can't you see that? Hasn't your much-vaunted experience—with your widowed college secretary—taught you to read the tea leaves?"

"*What?* I didn't vaunt my experience with her. You dredged that memory, not me. Maybe you're jealous."

In truth she was, but she only laughed. "Haven't we waited long enough? We don't need to go back to college."

"This will be learning of a different sort." As he said this, he laughed.

She giggled along with him, and the levity allowed her to relax and slip down into the bed and to receive him into her arms.

42

The first time. The dull ache between her legs proved it beyond doubt.

She'd slept with a man for the first time, yet she couldn't tell anyone. It was this confession or triumph she wanted to announce brightly, to push open the bedroom windows and shout across the city that a man had loved her this morning and that she'd loved him just as ardently. But her joy had to remain hidden. Were her parents to learn of it, her reputation and Henry's livelihood would be destroyed. No one must discover what they'd done. Stretching twice, she climbed out of bed, put on her robe with the white egret on the back, and stood at the windows, watching the late-morning sun illuminate the houses on the west side of the street. With electrified skin and breath like sparks in her mouth, she told herself over and over, *He is mine!*

Yet her chest tightened at the thought of how difficult it would be to keep this secret. When she and Henry returned to America, her parents would see it in her face, wouldn't they? They'd know she'd slept with him, that she hadn't returned untouched. Her mother had said she could tell about any woman, from the sway of the hips to the longer stride to a flicker of the eyes. Even if Laura attempted to take shorter strides and to keep her hips stiff as a board, her mother would realize what had happened and would tell her father. And then Henry would lose his job, and her father would do everything in his considerable power to prevent him from finding employment elsewhere. All these worries and fears, and yet . . . and yet what she most wanted was another night like the last.

Wasn't this the most basic human striving? To be loved in the golden light of dawn?

43

After having slept only three hours, Henry sat at the table in the library, writing an article about his experience in Metz. He left out everything about Alisha and didn't name her family. Instead he wrote of the area where they lived, the German flag over their house, the crates of MP 38s in the barn. The purpose of the story, Henry knew, was to frighten the French into preparing for war with Germany. It was a factual article with no flourishes, but the actions he reported would be seen as an affront to French sovereignty, a pulling of France into another catastrophic war, a commentary on the competence of the gendarmerie, and the participants would be labeled traitors—an explosive mix. Yet more reason to worry about the safety of his household.

When he removed the paper from the typewriter carriage, the time was 7:40. Laura hadn't come downstairs, and he presumed she was sleeping. He thought of her beautiful form on the sheets, with the bloodstain in the middle. He'd been the first to be inside her, and he wished that he could be the last but knew this was impossible. Already he felt jealousy for whomever she decided to marry. And yet . . . and yet an incredible exhilaration filled him. Even though he'd hurt her, he knew she didn't blame him. The pain couldn't be avoided, not if they were to make love. She'd enjoyed it, after all. And he'd never in his life known such thrilling love and fulfillment.

Love . . . he hadn't said the word, but he'd felt it. For her—someone he'd hated a month ago. How urgently he wanted to say he loved her, though he couldn't. He couldn't love her because the structure of their lives and families wouldn't allow it. But that didn't mean he couldn't love her in secret, expressing it, yes, but never confessing or admitting it. This was the only choice available, and it made him angry that he couldn't say and do the natural thing.

He reached for the telephone and called Levy, who seemed pleased to hear from him. They set up an appointment for eleven o'clock that morning at Café des Patriotes. After ringing off, he was slipping his article into an envelope when David walked into the room.

"Hi," the boy said, already dressed in light-gray trousers and a pink shirt. "You weren't here last night."

He reached toward David, who walked into his arms. "I had to be in Metz."

"Where's Metz?"

"It's a town near the German border."

David pulled back, unable to disguise his worry. "Why did you go to Deutschland?"

"Metz is in France, David."

"But you said it's close."

He nodded. "Too close. But I won't be going back. I'm going to stay in Paris with you."

David appeared relieved. "Really?"

He tousled the boy's wiry hair. "I'm certain of it. But first I have to see a man who'll get you a passport that says you're an American, and my son. Is that something you'd like?"

David nodded cautiously, as if this were too much to hope for, but then his eyes found Henry's. "The passport would say I'm your son, but I wouldn't *be* your son."

"I suppose that's true."

"But Mr. Henry, I wish that I could be your son."

"Would you?"

"Yes."

"I'd like that too."

David lowered his eyes. His voice grew quiet, just above a whisper. "Could I be?"

Henry considered this request. As he and Laura weren't legally together, he knew that one or the other of them would have to adopt David. Her parents would never allow such a thing—the burden on their social position and her ability to marry would be too great. *But how could I take care of a young boy forever?* he wondered. *I'm not married, and I have no money.* Slowly, he shook his head. "I don't know, David. I don't know how it would work."

The boy began to cry, and Henry reached for him and pulled him close, hugging him tightly, as if nothing could separate them, as if their make-believe family were real.

44

Henry arrived at the café, only to find Levy waiting for him. Levy's face had aged five years in a week. The bags below his eyes had darkened until they were almost black.

"You need rest," Henry told him.

Levy fished a pair of sunglasses from the breast pocket of his old brown suit and put them on, obscuring his eyes. "I worry, Henri. I worry about my newspaper and my reporters. And of course about France."

"Of course," Henry said and handed him the envelope containing his article. "Perhaps this will improve your mood. I wasn't planning to give you the story until my son had his passport, but I've changed my mind. After what happened last night, the guns will be moved, and I want the story printed now. I trust that you and Crescent will do as you've promised for my little boy."

"*Oui, très bien,*" Levy sighed and removed the sheets of paper.

Henry noticed the editor hadn't indulged in his typical espresso. He held up a hand for the waiter and ordered for both of them.

Levy read the pages deliberately. When he came to the end, he grunted. "You've done it this time. Our readers will be shocked, no? I'm most grateful, Henri. Our friends in London will be too. Your report shows that war is already here, in the shadows. We must increase spending on our defense. The British too. Enough of this willful ignorance."

When the espressos arrived, Levy drank so quickly it must have burned his mouth and throat. But he seemed immune to the heat of the drink or the day. "Summer will soon end," he said, "and in the fall, more trouble with Berlin."

Henry watched him, wanting to know what the older man knew. He asked, "What's your prediction?"

Levy lit a Gauloise. "Hitler will force Czechoslovakia into his jaws. He will eat Poland before he takes a knife to France. But then our time will come."

Henry leaned forward. "When Czechoslovakia?"

Levy exhaled up into the sunlight. "The Sudetenland in September, maybe October. Before Christmas."

"And France?"

Levy removed his sunglasses. "I think France is in danger now. There will be more guns in more barns. There will be groups in France who give aid to Monsieur Hitler. It's happening, Henri. It's happening now, and we need more from the Scarlet Pimpernel. You remember the story, yes?"

He nodded.

"'That demmed, elusive Pimpernel,'" recited Levy, leaving out the line making light of the French.

Henry stubbed out his cigarette. "Not so elusive, I'm afraid."

"Non?" Levy raised his eyebrows above the rims of his sunglasses.

"I didn't tell you before, didn't want to worry you. Already you don't sleep. But the Scarlet Pimpernel must take a holiday, because the Germans discovered him in Nice. Not his name or where he lives, but his general appearance."

Levy's forehead grew lined. "Why didn't you tell me, Henri? And knowing this, to Metz?"

"Yes."

"That was dangerous, *mon ami*. Perhaps you should not have gone. But I do thank you. And you'll be relieved to know that your boy's passport will be here in two weeks, according to Crescent. But we need a photograph."

Henry did feel relief. Soon David would be safe—or at least, safe if Cagney or Abendroth didn't learn of their house in the rue Dosne and try to take him away. This thought worried him, and he promised Levy, "I'll have photographs delivered to your office tomorrow."

"*Non.*" Levy waved away this offer. "Send them to Crescent, at Whitehall." Then he gave a rare smile. "I wish all Americans, and all Frenchmen, for that matter, had your courage and your sense of helping. *Helping?* Is that the word?"

"Yes, that's the word," Henry told him, "but I haven't done so much."

"Oh, but you have. You certainly have." Levy suddenly gripped his hand. "Be careful, Henri. You're safe if you live quietly, like a hermit. You might leave for Bordeaux or England. But if you stay in Paris, keep your eyes open, *oui*?"

"I'll be careful," Henry promised.

Levy released his hand. "You and your *femme et fils* must survive, even if some of us do not."

Another moment, and Levy set out sufficient francs to cover their bill. They stood and parted. Levy waved and walked along the rue de Clichy, toward his newspaper's offices.

45

Although the photo booth in the Victor Hugo Métro station was small and dingy, Henry hoped that it worked well enough. He saw that the operation was simple: one inserted a few coins, perched on the plastic seat, and smiled at the camera behind glass. After a minute or so a sheet of photographic paper would eject out the side into a narrow tray, with a dozen exposures on each page.

"I'll show you how to do it," Henry said, handing his suit coat to Laura and brushing his hair away from his face. He put a coin into the slot at the side of the machine and sat in the booth, staring at the camera as if he were threatening it, and as the machine's red light blinked, he said, "I'm a mean old man!"

This made them all laugh.

The red light in front of Henry blinked again. This time he smiled, with his lips together. The camera took another photograph. He grinned broadly, his white teeth exposed. Click, went the camera's shutter. Click, click, click. Soon the red light blinked a twelfth and final time, and he angled his head forty-five degrees from the lens.

When the machine dropped the sheet of images into the tray, David reached up and fished it out. He held it aloft for all of them to see. "It looks like you," he said. "But better."

This led Laura to chuckle. "Yes, much better."

"It might be wise," Henry told him, "to be generous with your praise until we see *your* photographs."

David looked up at him. "My pictures are going to be perfect. They'll be just like me."

Henry pointed at the seat inside the booth. "Take it away."

David grinned at him and lightly pushed his index finger into Henry's stomach. "I will, right now."

"Enough talk, buddy. Show us your smile."

David climbed into the booth, sat up straight, squared his shoulders, and smiled at the camera. The red light blinked, and the shutter opened and closed. He might have changed his expression, but he continued to smile for all twelve photographs. Then he jumped out of the booth and stood at the tray, waiting for them to develop.

"You'll have the happiest passport photograph in all of recorded history," Henry told him.

"I didn't want to look sad, because I'm not sad."

Laura put an arm around his shoulder and gave him a brief hug. "It's too nice a day to be sad."

"I'm going to be an American boy."

"Yes, you are, darling," she assured him.

Henry smiled at both of them. His chest warmed at the idea of an American safety net under this extraordinary boy.

When the sheet of photographs dropped into the tray, David reached for it and held it up for inspection. He laughed at himself. "I told you. It's me, exactly."

Laura looked carefully. "You're right. You photograph well, and you're so handsome."

He blushed and shyly averted his face.

"But even more handsome in life," she told him. Turning to Henry, who was examining the images, she asked, "Are they appropriate for his passport?"

He studied the clear images of David, who appeared so different now than when they'd met him aboard the *Île de France*. Clean skin and hair, good clothes, not frighteningly thin, a brightness to his expression. "Yes," he said. "These look great."

"He doesn't need to frown, does he?"

"Certainly not."

Henry tucked the photographs into the breast pocket of his coat. "We need to take these to the post office so I can mail them to my friend in London," he explained to David.

"Yes," the boy agreed. "But don't you think we should have photographs of Miss Laura?"

"No, no," she said. "I'm afraid I don't look good in pictures."

"Sweetheart, that isn't true," Henry said, pecking her cheek, suddenly hoping for a photograph for when they returned to Saint Paul and he could no longer see her or make love to her. "You're stunning."

"I don't like pictures of myself," she resisted.

David pulled at her arm. "But Miss Laura, I should have a picture of you. I want to put it in a frame and have it next to my bed. Wouldn't you, please, let me have a photograph?"

She looked at him, his expression of yearning. "Yes. All right, David. I'll take photographs for you. But I won't smile."

Henry deposited coins into the machine, and he and David waited while her photographs were taken. As she stared at the camera with an expression of genteel seriousness, her blond hair on the right side tucked behind an ear, Henry realized what was needed. Reaching down, he tickled her.

Laughing now, she lifted her feet and shrieked softly.

He'd wanted her to smile, and so she did, and the camera caught her looking downward and to the side, with a bright grin across her face. They examined the photographs, and while all of them showed her unmistakable beauty, it was this last that David claimed for his night table.

After Henry had mailed two passport photographs to Richard Crescent at Whitehall, they walked in the direction of the place Victor Hugo and home. There, Henry lingered in the street, lighting a Gauloise as he watched Laura accompany David into the house. He pretended to admire the swanlike wheel wells of a shiny Citroën sedan parked twenty meters from the front door. Leaning over the car so he could see the street and the houses reflected in the rear window, he exhaled copiously. As the smoke cleared, the street was plainly visible, as was a man who stood, stationary, in the doorway of the house across from his own. Not walking or smoking, the squat man wore a hat with the brim tilted down, obscuring his face, an open newspaper in his hands. Nevertheless, Henry recognized him. It could only be the man he'd seen directing the arms smuggling in Nice, the man who resembled James Cagney.

Henry stopped breathing.

The spying, he thought. *The articles for* La Gazette.

He knew that he'd disrupted one of the Germans' clandestine efforts that might be a prelude to war. His articles had brought increased scrutiny to arms smuggling and Nazi sympathizers in France, not to mention his killing—in self-defense—a farmer's son in a barn outside Metz. Now he realized the consequences might be all too real.

They tracked you via Levy, he concluded. *And what will they do?*

He waited, considering the best course of action. But no solution came to mind.

Then he threw the cigarette onto the cobbles and walked purposefully to his house, up the stairs to the front door, and inside. No footsteps sounded behind him. He closed the black door, glad it had no window and was two inches thick. It also had a dead bolt, which he set, and then he joined his family in the kitchen.

Laura was smiling at David, who spoke excitedly about his adventures with the photograph machine. Henry joined in their discussion, and the three of them laughed. Yet Henry's laughter hid a terrible worry, though he tried to obscure his fear and a new sense of panic that was like inhaling icy cold air filled with knives.

46

"My father has demanded that we sail for America next week," Laura told Henry late that afternoon. "Telegrams for both of us, with identical wording. I'm sorry for opening yours."

Sitting up in bed, resting his back against the headboard, he felt a thud in his chest. "Let me see it."

She reached into the pocket of her cotton trousers and gave it to him. He read:

> Europe dangerous.
> You must return Saturday on the Île de France.
> Le Havre to New York. Tickets held for you.
> No refusal possible. Credit halted.
> B. Powell

"Christ." He looked up at her and tensed his stomach muscles to ward off the sensation of falling into a bottomless hole. After seeing James Cagney across the street from their rented house, he knew that her father was right. Europe *was* dangerous, and it was especially dangerous for them. Yet he was torn by her father's demand and his own feeling that his life and his future were in Paris. He knew that if they returned to Saint Paul, he'd lose her forever. Touching her arm, he asked, "How will you respond?"

She sat on the edge of the bed, her expression grim. "I think there's only one thing to do."

"You'll refuse?"

"No." She shook her head. "I'll return on the *Île de France*."

He lost his breath. His body went rigid with desperation. His throat warmed, and he had to inhale slowly in order to speak. "I understand. And I want you to be safe, even if it means that I lose you. But, darling, is there anything for you in Saint Paul?"

"Very little," she admitted. "And it will be awful to give up my singing. But my father has stopped paying our bills. If we stay, you'd lose your job. How would we survive and give David what he needs? What if I never saw my family again?"

Henry glanced at the door to be sure they were alone. "What about David?"

At the mention of his name, she began to cry. "He has you," she said, touching his hand, her warm brown eyes on his. "You'll make sure he's safe. And I'll force my father to keep you here for the good of his company—I'll tell him via telegram tonight that I'll go home only if you can remain head of European sales for his company, at your current salary. My father wants both of us to return, but he'll be satisfied with me. And maybe when David has a passport, you'll bring him to Saint Paul, and I can be . . . his friend or his aunt."

"His aunt?" Henry replied, his voice showing his disbelief. But he was thinking not of David but of himself, of losing Laura and her affection, of never living with her again, of never holding her in his arms, of her finding love with another man. His anguish made him mute. He couldn't respond to her suggestion, couldn't think of anything. His pulse pounded in his temples.

He could see that she feared an argument. She stood, opened the door to the hallway, and shook her head, her downcast eyes a window into her torment. "I so want to stay here with you and David, but how can I? I love you! I want to marry you and have children with you, but how could we? Without your job, we wouldn't have money—not enough for a small apartment, let alone what children would need. I can't do that to you or David or our children. I'm sorry, Henry, but we've run out of choices."

His ear had caught the one phrase. "You love me?" he asked.

She gave him a mournful smile. "Of course I do. You're the only man I've ever loved. How can you not know?"

He watched her intently. While there were many things he could say, and one thing he knew that he ought to say, he couldn't find the words.

After hesitating briefly on the threshold, she left, closing the door behind her.

It seemed the meaning of his life, and all he loved, was vanishing. He wanted to shout to her that no, she couldn't leave, he'd be too sad and his life would end. But such a confession would show the traits no woman yearns for in a lover: woundedness, desperation, grasping. So he leaned against the headboard and silently responded that he loved her—that he'd loved her long before he realized it, that he'd always love her.

Then he lost the composure he'd bravely maintained while she sat on the bed. Hunching over, he drove the palms of his hands into his damp eyes until he saw crimson and black stars. *No,* he cried silently. *How could you leave? How could the world be so terrible? We have everything here—everything! And now it will be destroyed. Nothing will be left—not me, not David, maybe not even Paris. My God,* he thought, not picturing her but only the earth spinning in dark space. *How cruel . . . how essentially cruel.*

Laura didn't proceed into the kitchen, where she could hear David listening to a radio drama of *Twenty Thousand Leagues Under the Sea* on the BBC. She walked into the library and closed the door. Sensing that she'd fall or black out, she put both hands on the desk and leaned over. An incredible heat formed in her chest and migrated up to her head.

She could hear her pulse throbbing in her ears. She felt that she couldn't stand or sit, that she'd be ill. Forcing herself to breathe deeply, she was able to calm the bile in her stomach. She sat down at the desk, set her elbows on the wood, and pushed the palms of her hands into her eyes.

Sobs began in her throat and moved upward. She opened her mouth and released the sound of overwhelming sadness. Placing a hand across her lips, she muffled her cries. Her hands shook. These last weeks she'd reached for everything she could, and it was all turning to dust.

Now she'd just admitted that she loved Henry—something she'd never said to any man—and wanted to have his children. These words had been unplanned, and in a typical state of mind she'd never have said them. But they'd come out—she'd wanted to reveal the extent of her feelings, and doing so had brought happiness and relief, but also melancholy, because soon they'd cease to matter to anyone. He hadn't responded to these sentiments, yet she knew that he returned them. He must love her as absolutely as she loved him—this she firmly believed. But just as they'd begun a life entwined with that love, it would be wrenched apart.

Her body trembling, she silently acknowledged that nobody wanted to return to Saint Paul less than she. Who could argue that her family wanted to kill her dreams? She knew that in Saint Paul, without Henry or David or her life as la Perle, she'd lose all hope of becoming the woman she wanted to be.

"Miss Laura!" David called from the foyer. "Miss Laura! Do you think we could have dinner soon?"

She wiped off her face, pushed her hair back from her forehead, and tucked in her white blouse. When she opened the door, she saw him standing in the foyer, his handsome face tilted upward. She smiled at him. "Yes, darling. Let's have dinner. What would you like?"

47

Rain fell on the city, soft, insistent, impossible to avoid. It was a warm morning in July, and Henry had slept badly. Before going to sleep, he'd apologized to Laura and told her that he'd been angry because he loved her and knew that he'd lose her. Afterward, he held her, and they both wept openly.

The world, it seemed, was arrayed against them: European politics, her parents, their different histories, her money and position and his lack of these. The grim reality of the Great Depression hovered over everything. Lovers in a dream, they'd in life soon return to their previous roles as acquaintances, nothing more. He silently cursed the world, but it gave no response, not even a shrug.

And this summer had been a dream, one he'd hoped they could prolong forever. His life had become interesting and romantic and thrilling in ways that would have been impossible in Saint Paul. And he'd thought he loved Paris. But now that Laura was leaving, he understood that for him, she *was* Paris.

Once a soft rain in the old streets had been charming. Now it was dismal and enervating. Carrying an umbrella and wearing a trench coat, he walked to a newsstand in the place Victor Hugo, where he picked up a copy of *La Gazette*. Levy had changed few words in his article about the Koeppels' farm near Metz. His eyes flickered over his byline: *The Scarlet Pimpernel*. This was his mark on the world, his effort to do good. He was prouder of his articles for *La Gazette* than for all the work he'd done for Powell Manufacturing & Munitions, though he'd keep his position at the company—a concession Laura had demanded of her father. He'd be able to stay in the beautiful house in the rue Dosne. He could pay for the navy blue cashmere overcoat from Bergdorf's that was waiting for him at the Crillon. More pressing, given the imminent beginning of the academic year, David's future would be secure. He'd be tutored here at the house, at least until Henry was satisfied that he'd be safe at a French school with boys his age.

And James Cagney and Frederick Abendroth?

He hoped they'd slowly lose interest when they saw him behaving as an American tourist without political sympathies. They'd watch him less and less, and eventually they'd scan *La Gazette* for his articles, and if those articles failed to appear for a sufficient time, perhaps he'd be as safe as the moment he'd arrived in Paris.

He paid for the newspaper, tucked it under the arm of his olive raincoat, and on the way to the station, decided to stop by the Crillon to pick up his new overcoat. He went down into the Métro and caught the train to the place de la Concorde, where he walked the short distance to the hotel, all the while thinking of his reporting triumphs and the ache he'd suffer when Laura went to America.

The front desk at the Crillon had the box, sealed with tape and wrapped with twine, which held the overcoat. He thanked and tipped the deskman and then asked to use one of the lobby telephones for a local call.

Standing in one of the small booths behind a narrow oak door with a thick pane of glass, he called Levy at *La Gazette*.

The editor's secretary answered. "Who are you?"

"I'm a friend."

"Your name?"

"Henri."

"Last name?"

"He knows me quite well. Please tell him that Henri is on the line."

"I'm sorry, monsieur, but I cannot. Émile Levy died this morning."

Henry struck his thigh. *Damn!* He looked through the glass to the lobby, where the hotel's business continued without worry. *"Vraiment? Il est mort?"*

"Oui, monsieur."

He touched the side of the telephone and closed his eyes. "What happened?"

"He was beaten and stabbed. The gendarmerie has begun an investigation."

Henry was quiet for a minute, remembering the editor whom he'd come to appreciate and respect. Always he'd thought the life he was risking was his, not his friend's. "This is terrible news. Levy was a good man who helped me."

"Thank you, Henri," the secretary said, voice softening. "Monsieur Levy believed in my country's *liberté.*"

"Yes, he did," Henry agreed. *"Je suis désolé."* Having no other words, he hung up and listened to his breath in the small booth. He shook his head and sat with his elbows on his knees, staring blindly at the marble floor. At last he sighed and sat up. When he looked through the glass, he saw a large muscular man of about twenty-five, smoking a cigarette, watching him. The man had no expression, and he immediately strode off to the side, beyond Henry's vision. Now that Levy was gone, maybe he was next. But what could he do? After another minute, he called a London exchange, requested the ministry of war, and once he got the switchboard there, asked for Richard Crescent.

"Do you have a scheduled call with Mr. Crescent?" the operator asked him.

"No."

"Then you'll have to speak with his secretary."

"That would be fine," he said coldly, "but tell Mr. Crescent that one of his agents has been murdered."

Silence from the operator. Then: "One moment, please, Mr. . . . ."

"Salter."

"One moment, please."

He waited less than a minute for Richard Crescent's voice to come over the line.

Crescent sounded like he was eating something. "Salter?"

"Mr. Crescent."

"If you're calling about Levy, we know."

"When did it happen?"

"This morning, about eight o'clock. He was leaving for the office and got stabbed in the vestibule of his building. An ugly mess. Maybe he wasn't careful. How else would anyone know he worked with us?"

Henry didn't like the callous tone. "Maybe it had nothing to do with you. Maybe they didn't like my article and so they killed the editor of the newspaper that printed it."

"Yes. Maybe. But it was his idea to publish the reports. 'Good for *La Gazette*, good for France' was his justification. I'd have been happy keeping the information entre nous, but you can't tell a Frenchman anything."

Henry waited for more, but Crescent only made chewing noises. Levy's death had been his fault, he wanted Crescent to say. But the official from Whitehall didn't accuse him, only let the implication hang over the silence of the telephone line. Henry lowered his head.

"Salter?" Crescent grunted at last.

"Yes?"

"The passport for the boy will be ready soon. We think it's time you took another assignment."

"I'll consider it," he said, though he'd already decided to do no such thing. "But first," he said, "I must have David's passport."

"Sure, sure," Crescent intoned blandly. "In a few days. But be careful. The men who got rid of Levy might be looking for you."

48

Despite the rain he chose to walk home. He hoped that the cool air would revive him. Levy was gone forever, he mused silently, and soon Laura would be gone from Paris. A week of losses.

He opened his black umbrella and ambled through a mental fog. In his mind he pictured the last grains of sand falling through an hourglass. Three days until she left and their eternal separation began.

She cried whenever they were alone, though since they'd received her father's telegram yesterday, she'd made love to him feverishly, both last night and again this morning, climbing onto him and kissing him hungrily.

He'd held her hips, his thumbs brushing the edges of the soft hair between her legs, and helped her slide onto his sex. She closed her eyes and murmured. And then she began to move, first gently, then urgently, tilting her head up to the light flickering on the ceiling.

She hummed rhythmically and with pleasure and whispered, almost inaudibly. "I need you . . . I need you . . ."

Never had her desire been so obvious. Never had she been so vulnerable. This naked revealing of herself led him to respond with equally open lust and wanting and need. For a few moments their pleasure had consumed their worries, and then sadness had again enveloped them. Lovemaking was an escape from dissolution and death, but it lasted only a short time.

She had pretended to be cheerful with David. And the boy had been so caught up in playing with his football in the diminutive backyard that he hadn't noticed her eyes no longer lingered on him, her hands were never still, and her voice was filled with forced and unnatural emotion.

The rain was ruining the cuffs of Henry's trousers and his shoes, though he'd worn old pairs of each and didn't care. Water slipped off the parcel. Miserable weather for an awful day, and it seemed to be the end of sunshine and possibility. He wished he could reverse time and arrive once again with Laura at the Crillon, where their affair had begun. But life moved only forward, and there was no way to go back, no way to turn the hourglass over and start again. The wonder of his connection to her would end in days, in hours.

Along the Champs-Élysées the sidewalk seats were empty, the patrons having taken shelter under the awnings or within the buildings, which had taken on the grisaille of the clouds. At l'Étoile he turned west into the avenue Foch and walked under the lush green trees, the rain intermittent against his umbrella when he stepped out from under their canopies. Few cars traveled the street, and fewer people. The houses he passed were those of rich families, stately and expensively maintained. He stopped in front of one to admire its wrought iron gate in the shape of a centaur drawing an arrow across a large bow.

Even in his reverie he heard them before they entered his vision: two sets of feet, running toward him. He turned to look at whoever was approaching.

His head was knocked sideways, tearing at his spine.

The hit came so hard that he momentarily blacked out as he fell. Reaching out to the up-rushing concrete, he dropped his package and landed on his hands, his wrists. A sharp laceration drove into his left forearm.

He rolled to the side and tried to get up.

Another blow against his shoulders, causing pain of an unbelievable intensity.

He lay on the sidewalk, groaning, curled up, forearms over his face and skull, knees up near his chin to protect his torso and genitals as hard blows landed on his body. They hit him once more on the left side of the head, and the earth opened up.

He fell into a bottomless mine, in which he grew colder and colder and wind encircled him and dragged him deeper and deeper. He shivered again with the cold and tried to draw a blanket around himself, but the wind blew the blanket free, and it rose toward the surface like a bat. He watched it circle upward as he fell.

The wind lessened and stopped and then began again, blowing him up toward a pinpoint of light at the top of the mineshaft. As he neared the surface, he came to and tried to breathe and couldn't, tried again and could but a little, and at last gulped the air hoarsely. Light came onto his face, and rain as well. He remained on the sidewalk, the wrought iron centaur gate beside him, though the gate had swung open and a waistcoat-clad figure stood over him. The man, who must have been a valet, held an antique pistol in his hand.

"Monsieur?" said the man. *"Dois-je appeler une ambulance?"*

He tried to get up, stifling his nausea. Using the wrought iron posts, he pulled himself to his feet. He knew he looked very bad. Even in his dizziness he could feel a swelling wound between his forehead and his left ear. He touched his face, and his hand came away bloody. Crimson blotches had spread across his shirt, suit, and trench coat. Breathing was painful. Yet he could stand, he could hobble on his aching legs. He thought nothing was broken except a rib or two. His eyesight was good.

He attempted to smile at the valet, knowing he must be grotesque. *"Non, pas une ambulance, non,"* he said. *"Merci. Je vous remercie de m'avoir sauvé la vie."*

The valet nodded and replied in English: "You are welcome. I think the men who beat you were German."

He tried to smile. "They must know I don't like Krauts."

"Neither do I. That's why I shot at one of them." The older man gave a sly grin. "I might have gotten the short little bastard, but who knows? They ran off."

Henry surveyed the area around him and saw the box from Bergdorf's. Looping three fingers around the twine, he lifted it and found it immeasurably heavy, yet he limped along the sidewalk, thanking the valet once more as he went.

After a while he stopped and leaned against a tree, holding his throbbing head, forcing himself to go on. So tired he had to choose which foot to place in front of the other, he elicited many stares and numerous offers of help. He declined all of them.

Eventually he turned into the familiar street and in agony climbed the front steps to his house. With trembling and awkward hands, he used his key to unlock the door, leaned heavily against the oak slab, and as it slowly opened, fell over the threshold onto his knees and then his back.

He heard Laura scream and David shout, and the cool polished marble floor pressed against his cheek. He opened his fingers and tried to get them free of the twine-wrapped box. He saw Laura's white sandals and then closed his eyes and again fell into the mineshaft and down, down, the wind pushing him to the cold dark center of the earth.

49

Laura thought he was dead. It was like a sharp knife had cut into her, yet she didn't hesitate. She pulled the box from his hand and knelt beside him. Blood moved across the tiles, running from a cut above his forehead and from a puckering wound at the side of his head. She couldn't tell if he was breathing.

Looking up at David, who stood by with damp eyes, she said, "Go upstairs and get towels. As many as you can find."

He stared at Henry and didn't move.

"David!" she called. "Quickly!"

His eyes briefly met hers, and he backed away and ran to the stairs. She touched Henry's chest. It was warm and seemed to be rising and falling, but shallowly. She stood and left him there, going quickly into the kitchen and calling for a doctor and an ambulance. When she returned to the foyer, David was standing next to Henry with towels. His face showed terror.

"Here, sweetheart," she said, taking them from him.

David didn't answer, but Henry did. "No hospital."

He's alive, thank God, she thought, but decided his mind was foggy. "Of course you're going to the hospital. Your head is cut and you're bleeding like mad."

"No. The people . . . will get me . . . in the hospital. You can't . . . protect me . . . there."

"But you might need surgery."

"No," he said. "No surgery."

She tried to converse with him, to ask him what happened, but he was quiet and again seemed to be unconscious. He needed an ambulance and the hospital, she knew. But he was right: she couldn't protect him outside this house. At a hospital she could step away from his room or leave for dinner and when she returned, he might be gone—bludgeoned to death, which is what might have happened today, except they hadn't quite got him. At least she hoped they hadn't.

When the ambulance arrived, she told the medics to help him but leave him at the house. They protested, describing the severity of his wounds. She shook her head and asked that they carry him upstairs. Grudgingly, they lifted him onto a stretcher and brought him to the master bedroom, where they removed his trench coat and his other clothing, except his boxer shorts. His body, she was relieved to see, bore little evidence of violence except for deep bruises about his ribs. Yet she knew his head injury could be fatal. Keeping him here would be an enormous risk, one she didn't know if she should take.

The doctor arrived soon afterward, and David showed him upstairs. Dr. Roche stated his name to Laura and to the unconscious Henry. He was about Henry's age and very thin, as if he ate almost nothing and ran for the Olympic team. He wore gold wire-rimmed eyeglasses and had his light-brown hair cut short as a monk's. When the medics informed him of her desire to keep her husband—that's how she'd described Henry—here at the house and away from the hospital, his complexion flushed.

He turned to her. "This man, whose head has been hit like a piñata, needs to be in hospital. These men will put him on the stretcher and take him, *oui?*"

"*Non*," she said. "I'm sorry. He must remain here. He told me he must remain here."

"But madame," the doctor pleaded. "I don't have the equipment he needs. If he's hemorrhaging, I can't save him, not with the few tools I have in my bag. We must move him to hospital."

"*Non,*" she repeated. "He cannot be moved. You must do what you can."

"But he might die here, you understand? He might *die.*"

She looked at David, who hadn't heard Henry's request to be kept at the house, who wouldn't understand Henry's reasoning. The boy's forehead was wrinkled, and his skin had lost its healthy light-brown coloring and turned gray. He was terrified of losing the man who loved him.

She turned to Dr. Roche. "He will stay here. Please, do what you can. I'll pay whatever is necessary, but he will stay here."

Roche stared at her.

She waved her hand toward Henry's body. "Please, begin."

50

After a moment the doctor removed his coat, opened his bag, and put on a black smock. Laura watched him begin to pull vials, syringes, and bandages from his bag. He told the medics they could leave, and then turned to her. "Small towels, soap, and a basin of water. We're going to be in the eighteenth century, madame. Courtesy of your stubbornness."

"*His* stubbornness," she corrected him, nodding at Henry. She took David's hand, and they went downstairs together to get what was needed.

In the kitchen she found a large mixing bowl made of heavy crockery, a bar of soap, and soft old towels the house's owner, or her staff, must have used to dry dishes. As she moved around the kitchen, the house seemed unnaturally quiet, like a church. Or a tomb.

She forced the image of Henry's funeral from her mind. Her breath came in short bursts. She realized she was panicking and guessed that David was close to doing the same. Setting the basin, soap, and towels on the counters with shaking hands, she then opened a cupboard and took down a bottle of whiskey. She set a couple of tumblers on the counter and filled one halfway and the other with only a splash. Pushing the almost empty glass toward David, she said, "Drink it slowly, but drink it all."

His small white fingers wrapped around it and lifted it. "Whiskey?"

"Yes." She nodded.

"I've had it before."

"When?"

"On a ship. I was cold, and a nice old man gave me some from his flask."

"Well. You shouldn't drink it," she said. "But now it's okay if you have a small glass."

He sniffed it, wrinkled his nose, and drank quickly. As he put his empty glass on the counter, he coughed and his face reddened. He watched her drink. For her, it was strong but burned pleasantly in her throat and stomach. Her shoulders relaxed, and her breath came more easily.

"I'm going upstairs," she said. "But you should stay down here."

He shook his head. "I must help."

She saw that he wouldn't be kept outside the master bedroom. "All right. Let's go."

They formed a kind of relay. Dr. Roche, standing over the bed, dipped towels into the warm soapy water from the basin and cleaned Henry's wounds. Laura changed the water in the basin every few minutes, and David took the bloody towels downstairs and left them in the laundry.

Roche's smock was damp from his work. With rolled-up shirtsleeves, he set a hand on Henry's shoulder and another on Henry's hip and rolled him onto his right side, toward the middle of the bed. The ugly swelling above Henry's left ear was grotesque and frightened everyone in the room. As the doctor rubbed alcohol on a pair of scissors and then brought them toward the swelling, David cried out.

The doctor turned toward him. "I must cut the hair so that I can dress and stitch up the wound. *D'accord?*" After David nodded, Roche leaned over the wound and, with great care, snipped around the swollen area. Using an almost feminine gesture, he cupped a hand under the scissors to receive most of the hair clippings. When he'd finished, he backed away and asked for a wastepaper basket. David went for the one in the bathroom and returned a moment later, and the doctor dropped the hair in it. As the doctor stood at the dresser, sterilizing and threading the needle, Laura and David had a clear view of the wound.

She began to cry and reached over and rubbed Henry's shoulder. "Come back to us, darling. Come back to us."

David went around the bed and leaned over it. After a moment he moved closer yet. "Mr. Henry," he said in his bell-like voice. "Can you hear me? I'm beside you, and so is the doctor. He'll make you better, I know he will." David steadied himself, wiped his watering eyes, and touched Henry's warm cheek.

51

When the doctor had finished, he got up, rinsed off his tools in the basin of water, wiped them down with alcohol, and replaced them in a leather holder. He then removed his smock, folded it from the edges inward, and set it in his bag. After putting on his suit coat, he took out a pad of form bills. A glance at his wristwatch, and he wrote out the bill and gave it to Laura. Roche picked up his bag and stood in the doorway, behind her.

"I've done what I can," he said. "If he has internal hemorrhaging, he will die. If not, he will live. I injected him with penicillin but can do nothing else. If he wakes, give him water and chicken broth. If his pain is too bad, you may call my office in the day and my house at night. *Bien?*"

She nodded. "Yes."

"He may die," the doctor said quietly. "If so, my regrets."

Once again the thought of Henry's dying left her quiet. It seemed that if he stopped breathing, she and David would do the same.

"Shall I return tomorrow to redress his wounds?" Roche asked.

"Yes, please."

He left the room, his retreating footsteps sounding on the staircase and the tiled foyer. The front door shut loudly, and the house was silent. They stood looking down at Henry, whose chest continued to rise and fall.

"I should make dinner," she said.

"I'm not hungry," David told her.

"You will be."

"No. I want to read a story to Mr. Henry."

"Which story?"

"The book he's reading," David said, taking Henry's copy of *The Sun Also Rises* off the night table.

"That's very thoughtful of you. He's always liked your voice."

"He likes my voice?" David asked, looking up at her with doubt.

She reached over and rubbed his neck. "He often tells me your voice makes him happy. You have a wonderful voice."

"No, I don't. People make fun of my voice. They say it's little."

"It's clear and clean," she countered, "like the air on top of a mountain. The people who said your voice is little haven't ever heard you yell."

He laughed at this. "I can yell," he said.

"Yes, darling. You sure did when Henry came into the foyer and fell over. That wasn't a little voice, believe me."

"A big voice?" he asked, chest expanding with pride.

"A very big voice."

He sat in the chair where the doctor had perched and rested his legs on the edge of the mattress. After opening to the page where Henry's bookmark lay, he began reading: "In the morning it was all over. The fiesta was finished. I woke about nine o'clock . . ."

She listened and for a few minutes was entranced by the incongruity of a boy reading a very adult story to a man lying in bed with grievous wounds. Maybe it would help him survive; she didn't know. She saw the blood on the sheets and duvet, and the pillow under her lover's head was also dark and wet with blood. Her first impulse was to replace them with clean sheets and pillows. But she remained motionless, not wanting to move the injured head. For now, let Henry rest and listen, consciously or not, to the pretty voice of the boy who'd become his son.

Quietly, she left the room and went downstairs to the kitchen. She poured another whiskey. Down the stairway floated the murmur of David's words, which soothed her until she considered her departure three days hence. For a moment she considered telegraphing her father and putting off sailing for a month. But she knew he'd refuse. Henry's injury would have the perverse effect of steeling her father's resolve that she must return, France being too dangerous by far. Of course, if Henry didn't awake and recover, she'd stay no matter what her father demanded. But if Henry awoke and could care for David, she'd leave, for she was trapped.

It would be a cruel morning, certain to be painful. But it would be worse for David, who'd no idea that three taxis would come to the house and take her and her trunks to the Gare du Nord, and from there to Le Havre, and from Le Havre—via the *Île de France*—to Manhattan, and from there by train to Saint Paul. She'd no idea how to tell David that he'd soon be without her. The thought of leaving made her sad beyond words. She'd been unable to speak of her feelings with Henry, and she'd become distant from him not because she didn't love him but because she couldn't show her love without weeping. She pushed her hands against the edge of the countertop, the marble digging into her soft hands. But she pushed harder, until she cried from the pain.

Finished with the whiskey, she set the glass in the sink and went upstairs.

She brought a small wooden chair from David's bedroom into her own, where Henry lay immobile and unconscious. By the foot of the bed, she sat and watched him breathe. Into her mind came words she thought she'd forgotten: *The Lord is my shepherd, I shall not want.* She listened to David reading Hemingway's book in an intentionally cheerful voice, and it didn't matter that she had no faith. Her own childhood returned to her. *Yea, though I walk through the valley of the shadow of death, I will fear no evil.*

But despite these comforting words, she felt the shadow of death hanging over the room, muffling David's voice, which strained in a pure, clear melody to reach Henry.

52

The next morning—another terrible step away from her life in Paris. Another betrayal.

She made David an omelet and toast and set his plate on the patio table. She also brought him a glass of milk and sat down opposite him. In front of herself she placed toast spread with apricot preserves and a mug of espresso she made with the aluminum stovetop machine she'd found in the cupboards.

He ate quickly, she slowly. Before he finished one bite, he'd open his mouth for another, his fork like a steam shovel that never stopped moving. Her eyes focused on the rapidly diminishing omelet and the occasional stray olive that he'd spear and stuff into his mouth. When she dropped her eyes to remove lint from her sleeve, he took one of his toast slices and stuck it into his pocket.

She smiled at his appetite; she would miss it. After the single piece of toast, her stomach grew queasy. She pushed back her chair, crossed her legs, and reached for the package of cigarettes and the lighter on the table. Smoking, she felt better. She wished that she could blow away this discussion as she blew the gray smoke from her mouth, that the words she'd say to him would vanish into the air like nothing at all. "David?" she began.

"Mmm?" he murmured between bites.

"Honey, I need to tell you about next week."

"Next week?" He glanced at her and then down to the last sliver of egg and cheese.

"You see, if Henry recovers and can take care of you, I need to make a trip to America."

His eyes, though unworried, locked on hers. He finished chewing and drank some of the milk. "Why?"

"My family needs to see me."

"Oh." He took another sip of his milk, causing a white mustache to form over his upper lip. "How long will you be gone?"

"I don't know."

"But not too long?"

"I hope not too long. I have many things to do in Saint Paul."

"What do you have to do?"

Try to avoid getting married, she thought but didn't say. *Try to get back here by some method I can't even imagine.* "I need to visit my parents," she explained. "But I'll write and tell you all about it."

He nodded. "But when will you come back?"

She reached across the table and touched his hand. "I'm not sure of the exact date, honey. We'll just have to see."

He moved his hand away from hers and looked down. "You're leaving forever."

"No." She shook her head. "Not forever."

"Yes."

"No, darling."

He began to cry. "But what about Mr. Henry? He needs you."

"His injuries will heal soon, I'm sure of it. And he's a very strong man who'll take care of you."

"What if he doesn't? What if he leaves? What if he wants to be with you and goes to America? I have no money. I have nothing. I have no—"

"David, listen to me," she said, raising her voice. "Henry will recover soon. He'll be his old self. I'll be gone for a while, and you'll be here with him."

"No, I won't stay. I won't. I'm leaving with you."

She stubbed out her cigarette. "You have to stay here, David. And I'll be back soon."

"But when?"

"I've told you. I don't know."

"But when? When, Miss Laura? *When?*"

She saw that he was becoming hysterical. Getting up from the table, she looked down at him with what she hoped was a kindly expression. Forcing her voice to be soft, she said, "I'm going to hire a housekeeper who can cook and a man who can help you and Henry. I won't be gone forever, David. Everything will turn out all right."

"But you *can't* leave me!"

"I . . . I must go to Saint Paul for a while. You'll be with Mr. Henry. Don't you know he'll take care of you?"

"But I need . . . I need *both* of you."

Whatever she'd learned at Smith, it hadn't been how to deal with this situation. She realized this second abandonment might be one too many for him but was powerless to do otherwise.

"I know you need both of us," she said, getting up.

"Then will you stay?" he asked with wet eyes.

"I'll return, sweet boy. That's the best I can do."

She went into the kitchen and found the telephone number of Madame Bernard, the leasing agent who'd found them the house. Praying madame would know where to find a reputable cook and tutor who were Jewish, a distinction made for David's sake, she placed the call.

Madame Bernard recommended the Kislings, a Jewish couple in their sixties who'd fled Berlin after enduring a terrible loss. But David overheard her discussion with Madame Bernard, heard the words *housekeeper* and *tutor* and *live here at our house in the rue Dosne.* After letting out a single devastated groan, he ran upstairs to his bedroom in complete silence.

That silence was the worst noise she'd ever heard. She covered the telephone receiver with her hand. "Goddamn it," she said aloud. "Goddamn it."

53

Long after midnight Henry woke her. His hand pressed against her knee and pulled her out of a dream in which she was on an *Île de France* that had been cursed never to reach its destination, circling the Atlantic forever.

She turned toward him and pushed herself up on an elbow. "Henry? *Henry?* Are you awake?"

His eyes remained closed, but he opened his mouth very slowly. "My head feels like someone drove a spike through it."

Her heart jumped as she leaned over him, kissing his forehead, his cheeks, his lips. "My darling, my darling. I love you." She kissed him again. "I'm so happy you've returned to us. Would you like anything? Could I get you an aspirin?"

"Yes, please. More than one."

She went downstairs to the kitchen for the water she kept in the refrigerator, her pulse racing with relief and something like joy. Returning a moment later, she sat on the bed and handed him a full glass. From the night table she took three pills from the vial of aspirin and placed them in his upward palm.

As he awkwardly sat up, she caressed his bare back and placed her lips on his neck. When he'd finished drinking and set the glass on the night table, he took hold of her free hand. "Thank you," he said.

His expression of pain and general melancholy led her to say, "You needn't do anything but rest, my darling. I've hired a housekeeper, who'll cook, and her husband, who'll tutor David and manage things around the house. Both of them Jewish, so David won't be afraid."

He nodded gratefully. "Thank you."

Sitting on the bed beside him, she draped an arm around his shoulders, careful not to put pressure on his bandages. "Oh, darling. I'm so sorry."

"About what happened to me?"

"Yes, about your injuries, and about my leaving."

He placed a hand on her thigh and gently squeezed. "It's true you have to leave. It's not safe here. This"—his hand waved toward himself—"might have happened to you. And if it did, I wouldn't be able to forgive myself."

They sat quietly this way for a long while. She ran her fingers along his spine. He gently touched her thigh.

Then he said, "Would you get me the whiskey from the bottom of the armoire?"

Although she wished that he'd drink only water, she got up, took out the bottle of Jameson, and set it on the night table. In a ballet of silent protest, she wouldn't fill the glass. With his bruised hand, he poured the whiskey, the glass jittering nearly to the edge of the night table. He set down the bottle, picked up the glass, and swallowed greedily until it was empty. Then he set down the glass and again picked up the bottle.

"But darling."

"One more."

When he finished, he turned his head toward her. She could see the pain in his eyes.

He whispered, "You'll find a husband in no time."

She shook her head, her stomach churning at the idea of being touched by another man. "I don't want to find a husband."

"You have to. Even if you're pointlessly engaged to me."

She wondered if he wanted her to return the ring. Unless he asked, she wouldn't give it to him. *I want to keep it,* she decided, *in case . . .*

in case, what? In case I find a way to marry him? She'd already gone over and over the possibility in her mind and determined this couldn't happen. Disobeying her father, being left with nothing, and Henry left with no job and no way of living in a nation also suffering economic woe, a nation in which the French got whatever jobs there were before Americans were offered any—these were alternatives that would ruin them. Could she really cause Henry and David to live in the streets, to stand in the breadlines? Of course she couldn't. They must separate. Yet part of her would always be promised to him, though it would be a promise never fulfilled. "I'll always be engaged to you."

He laughed dryly and shook his head. "Always is a long time."

Her imagination failed when she considered never seeing him again, never seeing David again. Ignoring his sharp comment, she asked, "When will you come home?"

"But Laura," he replied, "this *is* home."

Her desolation grew. "But won't you return to Saint Paul?"

"I don't know."

"With David?"

"I won't go anywhere without David."

This wounded her. The necessity of her leaving David had broken her heart. Measuring how much she cared for him would have been impossible—it was as boundless as the pain she suffered now. But she was in a bind, and by sacrificing her own happiness, she'd ensured the livelihood of the man she loved and the well-being of the boy she considered her own.

Feeling her cheeks warm, she quietly drank the rest of her whiskey and looked away from Henry, at the painting of Mont Sainte-Victoire. She sensed that he was staring at her, but she didn't know what to say or how to explain her decision. She'd tried to make his life easier by hiring the housekeeper and tutor. And she'd reached an agreement with respect to his employment.

Turning back to him, she said, "I telephoned my father, who confirmed our agreement. He'll pay your usual salary, and you can remain here, in Paris, as long as you make adequate sales on behalf of the company."

"With that money," he said, "I can pay for the house."

"I don't know if you can pay for the house," she replied, "and also pay for your and David's other expenses."

"I'll fire the housekeeper."

"No, darling. You can keep the housekeeper and everything else. I'll send money from my allowance. I must do this. Please, don't refuse me."

He lay quietly. Again she thought he was asleep, but then he spoke. "Do you remember our second night at the Crillon?"

She blushed, recalling their first kiss. "I remember."

"Do you remember the other nights?"

"All of them."

"There haven't been enough."

"No."

"There won't be any more."

She said nothing, though he was right. For if there was something between them, there would have to be everything, and everything had led to this terrible day.

After a while she realized he was sleeping. She went along the hall to the empty bedroom and looked at her Louis Vuitton trunks and cases, lying open on the bed and floor, partly filled with clothes. How she wished she could close and stow them under the bed and in the closets, only to take them out when she and Henry and David traveled together.

Leaning over the bed, she folded the emerald silk dress she'd worn the day of their arrival and set it in the largest case. Then she couldn't do more without feeling nauseous.

After shutting the case, she ran her hand over its brass fixtures.

One more day, she thought. *Perhaps a miracle will happen and I can stay.*

54

But one morning later, Laura bathed and dressed and watched the taxis pull up in front of the house at seven o'clock.

The pain in Henry's head had eased—and for this she was thankful. Dr. Roche had come each noon since the injury to disinfect the wound and change the bandages. After Henry woke, his ribs remained sore, so he avoided coughing and spoke only softly to her and David. In the afternoon before, he'd sat on the brick patio, where he talked with David, read the detective stories of Maigret, smoked a package of Gauloises, and drank too much whiskey. He'd spent the day in his sky blue pajamas, a burgundy-colored bathrobe, and leather slippers.

That morning she woke and kissed him softly on the mouth. Head on his pillow, he watched with wounded eyes. She hugged him, touched the warm skin of his neck, and whispered that she loved him.

He moved a hand along the small of her back. God, how she'd miss his touch. Forcing herself to pull away, she went and stood for a moment in the doorway. Her lips wouldn't form the usual words— *goodbye, farewell, adieu*. On the bed where she'd found so much pleasure and comfort lay Henry, the man she loved. She knew that if she stayed a moment longer, she'd be unable to leave. So she shook her head and backed into the hallway.

"I'll wait for you," he called, his voice hoarse, his forehead lined.

"No, darling. You shouldn't wait for anything."

Wiping tears from her eyes, she went into David's room. Hearing her, he opened his eyes and climbed out of bed. Laura bent over to kiss his forehead. He felt warm and smelled faintly of soap. She hugged him tightly and for a long time. As they separated, he looked up at her. His eyes met hers for a second and then dropped to the floor. While she assured him of her return, he went to the window and saw the taxis in front of the house. She told him goodbye. He again faced her, his expression bereft. Sensing her resolve weakening, she said she loved him and left the room.

As the taxi drivers gathered her trunks in the foyer, an older couple, the Kislings, climbed the front steps, knocked on the open door, and gingerly entered the foyer. "Bonjour?" they called out.

"Thank you for coming," she said in English, entering the foyer. She offered her hand in turn to both of them, and each took it gratefully, almost bowing.

Herr Kisling was solidly built and in his mid- to late sixties, with thick gray hair and eyeglasses with tortoiseshell frames. His appearance was scholarly but pugnacious, until he smiled. Then Laura saw the light in his eyes, and his smile was easy, and his voice warm and friendly. Frau Kisling wore her curly gray hair in a bun. She was slender and short, almost fragile in appearance. Like her husband's, her smile was easy, but her eyes were dark and watchful and, Laura knew, hid a profound agony.

"Thank you, Mrs. Salter," Herr Kisling replied in English. In his thick German accent he presented himself as Max and his wife as Greta. Then he said, "You have saved us."

"No, no," she told them, blushing yet not correcting their belief that she was Henry's wife. "Your help is greatly needed here. While I'm in America, Henry and David will need assistance. I'm glad you could come with so little notice."

Herr Kisling nodded and looked about the foyer, with its high ceiling and marble floor. "A beautiful house," he said.

"Thank you, Herr Kisling. We've very much enjoyed living here, and I hope that you'll consider it your home as well."

"It will be excellent," he said.

"And if you'll follow me," she said, leading them along the hallway and into the kitchen. She stood at one end of the marble-topped island. "I hope this is acceptable. Henry and David like to eat." She smiled.

"A most beautiful kitchen," Frau Kisling said, touching the marble with one of her small hands. "Most beautiful."

Laura nodded in appreciation and turned to Herr Kisling. "David doesn't like school, but he's intelligent and must learn to have discipline. Without both of you, I'm certain he'd fall into very bad habits."

The older couple chuckled.

"We wish to work for you," Herr Kisling said. "Before, in Berlin, I was a professor. But the Sturmabteilung took our daughter, Tabitha, and I lost my position because I'm Jewish." He paused for an emotional moment, held a hand to his mouth, and then continued. "This is a new life for us, and we will take care of your family until you return. Please, trust that we will do our best."

"Our best," echoed his wife, her face watching his and then Laura's as she nodded vigorously.

"Thank you," Laura said earnestly. "Now, I must catch the train. Goodbye, Herr Kisling. Goodbye Frau Kisling." She kissed each of them on both cheeks, knowing she didn't have time to go upstairs a final time to see Henry and David.

After climbing into the first taxi, she looked up at the house and saw David standing beside the Kislings on the front steps. He was red eyed and teary faced.

And then behind David appeared Henry. His face was tanned from his time sitting on the back patio, and he'd changed into a sky blue shirt and tan pants. With unkempt hair pushing out from his bandages but somehow flattering just the same, he walked down the steps toward the taxi.

Heart rising in her throat, she swallowed, cranked down the window, and looked up at him. His emerald-flecked eyes watched her. Hands fidgeting, she said, "I'm sorry. I really am sorry."

He tried to smile. "Don't forget us."

She tilted her head. "You know I couldn't."

A moment of stillness between them, and he reached through the taxi window for her. His arms encircled her and held her against his chest, his left arm against her shoulders. She breathed his scent, felt his warmth, and appreciated the strength of his arms. And then he released her and withdrew.

He tapped the roof of the taxi, and the car began to move, away from him and David and the Kislings. Away from the life she loved. She wept silently.

Turning, she gazed through tears out the back window and saw Henry standing in the middle of the street. Down the steps came David, shouting and running after the taxi. She couldn't make out his words but knew he was crying and shouting for her to stay. As the taxi accelerated and turned north toward the avenue Bugeaud, he seemed to trip and fall onto the cobbles.

55

It all seemed possible until she reached coastal Le Havre after a long train ride from Paris.

As her three taxis pulled up to the dock and stopped near the gangway, sharply dressed porters surrounded the cars and began removing her trunks, which had been strapped to the roofs, and her cases from the boots. The porters had brought several long dollies alongside the taxis and set the luggage quickly but carefully onto them, with Laura watching the operation to be sure nothing was missed and nothing went missing. She knew that the Louis Vuitton luggage itself, without the wedding gown from Vionnet or the rest of the wardrobe she'd brought with her and the things she'd found in the shops on the place Vendôme, cost more than a porter would earn over several years of difficult labor. She watched them prepare to take her things off European soil and felt her spirits sink as she became dizzy and disoriented.

Hard clanging came from the next pier. Turning slowly to look, she saw a French destroyer taking on ammunition and supplies. No elegantly uniformed porters loaded that ship, only sailors dressed in navy blue work trousers and black boots, their bare shoulders and chests straining under their loads.

War, she thought. *How many of these sailors will it claim?*

She'd read about the Great War and expected a second slaughter to be worse. That's what her father had been telling her for several years, and on this point—and on this point only—she assumed he was right.

The rhythmic knell from the destroyer made her head hurt, but she didn't cover her ears.

Walking over to one of the dollies, she reached out and rested a gloved hand on the brass fitting at the corner of one of her trunks. She looked up at the enormous *Île de France* and recalled how she and Henry had been on this very ship only weeks earlier. How happy she'd been then. How the world had been filled with possibility. How la Perle was born as she'd sung in the lounge and received such applause. How she'd felt the faint stirring of desire for Henry, desire she'd believed at first to be dislike and disdain. How she'd changed her view of him, and how she'd allowed her desire its full expression. How she'd met David, learned his name, and cared for him.

David.

She looked down at her chest and the dragonfly pin of sapphires he'd stolen for her. Pulling off her right glove, she reached up and ran her fingers along the curved platinum that held the blue stones in the shape of a dragonfly, touched the silver wings and the diamonds that formed the creature's eyes. But after a moment she was seeing not the pin but David, his warm brown eyes that watched her whenever she entered a room, the smile he gave her almost every time she saw him. Feeling his arms wrap around her neck when she picked him up or hugged him before he went to sleep in the spare bedroom. The red mark of the sheets on his face when he awoke in the morning and came downstairs to greet her.

Everything she loved remained in Paris.

She, herself, the woman who sang as la Perle and was a mother to David and a lover to Henry—she remained in Paris.

If she were to leave now, she'd gain money and maintain her position in a provincial society but lose what made her the person she'd become. And Henry? He was handsome and smart, exciting in and out of bed, and would he remain unmarried and alone?

No, she understood that it wouldn't be long before he found another woman, and he might be happy. Yet she knew that by marrying an unimaginative businessman from her family's old money social set, she'd never be content, let alone joyful. And she'd spend the rest of her life wondering what might have been and wishing that she'd made a different choice. Permanent regret—this would be her lot when she returned to Saint Paul. A prison of regret that would encircle her until her final day, when at last she became free.

Was that it—was that finally it, the cause of the present shifting that she felt within her, the recalibration of all she'd believed, the sudden understanding—the understanding of death?

Death, its nearness, its finality, the certainty of doom, existing within her, alongside the very human wish to live and to have her own life. After years of frustration at home, she'd grown happy in Paris. Yes, at twenty-three she'd learned that living someone else's life would be a crime against herself, against how she was made, against the life that she'd imagined and, in Paris with Henry, had created for herself. Understanding all that she did, could she truly take this step and commit such a crime? Would the consequences be worse than those she'd suffer by remaining in France? *Was* there a consequence worse than a living death?

Her body abruptly feverish with her decision, she lifted her hand from the case and approached the lead porter. "Sir? Sir?"

He didn't hear, as he was speaking to his men, urging them on to greater speed and effort.

She walked over to the dolly he was helping to load. "Mr. Porter, sir!" she called.

He turned to her, pulled a white handkerchief from the back pocket of his trousers, and wiped his forehead. "Almost done here, ma'am. You can go aboard, and we'll get everything to your stateroom quick."

She didn't respond.

He held up a hand to his team of porters. "You *are* going aboard the *Île de France*, aren't you?" He stared at her, questioningly. "Ma'am?"

56

The taxi turned from the boulevard de Clichy into the rue Houdon and then stopped.

Stepping out in the cool air of night, Henry turned up the collar of his navy overcoat and walked out into the rain that glittered in the streetlamps and ran in the troughs between the cobbles. This was his first visit to the underside of Paris: the Pigalle district, home of the Moulin Rouge cabaret and seedy bars and brothels and drugs and young girls who did all manner of things. He'd read and heard about this neighborhood, though he was here for a meeting rather than an assignation.

He thought Proust had been right: *Les vrais paradis sont les paradis qu'on a perdus.* True paradise is the one you've lost.

In the five days that Laura had been gone, he'd felt as if his future stretched before him like a lifeless desert. He could find nothing to interest or comfort him, even as his head wound was healing rapidly and the volume of bandages that Dr. Roche used decreased by the day. *Un miracle,* Roche had told him. But he wasn't so sure.

Despite Roche's advice, he'd been drinking too much, and he'd been surly with David. Probably the two mistakes were connected, but his anger had no outlet except through whiskey and the boy. In a quiet rage he'd thrown into his dresser drawer the photographs of Laura they'd taken in the Métro station at the place Victor Hugo, yet his fingertips touched the smooth silver frames each time he reached for a pocket square. He'd tried to hate her and then to forget her. Neither had worked.

There it was—Bar Frida. The name in bright red, childish letters. He walked into the small, dimly lit establishment, filled with blowsy patrons smoking and drinking. Several looked up at him, focused on the bandage on his head, and then turned away. *Best not to get involved.*

At a table in the rear sat a man of perhaps twenty-eight, whose suit coat was wrinkled with casual wear and whose tie was askew. This young man raised his chin and glared.

Émile Levy's replacement, Henry thought. *And will he die just as Levy did, as I nearly did?*

"I'm Jean-Baptiste, assistant editor of *La Gazette*," the young man said, not getting up. He wore his dark hair rakishly long, and his face was unlined and pale. "You're Henry Salter?"

"Yes," Henry confirmed, offering his hand as he sat down. "How do you do?"

Jean-Baptiste's handshake was firm but very brief. He blushed when his eyes met Henry's. Or perhaps it was anger Henry saw in the younger man's face.

"The war will begin soon," said Jean-Baptiste. "The Germans will finish their business in the East and come for us. They'll have your help."

"*My* help?" Henry thought for a moment this new editor wasn't aware of his work as the Scarlet Pimpernel. "You'd better explain."

Jean-Baptiste eased forward. "Do you know a man in your firm called Barton Powell?"

Henry thought of Laura's father—prosperous and intimidating, a capitalist who made things and people do what he wanted. The man who'd taken Laura from him. Henry gulped his whiskey and said, "He's the owner of the firm, and he works out of our main office in Saint Paul. When I receive orders from Whitehall, I send them to him."

"You have no further connection?"

"None."

Jean-Baptiste looked at him intensely. "We've learned that Barton Powell is selling to the Germans."

"No," Henry replied instinctively, "that can't be." He sat up straighter, until he was looking down at Jean-Baptiste. "The firm supplies British and American forces. And under the United States Neutrality Acts, there's an embargo against Germany. Powell would have to smuggle the arms from Minnesota to New England and then aboard a ship to—where? I don't think it would go unnoticed."

"But, Monsieur Salter, it hasn't gone unnoticed," said Jean-Baptiste, eyes widening. "Powell has been selling to the Germans for at least six months, but not in the way you describe. They sell to a Swedish company in Göteborg. Sweden is neutral, so that is permitted under American law. The Swedish company sends the goods down the Baltic to the town of Wismar, in Germany, but the profits go back to Barton Powell in Saint Paul."

"You're certain the armaments leave Sweden?"

Jean-Baptiste sneered, glanced around the room, and said, "Do you think I came to this shithole for no reason?"

Henry narrowed his eyes. "Why would Powell do it?"

"Money," said Jean-Baptiste. "Isn't that what Americans care about?"

He thought of a sharp reply but made none. He knew his face had turned red with embarrassment, because he believed Jean-Baptiste. Barton Powell *was* mercenary. Profits were profits; a war in Europe didn't involve the United States; every country had the right to arm itself for defensive purposes. He'd heard these arguments in the past as Barton had pontificated in the firm's plush offices in Saint Paul, and he'd often agreed with them. But now he realized Laura's father had no moral compass. Barton was arming the Nazis, and it didn't matter to Barton how the weapons would be used. The firm's specialty—antitank and antiaircraft guns—would be used to kill French citizens and, if a war came and Americans fought in it, maybe even the boys he'd known growing up, maybe even him. And Laura's father didn't mind.

He nodded to the waiter, who brought him another whiskey. As he drank, he kept his eyes on the table and considered what Jean-Baptiste had told him. Distinct from the noise of the bar, something became clear to him then.

The men watching the house, he thought. *They aren't in the rue Dosne only because of my two articles for* La Gazette. *No, they're Germans. They know that Powell Manufacturing & Munitions is selling arms to their government. Yet they wonder why I, the director of European sales for that very firm, write articles exposing a smaller but still important traffic in arms via Nice and Metz? I'm double-dealing, they must think. Or Laura's father and I are working to eliminate the competition. Or there is another reason they don't understand. But as they don't have the answer, they'll watch my house until they find it or until my journalism ends by their own brutality.*

His face warm from the heat of the bar, he looked earnestly at Jean-Baptiste. "I'll find out," he promised. "And if it's true Powell sold to Berlin, you have my deepest apologies. I believe you know that I've been working against the Germans not only through my arms sales to Whitehall but through my activities here, in France."

"We know of the Scarlet Pimpernel," Jean-Baptiste told him. "And we don't question your loyalty. But will your loyalty compel you to stop Powell's company from selling to Berlin? If you can't stop the sales, we—and I mean *La Gazette* and our contacts in the government—will consider you our enemy and you won't be welcome in my country."

This wasn't the approach Levy had taken with him. Levy had demanded much but had been kind and solicitous and complimentary. But perhaps the era of the gentleman had ended, making room for millions of Jean-Baptistes. Or maybe everyone had to discard his manners in order to survive in the hard new world. He shook his head and, without looking at the editor from *La Gazette*, left a few francs on the table, went outside, and stood amid the colorful and lewd signs that glistened in the rain.

He clenched, then loosened his hands. He breathed deeply, in and out, just once. A stone on the cobbles caught his eye, and he walked a few steps out of his way to kick it, hard as he could, up the street. It skipped haphazardly until it stopped by a shadowy doorway. From the darkness stepped a young woman in a tan raincoat and a dark hat. When she began to open her coat, he turned away and descended from the hill of Montmartre in the direction of home, and David.

57

A week after Laura's departure from Paris, she returned on a train, which pulled into the Gare du Nord in early evening.

During the journey from Le Havre she'd considered whether it would be best to take a room at the Crillon and telephone Henry, or to appear at the house in the rue Dosne and greet whomever was there. Caution urged her to take a room at the hotel so that Henry and David might grow used to her return. How desperately she wanted to see them again! Wanted Henry to hold her and make love to her. Wanted to look into his dark eyes and touch his jaw and feel his shoulders above her. If he were to refuse to see her—no, that would be impossible. Her heart told her that even after her departure, their love remained strong. But if he did refuse—perhaps because he'd fear she'd leave a second time, or because he'd wanted her to leave in order to be safe in Saint Paul— she'd wait a month and try again. She would stay. This time, she'd be determined.

At the station she directed the porters to carry her three large trunks and the other cases to the taxi stand outside. It was a pretty evening in early fall, the air limpid and cool, the familiar avenues wide and welcoming. She climbed into the first of the taxis and retraced the route she'd taken with Henry less than two months before. Now she existed between two worlds, her position uncertain in both. And she couldn't know Henry's reaction to her return or if her father had learned that she'd failed to disembark in New York that day.

As she settled into a suite at the Crillon—again her rooms had views of the obelisk in the place de la Concorde—she thought about whether taking money from her trust fund had been right. Her parents would have given it to her husband if she'd married a Saint Paul businessman from their social set. But if she married Henry, well, she'd receive nothing. She remembered very clearly the telephone call from the hotel in Le Havre to her contact at First Bank, in Saint Paul, which she'd made six days earlier, and she blushed even now at her temerity and the ease with which she'd lied.

"Mr. D'Acquila, please," she'd said. "Laura Powell calling."

A moment later his deep voice came over the line. "Lorenzo D'Acquila. How may I help you, Mrs. Powell?"

Mrs. Powell. He mistakenly believed that she was her mother. No reason, she decided, to disabuse him of the idea.

"Good morning, Lorenzo. I've a favor to ask of you."

"How may I be of service?"

"My daughter, Laura, is leaving Europe for America over the next few days, but she needs to pay the many couturiers she engaged while in Paris. And she must also pay for the expensive, the *very* expensive, Louis Quinze chairs and three nice Renoirs she bought from an auction house, you understand?"

"Yes, of course, Mrs. Powell. How may I help?"

"I need you to transfer, from my daughter's trust account to her account at Banque de Paris, the amount . . ." And here she named a king's ransom, the equivalent of Henry's salary for eight years.

There was a pause on the other end of the line, and for a moment Laura believed her ruse was discovered.

"So much," Lorenzo D'Acquila said, obviously surprised by the number, but then he regained his manners. "But of course clothing for your daughter and the furniture and the paintings, of course all of it must be of the highest quality and very beautiful."

"I'm hoping it's as nice as she's described in her letters," Laura had replied, laughing indulgently as if at her daughter's being a spendthrift. "When will the transfer be complete, Mr. D'Acquila?"

But now, installed at the Crillon and without the funds to pay for it, the next morning brought great anxiety. It wasn't until after she bathed and dressed that she had the courage to telephone the Banque de Paris. Yet a brief conversation confirmed that she was affluent. She sighed and thought of the money. Perhaps when the war ended, her parents would forgive her and she'd inherit. Perhaps not. These would be worries for another year.

After setting down the telephone receiver, she again took it up and asked the hotel operator to connect her with the house she'd rented in the rue Dosne.

"Bonjour," she said when Frau Kisling answered.

"Bonjour," came the automatic response. And in the pause that followed, Frau Kisling seemed to recognize the voice she'd heard only the morning Laura had left Paris with her many trunks. "Fräulein Laura? *Wie geht es Ihnen?*"

"Yes, Frau Kisling, it's Laura. I'm well."

The housekeeper cried with delight. "Where are you? You couldn't be here, could you?"

"Yes, I am here. I couldn't return to America."

"Wunderbar! Wunderbar! Where are you?"

She smiled into the receiver. "At l'Hôtel de Crillon."

"Oh, you must come see us."

"I'd like that very much. But I must know what I'll find at the house."

"We are here," began Frau Kisling, before growing quiet.

Her chest tightened involuntarily. "Is David well?"

"Yes, yes. He is well. But like any ten-year-old boy he doesn't pay sufficient attention to his studies. Though he's very smart. Sometimes, too smart for his own good."

Her nervousness lessened a little to know that David was healthy. Now it would be appropriate for her to inquire after Henry, but no words would come.

Mercifully Frau Kisling broke the silence, speaking lightly. "Herr Salter is well, and his injuries heal, and his bandages are smaller." She paused a moment and then added: "Herr Salter is alone."

"Thank you," she told Frau Kisling. "Would you let Henry know that I'm here and that he shouldn't speak about it with David until he sees me?"

"Yes, yes, Fräulein Laura. But when will you come to the house? I want to see you. David will want to see you. Please, visit us."

"I hope to visit you," she said, worried now that Henry would demand that she leave Paris for the safety of America. "But first I must see Henry."

58

Arms filled with paper shopping bags, Henry and David walked into the foyer of the house. The way Frau Kisling looked at Henry when she came out from the kitchen to close and lock the door and help with the bags, he knew something important had happened. Her silence in front of David indicated the news was appropriate only for him.

Recognizing her expression, he called for Herr Kisling, who was reading in the library, and asked him to take David by taxi to the Eiffel Tower. See how high David will go, he asked Herr Kisling, but not so high he's overly frightened. Kisling set down his volume of Goethe and stood up quickly. David ran upstairs for his most comfortable shoes. A moment later they were gone, and Henry strode into the kitchen, where Frau Kisling was putting away the groceries in the pantry and adjoining scullery.

"What is it?" he asked.

With effort, she set down two heavy jars of crushed tomatoes. Staring at him, she crossed her hands in front of her. She breathed deeply and said, almost softly, "It's Mademoiselle Laura." And then she couldn't help but smile. "She has returned to Paris, to the Crillon."

"Here? Now?"

"Yes, Herr Salter. She never went to America."

"You're sure?"

"I haven't seen her, but she called on the telephone."

She wouldn't have telephoned from America, he knew. Laura, at the Crillon, not four kilometers from here! Had she decided that she wanted to stay with him and David, no matter the personal cost? Despite his trepidation, he couldn't keep the joy from his voice. "The Crillon, you said?"

Frau Kisling nodded.

"I'm going out," he said. "Please tell no one about Laura."

"*Natürlich*, Herr Salter."

59

After climbing out of the taxi by the Crillon's entrance, he walked through the large doors of polished brass and into the lobby, where he approached the reception desk.

"Would you ring a guest named"—here he paused to consider the name she'd use if she were truly opposing her father's command—"a guest named Laura Salter?"

The clerk looked at the hotel records, smiled at him, and said, "*Un moment*, monsieur." She picked up the telephone and dialed. "I have Mademoiselle Salter on the line. May I give her your name?"

"I'm Henry Salter, her . . . husband."

"Oh, monsieur, I did not understand. I am sorry." The clerk then spoke into the receiver and listened for a moment. "Your wife asks that you come to her suite. Number three seventeen."

He thanked the clerk and took the elevator to the third floor, where he tore along the hallway and thought about Laura's intentions. Was she using his name only to hide from her family? Or was she hinting at something else?

As he stood at the door to room 317, he rapped on the enameled wood and waited.

All was quiet. He knocked again and heard footsteps moving across the rug within. The door remained closed. He could almost hear her breathing on the other side of the door. He made to speak, but his mouth was so dry he managed just to clear his throat. After swallowing twice, he said, "Laura?"

A pause. "Henry?"

"Yes."

"Are you angry with me for returning to Paris?"

"No, but I don't understand why you're here."

"Oh, Henry," she said with a sigh. "Leaving was like dying, and I'm just not ready to die."

He breathed deeply, stared at the door, and asked, "Are you alone?"

The lock turned, the handle pivoted downward, and the door was pulled open.

She wore a navy blue dress with white polka dots—her pearl necklace and pearl earrings visible because she'd pulled her hair back into a barrette—and blue heels. On her finger was the ring she and David had bought at the shop in the rue Saint-Honoré. Seeing it gave him confidence. At the same time he realized that he needed to hold her, whether or not she returned his feelings.

He stepped toward her and kissed her briefly on the lips and then held her tightly, bending slightly so his nose was close to her ear. He could smell her Chanel No. 5. He could sense her nervousness. Relief and joy filled him as her arms wrapped around his back and pulled him hard against her. He felt her slender frame, her breasts and waist, her slight shoulder bones. Warm tremors of love and desire infused his body. He held her even more tightly, before loosening his arms and moving apart from her.

"Come in," she said, and when he passed by her into the sitting room, she closed the door and turned to him.

For a moment he feared that he'd made his emotions too obvious, so he went over to the windows and looked out at the leaves that had fallen onto the paths through the Tuileries. Why stare at her with an expression of yearning, when he didn't understand her motives? He touched the bandage over the left side of his forehead, pushed his longish hair over it, and listened to her go to the bar and pour two bourbons over ice. As she approached him, he turned, took the glass from her, and looked at her intently. "Why didn't you go to Saint Paul? What about your inheritance and your family—and your safety if there's a war?"

Her pink lips curved along the rim as she drank deeply. When she lowered the glass, her wet mouth appeared almost swollen, as if he'd kissed her for hours. "As for my safety," she said, "I choose to believe that we'll be safe. Maybe that's a naive and silly belief, but together—the two of us and David—we'll survive. Somehow. And I might as well confess that I took most of the money from my trust account. I called First Bank and had it sent to the Banque de Paris—they thought I was my mother. So I have something to live on, for a few years."

"Your father won't try to find you?"

"He doesn't know where I am. Anyway, what can he do? I'm an adult. I have the money that was to be mine, or more likely my eventual husband's, upon my marriage. They don't own me, no matter how much they believe they do. But I'm sorry, Henry, I'm very sorry."

He watched her compassionate eyes. "Sorry for leaving?"

She gave a slight smile and shook her head. "No, my darling. You see, when I chose not to go back to Saint Paul, it meant that my father would sack you from your position at his company. If you haven't heard from him, I'm sure you will. Or maybe you won't, but you no longer have a job. So my choice has taken away your livelihood." She held up a hand to keep him from speaking. "Yes, you'll say that you don't care, that other things are more important, but your job is important too. It's true that I have enough money to support . . . to support the three of us, if you want to be with me, but eventually, in several years, we'll run out. And so I'm sorry for causing you to lose your position."

He considered all she'd said. The loss of his job, especially after he'd learned from Jean-Baptiste that Powell Manufacturing & Munitions was arming the Nazis, was a sort of relief. That he was no longer compromised by working for such a firm made him feel lighter and led him to assume that other jobs, other positions might become available. His shoulders seemed to rise, as if a burden had been lifted. "It's all right," he told her. "I . . . I don't mind. Another time, perhaps I'll explain. But you should think about your safety at this hotel. Wouldn't your father, or his agents, search for you here?"

Uncertainty spread across her face. Within her string of pearls, her neck flushed like a rose. She raised the tumbler to her mouth and drank the bourbon until it was gone. "I don't know. I . . . I don't know where to go. Wouldn't they find me at any hotel?" She sat on the sofa, covered in pale-green silk, and lit a cigarette. After exhaling, she leaned over, slipped the straps of her shoes from around her heels, and tucked her feet beneath her. She looked at him with an expression he took for courage and, perhaps, hope. In a soft voice, she asked, "Would you still have me?"

He sensed his body warming. "That would depend on many things."

"You see, I still love you," she said nervously. "I thought I might love you less when I'd left and was about to board the *Île de France*, but I was wrong. I saw things more clearly than ever before. I saw that my family likes me only when they approve of me, which is when I do exactly what my mother did at my age." She shook her head and reached forward and stubbed her barely touched cigarette in the ashtray on the coffee table. Her eyes filled with tears. "What you can't know is that I'm sorry for leaving you, even if we thought it was forever and it turned out to be only a week. I felt that I'd die if I didn't return to Paris, and to you."

His heart throbbed with excitement. He said, "What do you want now?"

"Henry, I've loved you every day I've been gone. I've loved you more than when I was here." Great emotion washed over her chest and shoulders. She breathed deeply and tried, with only mixed success, to prevent herself from weeping. "I couldn't," she said. "I could not leave you for more than a few days. I couldn't leave you again. No, never."

Seeing that he didn't respond, she quietly stood and straightened her dress. In her bare feet she was a few inches shorter than he. Moving closer, she tried to smile faintly, her face flushed with pink, and put her hands on his shoulders. Slowly, she pulled him close and pushed her face into his shirt.

"Gather your things," he said. "I'll take you home."

She looked up at him, her eyes vulnerable and showing fear. "Are you certain you want me?"

"You're the only one want I want, the only one I'll ever want. Are you prepared to be with me?"

She stood and put her tremulous hands together. "I am."

"In sickness and in health?"

"Yes."

"Children?"

She flushed again. "I want to have your children."

"Till death do us part?"

Her stomach tightened. "Yes, but I don't want to think about death. We're too young."

He nodded. "And your family?"

"I don't care."

"They'll despise us."

"I'd rather be despised than miserable."

"You're willing to live here during the war?"

She raised her chin. "I am."

"It will be dangerous. It might be fatal."

She nodded once. "The price of living."

He looked out again. Sunlight dappled the colorful trees around the place de la Concorde.

This is heaven, he thought. *But for how much longer? And can I keep all of us together if the Germans invade?*

He said, "I haven't told David of your return."

She faced him. "Will he be upset?"

"I think he'll be happy but afraid of loving you too much, too quickly."

"Yes," she agreed. "I know he loved me and I abandoned him. But I will tell him—and I'm telling you—that I'll never leave him or you again."

"He might not believe you."

"Maybe not," she said. But then she lifted her face. "But I'll prove it to him. And to you."

60

That afternoon when Henry and Laura walked into the foyer, Frau Kisling heartily embraced her. Three inches shorter than Laura (more when Laura was wearing heels, as she was today), she pushed her face into Laura's upper arm and squeezed until the younger woman thought she'd pass out from lack of breath. Herr Kisling came in from the library, where he'd been listening to the news on the radio, and called out to her: "Laura? Laura!" His face and eyes warmed with emotion as he hugged her with gusto and kissed her cheeks. She could only smile and tell the Kislings how happy she felt at seeing them again and how much better she hoped to know them. Then she turned to Henry. "I need to see David."

Henry looked concerned. "Alone?"

"Yes. But would you join us in a few minutes?" She touched his arm and then walked up the wide staircase to the second floor and past the hallway bathroom and the master bedroom to David's room. She hesitated. Did his anger at her abandonment remain? Would he ask her to leave, to return to America? Though she suffered many doubts, she also couldn't ignore her compulsion to see him: she was certain of her love for him. With only a door separating them, she couldn't turn away. Her lungs seemed to swell with emotion, and her hands grew warm. Knocking briefly but loudly, she pulled down on the latch and pushed open the door.

He lay on the bed, resting on his elbows, reading a book. His face was away from the door, but she could see his short hair and shoulders, which seemed to have broadened since her departure. "David?" she said quietly and moved closer. "David?"

He closed the book and then was still, as if her voice resonated in his ears for a moment before surprising him. Pushing himself up and turning his head in one motion, his eyes wide and his expression filled with delight, he called: "Miss Laura! My God! You're here!"

Seeing his face again was like breathing joy. "David!" she called. "I'm so glad to see you."

They embraced, and she sat on the bed, beside him. He kissed her cheeks, hugged her, and kissed her cheeks again. Her body flushed with warmth. As he pushed his head against her shoulder, beneath her jaw, she smelled his boy smell and kissed his hair, closing her eyes and enjoying how his arms had gone around her and held her with such excitement. He was just as she'd dreamed over her week of travel. His scent she knew as well as Henry's, as her own.

"I can't believe you're here," he said. "Did you go to America already?"

"No, darling, no." She shook her head with a smile. "I never went to America. I decided that I couldn't go."

He seemed confused. "But will you be leaving soon?"

"No. Not soon. Not ever. David, I'll never leave you again."

His face brightened, and then he frowned. His eyes darkened as he watched her, his mistrust obvious. He looked down and began picking at a fingernail.

"You're my son. I couldn't leave you."

"Really?" he said, raising his eyes to hers. "You want me to be your son?"

"If you'll have me as your mother."

He leaned forward and hugged her tightly. "You know I will."

The door opened wider, and Henry entered the room. "David, are you all right?"

"Miss Laura's here," the boy said. "Did you know she'd come back?"

"Not until this morning. She surprised me too." He leaned down, kissed Laura's cheek, and playfully squeezed David's shoulder. "But this time we're going to stay together, no matter what."

"We are?"

"You're damned right we are," he said with grave certainty. "Why wouldn't we? And as soon as we've worked it out with the authorities, we'll adopt you as our son."

"But I thought I've been your son since I met you."

"Of course you have. But when you're adopted, you'll be connected to us legally, a connection that can never be severed. Never. And that's something I want very much."

"Me too," David said.

Laura touched his cheek, thrilled by its warmth and how it was, in a way, now hers.

61

At sunset Henry closed and locked the door to the large bedroom. In the fiery light coming through the tall windows, he watched Laura, now dressed in a light-gray skirt and a blouse of sky blue, turn toward him. Her gaze was direct and loving but uncertain and apologetic.

He meant to assure her and to show that he loved her. His hands were warm, and he sensed a drop of perspiration fall from his underarm within his shirt. He felt winded and dazed at what would happen, at the intensity of his need for her, at the suddenness with which he'd regained love after losing it completely and forever.

Moving toward her until they were standing inches apart, he gazed for a moment into her light-brown eyes, made even lighter in the sunlight, her irises glittering as if they had specks of amber and onyx floating in them. He saw her rosy lips, damp and perfectly formed. And then he kissed her, his mouth remembering hers. Reaching for her, he touched the string of pearls round her neck, the soft collar of her blouse, and then down along her spine and narrow waist. For a while he held her this way, his lips touching her mouth, her face, her neck, before he pulled her toward him.

He put his hands on her waist and held her tightly, felt her tremble at his touch. He kissed her gently, then insistently. He pushed her against a sun-drenched wall and ran his hands along her legs, pulling down her panties. She leaned back, putting one arm behind her as the other held the hem of her skirt above her navel. He let down his trousers, the silver belt buckle landing with a soft click on the oak floor, and with his hand caressed the arch between her legs, causing her to make a faint cry at the back of her throat.

He was gentle as he pushed himself into her, holding her legs, holding her everywhere as she leaned against the wall and closed her eyes.

"Oh, Laura," he whispered. "My darling. My God, do I need you. If you hadn't come back . . ."

"But I have," she assured him. "I have."

62

They were in love, but they weren't innocent in the ways of the world.

The next day she moved the funds she'd taken from her parents over to Henry's account at the Banque de Paris. She'd decided the money was safer if held in his name—less chance of her father trying to seize it. Then Henry withdrew a large sum of that money, fearful that if the Germans occupied Paris, they'd halt all bank activity, perhaps even loot the banks of currency.

He hid the money around the house, enough for them to live comfortably for a couple of years. All crisp new bills, dry as leaves, which he rolled into little bundles. Some he stashed beneath a pile of winter sweaters in his chest of drawers. Others he lodged beneath one of the library's loose floorboards and covered it with a Persian rug. Smaller rolls filled every breast pocket of each suit he owned. At night he sometimes wandered the house, dividing the money into ever-smaller increments, finding new methods of hiding it. Bills lined his shoes, so that he could hear a faint crinkling when he wiggled his toes. The rest he kept in his money clip.

He knew that wads of franc notes couldn't buy happiness, but he guessed that in wartime they could buy everything else. He and Laura and David were as secure as they could be, living just over two hundred miles from Hitler's Germany.

Not far, he realized, if the Wehrmacht—the German war machine—attacked. And if the defensive Maginot Line didn't hold, it would be months, but no longer, before the Nazis overran Paris. He feared what might happen to Laura, but he had the recurring nightmare that David would be captured and all the money in the world wouldn't be enough to save him.

Yet he learned to live with those fears, and for many months all seemed well. Once it became clear that the Scarlet Pimpernel had ceased writing, the men who'd stood across the street, watching their house, vanished. The lives of his new family grew more intertwined, and deepened. Paris and the house in the rue Dosne began to feel like home—a home they might never leave. He knew that all of them—Laura, David, and the Kislings—came to believe that their existence would go on in this way, all dangers having receded more or less permanently, with peace remaining in their part of the world. Each month, the fear of war faded somewhat, until it returned in a new and terrible form.

PART II

63

Twenty-one months later

Europe had changed, and David's life was in danger.

Henry gathered his makeshift family in the dining room of the house in the rue Dosne. This would be a serious conversation, and to mark its importance, he'd put on a somber gray suit and a plum-colored tie. He was dressed like a banker, but instead of counting money he was counting lives.

Late the September after Laura had returned, they'd heard on the wireless that Chamberlain, the prime minister of Britain, had signed the Munich Agreement, giving Hitler the Sudetenland. "Peace for our time," Chamberlain had told his nation. Henry had hoped the prime minister was right, but he'd had his doubts. Two months later, they'd read news reports of Kristallnacht, the pogrom in Germany led and coordinated by the Nazis, who sent tens of thousands of Jewish citizens to concentration camps. And only seven months ago the Wehrmacht had invaded Poland, bringing France into the war. Although the French military hadn't fired a shot—although the fields between Paris and Berlin were green with crops while the Germans were busy in the East, fighting the Poles—France and Germany were at war.

Night covered the city like a stifling blanket. The dinner plates and silver had been cleared away and washed, the drapes closed. The chandelier over the table he'd switched off, leaving the room partially lit by a floor lamp in one corner. Standing around the rectangular walnut table with him were Laura, David, and the Kislings.

He lit a Gauloise and looked up. His head had completely healed from his beating in the summer of 1938. His thick brown hair had grown over the scars, and it was only he and Laura, who touched him in the night, who felt the rough skin above his temple, who knew how close death had been. "It's April 1940," he began, "and soon the war will reach Paris." He saw that his prediction surprised nobody, and he continued. "Like you, I read the newspapers, and I hear talk in the cafés. Smart people think Hitler is afraid to attack France and that he's satisfied with the Drôle de guerre, the Phoney War in which there isn't any fighting. But do you know what I think?"

The Kislings and Laura nodded somberly.

David said, "Hitler is the worst person in the world."

Henry didn't smile, for David wasn't joking. Neither was he. "Hitler *is* the worst person," he agreed. "And it doesn't matter that France's Armée de terre waits behind the Maginot Line. Nobody can stop the Germans. And nobody in Paris will be immune from their brutality."

He didn't remind everyone of *Le Figaro*'s reports of women and children being evacuated from London, in preparation for an attack from the air. He didn't point out that his little family was stuck in France. He'd told only Laura that Richard Crescent, of Britain's ministry of war, had used his influence to halt America's issuing a passport, visa, or any kind of papers for David. Crescent had explained: Chamberlain hadn't given Whitehall the resources it needed, so it must rely on unpaid observers, or *informants*, or *spies*—whichever term one used—like Henry. Not forever, no. But for a while longer, Henry must continue his work and not leave the Continent.

For months Henry had refused Crescent's demands, and the date of his firing from Powell Manufacturing & Munitions receded. Perhaps for these reasons the house in the rue Dosne ceased being watched.

How peaceful it was to live free of surveillance. Grateful that his articles for *La Gazette* were forgotten, he studied the daily press reports on the German war effort in Poland and the occupation of the Sudetenland, on the strength of the Maginot Line, and on the buildup of the British defenses, and he decided that he had nothing to add.

But then he grew angry—at the way Laura's father had been arming an evil force that was striving to destroy the Poles and Jewish people like David—and bored, as her father had sacked him when she'd decided to live with him in Paris. Her parents blamed him, and perhaps more than anyone, he was to blame. She also wrote them about David, but they couldn't or wouldn't understand. They'd called her a thief and a whore and then ceased replying to her letters.

Only a week ago, after months of using his former business contacts to verify numerous clandestine arms shipments from Powell Manufacturing & Munitions to Hitler's army—just as Jean-Baptiste had alleged at Bar Frida on the place Pigalle—Henry had described Barton Powell's criminal affairs in a third article for *La Gazette*. His piece had led to an investigation of Laura's father by the Federal Bureau of Investigation, something neither Henry nor Laura regretted, as well as the cessation of international sales by Barton Powell's firm.

"The war will reach the *seizième* and our street," he told them, his voice low. "If not now, then very soon. Even though Paris hasn't been attacked, we've heard the fighter planes and the bombers. This is bad news. Three of us are Jewish. And if Hitler invades France, then America will enter the war and Laura and I will be enemies of the Third Reich. I'm already a marked man, due to my articles for *La Gazette*. They almost killed me once, and they'll probably try again. So we must be careful, and we must prepare. I've thought about these things, and you may have suggestions, but these are my . . ." He struggled with the word *orders*, not wanting to sound like an army general. "These are my requests," he said.

"I have an idea!" David raised his hand as if he were in a tutoring session with Herr Kisling, though his voice had broken earlier that year and now sounded almost like a man's voice. "We could barricade the door with wooden boards."

"Yes." He smiled at David. "That's a good idea. I'll add that to my list. All right?"

David nodded with a bit of pride. "Yes."

"So beginning tomorrow morning we'll leave the house in groups of two or more. If all of us try to leave at once, or if we take suitcases and have taxis pick us up, or if we purchase train tickets, we'll be followed and our new location will be noted by German agents. It might seem easy to run, to escape, but it's impossible now. We'd be moving locations but watched just the same. So we must wait for the right opportunity. Until then, don't leave the house alone, because we're under surveillance. Whoever is watching will be less likely to hurt us if there are two rather than one. We must show that we intend to stay forever, that we're not considering leaving the city. You understand?"

"Who has us under surveillance?" Herr Kisling asked, tightening his mouth and furrowing his brow.

"It can't be true," said his wife. "How are these people watching us?"

Henry didn't explain that he regretted his article exposing Barton Powell's sale of arms to the Wehrmacht—and not because he'd destroyed Germany's method of acquiring American armaments. No, his regret stemmed from the unfortunate change in the rue Dosne.

The day after his final article for *La Gazette* was published, and for each of the six days since, a series of young men began to stand in the doorway of the house across the street. These younger men were thin, with military posture. Schoolyard brutes like Cagney had been sent on other errands; professionals had taken over.

Now, he silently told himself, *they're certain that I'm a spy. They want to discover my sources, my agents. Where I've done nothing but research as the basis for small-time journalism, they've seen spy craft and running agents they can't find. They've come to believe that I direct spying operations that might reach into Germany, into the command of the Wehrmacht and into the chancellery itself, while in fact I'm nothing but a freelance reporter.*

How do I convince them I'm not a spy? he'd wondered over and over. But he couldn't imagine a way to do it, at least not one they'd believe.

He also understood that Frederick Abendroth's patronage of La Pomme might have been a way to threaten Laura's father. No more arms shipments to the Wehrmacht, the Germans may have hinted to Barton Powell, no more Laura. Or perhaps the patronage was innocent and Abendroth had happened upon la Perle and fallen under her spell. How could Abendroth have learned that she was the daughter of an arms manufacturer?

The reasons for the surveillance didn't matter, he'd concluded. It wouldn't stop, not after the damage his final article for *La Gazette* had done to the German war effort, not until after the invasion.

If his family and the Kislings left together, he was certain they'd be stopped. If all of them left in stages, the last one would be captured. He guessed the men kept count of who was in the house and how many had gone. After setting the burning Gauloise in a crystal ashtray, he said, "I thought you'd noticed."

"What? Who is there to see?" they asked.

"Come with me," he said. "But be careful on the stairs—we'll keep the lights off."

64

Henry led them up to the second floor and up the narrow back staircase to the maid's quarters on the third floor, which had been taken over by the Kislings. The room was clean, and the glass doors built into the mansard roof were swung inward to let in spring's cool night air.

"To the left," he said to David and Herr Kisling—the first to stand on the narrow balcony.

David leaned over the railing. "There's nothing."

"Look more carefully."

"*Scheiße*," Herr Kisling muttered.

"I see him!" David said in an excited whisper. "I see him! The cigarette he's holding! Doesn't he know we can see him?"

"Oh, I think he does know," Henry said. "What should worry us is that he doesn't care."

Frau Kisling took her turn at the window. "*Mein Gott*," she said and looked away while gripping her diminutive hands together as if in prayer.

Laura stepped near the window, saw the shadow across the street and the suspended orange disk of the burning cigarette, and left. She went out into the hallway and turned around.

All watched Henry, waiting for him to say something. "Come inside and close the windows and drapes," he said. When this was done, he switched on the nightstand lamp and continued giving his instructions. "There is a man watching our house at all times. I don't know if he works for the Nazis or their sympathizers, and it doesn't matter. Never leave the house alone, and never at night. David, I don't want you to go out unless you're with me. Do you understand?"

"Why can everyone leave but me?" David complained. "I'm twelve. I can go out by myself."

"You know why. We don't need to talk about your lack of papers and your Jewish . . . background. And I said you could leave, but you must be with me. Do you understand?"

With a sour expression David said, "Yes."

"Tomorrow morning we're going in twos to buy provisions. We're going every morning for a week, and we'll bring back as much as we can carry, but we won't use taxis or delivery services. We don't want them to see what we're doing."

"But what *are* we doing?" Herr Kisling asked, head tilted to the side.

"We're buying food that will last, in addition to perishables like milk and eggs. Buy coffee, buy as many Swiss chocolate bars as you can. Buy wine and drinking water, salt and pepper, lots of sugar and cooking oil, flour and canned vegetables. Buy provisions for the house like bleach and soap, everything we need to live for three months."

"Three months?" David said. "You want us to stay in the house for so long?"

He shook his head. "Not unless we're forced to remain inside. But if war comes, there will be shortages. The Germans will take everything. Everything, you understand? How else will they feed themselves? So we must be sure to get what we need. Laura and I will give you money to buy everything. Herr Kisling, please find all the books David will need for the next six months, *bien*?"

"*Bien*," Herr Kisling said and looked at David, who groaned.

"School, school, school. I hate it."

"Everyone," Henry told him, "hates school. But at least you're learning from Herr Kisling, or you'd be learning from me. And since I don't know anything, that would be a very bad predicament."

A few smiles from the group. Already the small room had become warm, and the possibility of virtual imprisonment weighed on their minds.

"A moment longer," Henry said. "The Germans haven't invaded, and their agents won't try to take us while the French govern this country. And perhaps my worries will fade if the Maginot Line repels the Wehrmacht. Nothing will happen quickly. So, we'll continue living here in Paris while I find a way to escape somewhere all of us will be safe. We'll wait and see what happens. If we need to escape, we will."

"How?" asked Frau Kisling. "Where? When we tried to leave Berlin, it took six months. It was horribly difficult."

"I think we could climb out these windows, which after all are set within the roof. We could climb up onto the roof and walk to the end of the row of houses and then get down. Somehow."

"I cannot fly," said Herr Kisling.

"I will think of a way out," Henry promised them, patting Herr Kisling's shoulder. "And where we'll go. But for now we must be careful and we must prepare. In that respect, Herr Kisling, I have one further request of you."

"I?" the older man asked.

"Yes." And Henry leaned over and whispered to him.

"I'm not sure," Herr Kisling replied, shaking his head. "Escaping once might have been luck. But twice? I don't know."

Ignoring the old man's fatalism, Henry said to the group, "I hope we can stay here always. With luck, the Maginot Line and the French Army will keep the Wehrmacht where it belongs."

"Yes, *bitte*," came low voices.

"Thank you for listening to me. Perhaps we could go downstairs and drink to the success of our family. Whiskey for everyone? Or will it be wine?"

"Why not champagne?" Herr Kisling asked, expressing optimism he might not have felt.

So they went down the narrow staircase from the attic room and down the wide staircase from the second to the ground floor. They followed Herr Kisling into the kitchen, where he withdrew a cork from one of the bottles of Veuve Clicquot that Laura had bought upon her return. After filling five glasses, he pushed them across the marble counter to the waiting hands.

All smiled at each other and held aloft their glasses.

"*Santé*," said Henry.

"*Santé!*" they echoed.

More champagne was poured and another bottle opened. They became so focused on their good cheer in the face of danger, so enthralled by the tonic of the drink and of their conversation, that they didn't see David guzzle another glass and disappear up the wide staircase to the second floor.

He didn't stop but charged up the back staircase to the attic room. After switching off the light on the nightstand, he pulled open the drapes. Nervous, but made courageous or reckless by alcohol, he unlatched the doors and pulled them open. Inhaling the cool air of night, he moved to the railing and peered down.

The figure hadn't moved. The orange glow of a cigarette faintly illuminated a man's face.

He felt compelled to *do* something and not to hide like a fugitive, the way the rest of his family had done. He wanted the man to see him, to know he was here and unafraid.

Stepping back to the nightstand, he turned on the lamp and returned to the railing. He bravely surveyed the rue Dosne. But he didn't look at the man across the street—not at first. To the north and south his gaze wandered, until, throat swelling and palms hot, he looked directly at the orange face behind the cigarette and didn't blink. The man lowered his cigarette, dropped it on the concrete, and stepped on it, causing him to vanish from David's sight.

But David held his head steady in the direction of the man, who'd become less than a gray wisp of shadow. He counted to thirty and then moved away from the railing, into the room. After closing and latching the doors, he closed the drapes.

Nearly trembling with excitement and wanting to shout or groan in relief, he left the room and ran downstairs to the warm sound of the voices in the kitchen. There he had more champagne and talked and talked, but said nothing about his appearance on the upstairs balcony.

65

A month later in the early morning darkness, Henry and Laura held each other in the large bedroom. Sirens pealed near and far. He sat up and climbed out of bed. Herr Kisling pounded on the door and called, "It's the Wehrmacht! The BBC says they've gone into Belgium and will head south later today, toward us!"

Henry considered the Maginot Line along France's eastern border with Germany. Worthless, he knew, if the Germans truly were advancing from the north. He needed to determine what was happening.

A half hour later he left the house, ignoring the man across the street. He walked over to the place Victor Hugo, found a taxi, and asked the driver to take him to the place de la Concorde and back.

He glanced at the Arc de Triomphe and then the buildings lining the avenue des Champs-Élysées. All of it the Germans would take for themselves. Who could stop them? There were lines out some of the boulangeries, the markets, and the stores of the *cavistes*—it must be true that Germany had invaded Belgium. People were frantic, buying what they could, deciding too late to hoard food. How quickly things changed.

Yet Paris remained free, though panic had filled its inhabitants, and who could say the panic was unwarranted? He felt grim satisfaction in having purchased great amounts of food and wine. Yet he silently warned himself against complacency: things would undoubt-edly become bad, and life would be dangerous. What worried him most wasn't his or Laura's safety but David's. The boy had no papers, no passport, and an independent mind that might play the wrong card at the wrong time.

66

The next month was paradise within an inferno. All members of the family went out by twos or threes, ignoring the men who took turns watching the house from the sidewalk across the rue Dosne. Sometimes randomly, for several hours, the men were absent, and the family hoped they wouldn't return. But they always did.

When Frau Kisling visited the boulangerie at the corner of their street and the rue de la Pompe, there was still bread for sale. But when she walked to the *marché* on the place Victor Hugo, she found limited perishables and almost no canned food. Other housekeepers had whispered that a thriving black market existed on the place Pigalle. Early one afternoon she ventured there and couldn't believe that the prostitutes worked in the middle of the day. Yet she found potatoes and bread, greens and butter sold by a gangster from the back room of a café. Part of her wanted to flee the café and this dirty part of the city, but her family's nourishment was worth all indignities.

Herr Kisling walked along the Seine, browsing the used books for sale in the small kiosks. He also wandered into the Bois de Boulogne and, in the route d'Auteuil aux Lacs, found the riding stables. From a supplier there he found a length of thick rope that met the criteria Henry had given him. He also bought a large canvas sack and used it to transport the rope back to the house in the rue Dosne, a task that left him exhausted. He was relieved when Henry took it upstairs and stowed it in the attic room under the Kislings' bed.

Another day Henry went to the *caviste*, where little table wine remained, and bought expensive bordeaux. Walking around the neighborhood, he noticed the city had grown quiet. Although cars, delivery trucks, and autobuses continued to fill the streets, fewer patrons sat under the colorful umbrellas of the sidewalk cafés. Fewer yet wandered the streets with their children and dogs. He saw that shopkeepers were shorthanded, their employees perhaps gone to join the army or to return to the provinces in an attempt to elude the onrushing Wehrmacht that, each day, drew closer to the capital. In fact thousands were leaving their homes in Paris for the hoped-for safety of the south. In a day, many of these proud citizens of Paris had become refugees, traveling in overloaded cars and trucks and even on foot, pushing small carts with clothes, food, and personal or religious treasures. The exodus began in the northern sections of the city—the seventeenth, eighteenth, and nineteenth arrondissements—and spread southward, until the city center and the southern arrondissements began to lose people by the week.

One day, Henry and David took the Métro to the northern and eastern sections of the city, walking Pont-de-Flandre and Saint-Fargeau, where they saw barricades being erected by the French Army, aided by men from the neighborhoods. Henry explained that the same thing had been done during the French Revolution, in 1789, with only mixed success.

"They won't keep out the Wehrmacht, will they?" David asked.

"For an hour or two or three, maybe. But not much longer."

David stared. At last, he said, "The men who killed my family are coming for me."

Henry put an arm around him. "I'm working on a way for us to leave, to a place we'll be safe. We need to go far from the city where we can be isolated from others and where we can trust the people hiding us. It's not easy to find such safety."

Although David took his hand, his young, unlined face seemed hollowed out with fear. "I'm afraid, Mr. Henry."

He kissed the top of the boy's head. "All of us are afraid."

Closer to home, in the lush and leafy *seizième*, Henry and Laura walked the calm streets with David. They spoke compulsively about their lives and the war and the German soldiers who were coming to the city. They spoke of the bright days, the limpid nights, and when and how they might leave Paris. David asked again and again where they'd go, and Henry told him he hadn't decided, though of course he had, and he'd begun to make arrangements to flee. With the men watching the house for the past several weeks, he knew they were trapped, at least for a while. His plan—so carefully wrought—was to escape in the single moment when no one thought they could.

Within the gaps of their conversations came the sound of wireless radios through open windows as they walked under the trees lining the rue Saint-Didier. Voices from those radios came from Paris and from the BBC, reporting of German triumphs in the Ardennes. Once, they stopped below a window and heard of blitzkrieg. To David it sounded like his parents' burning shop and apartment. Henry pictured bodies torn apart by hellish machines. Another afternoon they went as far as l'Étoile, and as they returned along the avenue Foch, having passed the gate with the centaur where Henry had been beaten, they heard staccato wireless reports of the British Expeditionary Force retreating to Dunkirk, where they'd soon be surrounded by the German Army. Henry knew the Germans would wipe out the British, who had nowhere to go.

Within Henry's family, ordinary life continued. Laura fulfilled the role of mother and manager of the household. Never did she mention America or returning to Saint Paul. Frau Kisling enjoyed her company and followed her instructions with good nature. David's teenage sullenness became less frequent. He read and did the mathematics given him by Herr Kisling, and he enjoyed the comfort of playing on the patio and in the small backyard. Henry and Laura experienced again the passion of nearly two years ago, making love with a frequency, an urgency that surprised both of them. It was a living household, made intense by the notion that the peaceful city might soon be under Nazi control.

67

On the fourteenth of June they stood in the library, listening to the news coming over the wireless. Henry leaned against the bookcase and watched the others stare at the device encased in burled oak that sat on the edge of the desk. Frau Kisling's small hands made a steeple as her usually sunny expression darkened. Her husband shook his head at every new detail. Laura crossed her arms over her chest and shifted her weight from one high heel to the other, while David sat in a chair and rested his chin in his hands, his eyes dropping to the floor.

They heard a man's voice telling of the Wehrmacht's march into Paris. There was no fighting in the famous streets, the French forces having withdrawn to prevent the city's destruction. Yet thousands of jackboots pounded the cobbles of the Champs-Élysées. Tanks shook the Jardin du Luxembourg, where David had once sailed his toy boat, and trucks filled with Hitler's troops thundered past the stunned citizens along the rue de Rivoli. Would this bloodthirsty war machine destroy their homes? Take their wives and daughters? Eat food that rightfully belonged to the French? *Our government has retreated to Bordeaux. We are defenseless, at the mercy of a tyrant. Now, I will read instructions from Marshal Pétain.*

Henry went to the desk and switched off the wireless.

The others looked up at him. They heard birdsong through the open window.

"No," he said to them. "Don't listen to the news reports."

"But Henry, we need to know what is happening," protested Herr Kisling.

"We know the Wehrmacht has occupied the city. Everything else comes from that simple fact. The Germans are brutal. It may appear they'll use a gentle hand with us, but they won't. We're in terrible danger. I've been working on a plan to leave the city. For the past three weeks, I've been speaking with Madame Bernard, the woman who leased us this house, and she has agreed to help. Escape will be expensive. But I'm planning for us to leave at the right moment, at the only moment when we might have success."

Laura's voice was low and soft. "Where will we go, Henry? The report said the Germans have encircled the city."

"I've found us a safe place. We should prepare to leave. Another day, another week. No longer."

What at first seemed to be the sound of a truck rose in pitch and volume. A screeching noise filled the house, overwhelmingly loud. The library's heavy furniture seemed to rumble on the oak floors. They hurried to the open window and looked up. Above the city flew a formation of German fighter planes, Stukas, the undersides of their wings emblazoned with the black cross of the Luftwaffe.

David returned to the floor and sat with his hands over his eyes. Laura touched one of his trembling shoulders. Herr Kisling turned his back to the windows and went over to the desk and sat on the edge of it, wiping his brow with a wrinkled handkerchief.

Powerful and menacing, the Stukas crossed the sky like an arrow with a hundred tips, the first formation followed by another and another and another. How could anyone, even the Americans, drive them out of France? Henry shut and locked the window and looked out once more. He saw no soldiers, but across the street a man watched their house. This man had his hands in the coat pockets of his suit and a hat over his eyes, even in the heat of the afternoon, and he didn't look up at the fighter planes.

Henry cursed under his breath. He'd assured the others that they were waiting for the only possible moment they might escape, but he'd no idea when or if that moment might come. If it never did, he knew they'd die—and he'd be the first to be shot. An advantage, for he wouldn't have to witness the deaths of the others.

68

"I'm going to work," Laura told him at eight o'clock that evening. She'd bathed and put on a sheer black dress, her string of pearls and her pearl earrings, and her engagement ring.

He was behind the desk in the library, thinking how to move his family out of the city. Her announcement led him to sit up. He shook his head, wondering at the risk she was willing to take. "Honey, it's too dangerous. We don't know how badly the Germans will treat people, and there's a curfew. You shouldn't leave the house."

Her face flushed. "I *am* leaving the house, and there's no point in arguing about it. Monsieur Bellegarde said over the telephone that La Pomme is open and people are out in the streets and there isn't any danger. I've thought about it, and my singing is too important to give up. It's one of many reasons I came back to Paris, and it will be my protest against the Germans."

"But what if you're stopped and questioned?"

"I'll show them my American passport. America is a neutral country. What could they do? Nothing will happen to you or David, and I'm sure I'll be safe."

Henry decided that she'd go, no matter his objections. "Give me five minutes to dress," he told her. "I'll take you to the club."

He saw that her smile showed not triumph at winning the argument, but relief.

69

It was ten o'clock when the Kislings and David went to bed. Herr Kisling stood in David's room, wished him good night, and went out to the hallway, closing the door behind him. Then David heard the old man's heavy tread on the staircase to the third floor. David lay in bed, waiting, fidgeting, yearning to break free of the house. He listened as Herr Kisling's footsteps moved across the attic room and as the bed squeaked briefly when the older man climbed in beside his wife.

Ten minutes later Herr Kisling's rumbling snore carried through the ceiling of David's room. David jumped out of bed and began to dress in a gray suit and blue shirt. It wasn't right that he'd been left at home with the Kislings. Not with the German armies marching in the streets. What if, he thought, the Gestapo came to the house, looking for him or for Mr. Henry? Wouldn't he be trapped with two Jews from Berlin whose daughter had already been taken away somewhere terrible? As he threaded a pair of barrel links through the slits in his cuffs, he decided that just as he'd escaped Berlin in the past, tonight he'd escape the Kislings. He must join Henry and Laura at La Pomme, he decided. Only by taking a small risk would he have the safety he needed. He could do it, he told himself. He'd grown much stronger recently, and he was becoming a man in other ways. His voice. His shoulders and hands. Other parts of his body. Yes, he could go out alone, despite Mr. Henry's advice.

So he pushed open his bedroom window and looked down. After a moment of planning, he climbed through the opening, shuffled across the frieze above the library window below, and down the drainpipe. After landing on the flagstones, he looked across the street at the man who stood in the shadows, smoking. And then he ran, fast as he could.

But he never reached La Pomme.

70

"David?" came Herr Kisling's voice. "David, we have Latin this morning."

At first Henry thought the old tutor was having difficulty waking a boy who'd rather sleep than work on his Latin declensions. He didn't blame David, remembering how little he'd enjoyed his own Latin classes. Having returned with Laura to the house in the small hours, he turned over, hoping to sleep another hour or even two. Beside him, he could hear Laura's regular breathing.

Soon, he heard Herr Kisling's heavy tread on the stairs, and his mind softened and sank into sleep. But only seconds later, or that's how it seemed, he heard loud knocking on the bedroom door.

"Henry!" Herr Kisling called out. "David is gone!"

Henry climbed out of bed. He thought quickly. Going to the bedroom window, he looked out. In the doorway across the street from which the young men with military bearing had watched their house, there was no one.

Its emptiness told him everything.

A half hour later, after a frantic but hopeless search of the house, after observing that David's window was open, Henry and Laura sat in the kitchen, going over ways they might regain the boy they loved.

Weeping, Laura said, "Because of me, he's lost to us because of me. If I hadn't insisted on performing last night, he'd be here, at the breakfast table with us, safe."

"You couldn't have known what he'd do," Henry told her. "And we're not certain where he went."

She shook her head. "I'm certain he tried to go all the way over to La Pomme in the boulevard Raspail, to hear me sing. I should have known. And the man across the street took him. My God!"

Herr Kisling, sitting with a cup of coffee, removed his tortoise-rimmed eyeglasses, as he did when making an important point to students. "David climbed out his window. There is nothing you could have done. This is not your fault."

Shaking her head, she dabbed her eyes with one of Henry's linen handkerchiefs. "It *is* my fault. You must see that."

Frau Kisling was a few feet away, sitting on the patio steps leading down to the garden, mumbling to herself in distress.

"No," Herr Kisling disagreed. "It is not your fault. It was an accident."

"An accident," Henry repeated and stood from the table. "And we'll find him, Laura. We'll find him today. The office of the gendarmerie must be open. We ought to go and inquire—they have an understanding with the Germans." Having dressed in a blue pin-striped suit and a solid tie, he appeared to be a wealthy businessman whose son had gone missing. He'd hint at a reward for whomever found his son. Perhaps he'd do more than hint.

Laura shrugged helplessly and got up from the table. At Henry's request, she wore her pearls and the emerald green sundress from the day they'd arrived in Paris in June 1938. She put on her ring and her high heels and carried a small white handbag with a silver handle. Soldiers would either respect or hate people with money, he wasn't sure.

They left the house and climbed into a taxi that Herr Kisling, himself weeping, had called. Henry gave the address of a commissariat, at sixty-two avenue Mozart. When they arrived, a beefy German officer was pacing on the sidewalk, his polished black boots with metal heels striking the concrete. He was speaking in French to a group of gendarmes, who were slender and appeared feeble and disheartened in their wrinkled uniforms. The officer squinted into the morning light, but his expression and voice were firm. Behind him, in a row along the building, were his men. Shaved, well groomed, with blue dress uniforms, the soldiers of the German Army appeared invincible. They arrogantly stuck out their chins, held rifles at the ready, and wore handguns in holsters attached to their belts. They seemed alien on the pleasant street, from a different, much harder world.

"*We* give the orders," the officer said loudly to the gendarmes. "You follow them."

"But you don't know our city," a gendarme officer complained. "You don't know the French procedure."

The German soldiers snickered, and their officer answered the gendarme: "Now there is only the procedure of *Nationalsozialismus*. We will work with the Gestapo to maintain order, and you will help us. If you refuse, you will be charged with insubordination and dealt with in the German way. Begin your patrols, little gendarmes, and remember your place."

The gendarmes wandered off, along the street, listless and indifferent. The officer of the Wehrmacht turned to Henry and Laura, the only civilians present. "What?"

"Bonjour," Henry said, attempting to be excessively polite, as it was clear the officer felt he was owed enormous respect. "I understand, sir, that you are very busy, but we'd like to make an inquiry if you have time to consider it."

The officer shrugged. "That would depend on its subject."

"Sir, last night our twelve-year-old son left our house and didn't return. My . . . wife . . . and I are here to see if you've found any missing boys."

"Please, come with me," said the officer, who led them into the station—the exterior flagpole already flying the swastika—and extended his hand toward the largest office, whose nameplate had been removed and replaced by a hand-printed sign reading STURMSCHARFÜHRER HANOVER.

As they entered, they saw that a soldier stood at each side of the doorway within the office, where two wooden armchairs faced a large desk. The room was in partial darkness, with dim light coming through the single window and a torchère casting a faint yellow disk upon the ceiling. The walls were painted a pale blue, and pinned to them were yellowing maps of Paris.

Hanover removed his cap and set it on the desk. He sat down and looked at them. "You're American?"

Henry thought about lying, saying he was from Montreal, but what good would it do? He was from a neutral country—if you didn't look closely at the massive arms shipments the Americans were sending to Britain—in the prosecution of the war. "Yes," he said.

Hanover opened the center desk drawer and withdrew a fountain pen. He began writing on a pad of paper.

"Why are you in Paris?"

"We live here."

"Occupation?"

"I have independent means," Henry said.

Hanover looked up from the paper and stared at him.

Henry didn't blink, but he felt his face warm at this half truth.

"Where did your money come from?"

"My father was a surgeon, in the city of Saint Paul."

"Is your money here, in France?"

"Some of it, yes. At the Banque de Paris."

Hanover nodded and made a note.

"Your name?"

"Henry Salter."

"Address?"

Laura began to sob, almost hysterically. Henry turned to her. She reached for his hand and dug her fingernails into his palm. She bent over and theatrically dabbed at her face. She wasn't really crying, he determined. Her knifelike fingernails were warning him. He pulled back his hand.

"We live at three forty-nine avenue Kléber," he lied.

Hanover wrote the address. "The boy's name?"

Henry considered lying, but he'd already given his own name. "David Salter."

"When was he last seen?"

"Last night, perhaps ten or eleven o'clock. He was in his bedroom, reading. We thought he'd gone to bed, but in the morning his room was empty."

Hanover nodded. "Does this happen often?"

"No," Henry said. "Never."

"He's never stayed out all night?"

"No."

Hanover set down the pen. "Your son is twelve. Maybe he is testing your failure to impose discipline. Maybe he grew excited by the presence and strength of the Wehrmacht and went out with friends to watch us secure the city."

"Yes, sir," Laura said. "I'm sure that's what happened. We'll go home and wait for him." She stood and tucked the handkerchief into her sleeve. "I'm very sorry for taking your time. You're an important man. We shouldn't have come."

Hanover gave a false smile. "Before you leave, you must give me your telephone number so that if we find your son, I'm able to contact you."

"Of course," Henry said, also standing and taking Laura's elbow, a gesture that in normal times would earn him a jab to the ribs. He recited an imaginary number and then thanked Hanover, bowed with a show of deference, and escorted Laura between the two soldiers and out of the office. For a moment he let her walk ahead as he lingered in the hallway and listened carefully.

"Check on those people," Hanover said, having switched to German. "The Americans may be rich, but they are not tourists. When you have learned where they live, I will tell the *Obersturmbannführer*. He will decide what to do with them."

71

Henry joined Laura, who was waiting near the doorway to the street. A panic took hold of him that made breathing difficult. Yet he forced air in and out of his lungs to lessen his dizziness. "Let's go," he said, taking her hand and pulling her along. *"Hurry!"*

He was relieved that she kept up with him, in spite of her heels. A vise seemed to close around his throat.

Laura looked up at him. "If the Germans have David, we'll never see him again."

Instead of responding, Henry flagged the first taxi they saw. Not looking behind them—they were certain one of Hanover's men was following—they climbed into the back seat.

"One hundred francs," Henry told the driver, "if you outrun the man behind us."

The driver nodded, glanced into his mirror, and tore away from the curb. Under his breath he cursed Adolf Hitler.

After a moment Henry turned to look through the rear window. A soldier jogged after them, but there were no other taxis. As they turned left into the rue de la Pompe, the soldier disappeared from view. "We've lost him," he told Laura. "They won't find us, at least for a while."

She turned to him, her face no longer composed. In an instant her cheeks had become wet. Her voice was a quivering whisper. "Henry, they're going to send him to Germany or worse. Oh, God. How could this happen?" She tucked her shaking hands under her arms, as if she wanted a straitjacket, and continued. "If I hadn't gone to sing last night, if I'd stayed at home and read to him, he'd be with us; he wouldn't be hurt. What can we do, Henry?"

"Shh," he said, putting his arms round her, holding her tightly against him. But he could think of no words to comfort her that weren't obviously false.

"I should have stayed home last night," she sobbed in his ear. "None of this would be happening."

"Nothing *is* happening," he told her. "Nothing. He broke the curfew, and we'll get him back. David has never tried to go to La Pomme on his own. You couldn't have known he'd try last night, if that's what he did, and I'm not at all sure of that."

But silently, Henry cursed himself. He hadn't taken David with him to La Pomme. It was his fault, not hers, that their son was lost. The unstoppable German machine would grind him into pieces. And then it would come for him and Laura.

As he separated from her, he saw that her eyes were filled with the fear of a hunted animal. He looked forward, into the driver's rearview mirror, and saw that his own eyes had widened with alarm. His dread of what would happen lined his face.

72

David breathed the warm damp air of his cell.

In the near darkness—the only light came from a fixture in the hallway beyond the bars—he sat on a stone floor with several men and boys. Two of the men smelled, and from their rags he assumed they were beggars. The other three men wore suits, though theirs didn't fit as well as his did. He wiped his bloody nose and lips on the cuff of his coat, thinking it had been an hour or two since he'd last been questioned, but he couldn't be sure. *Who was the Scarlet Pimpernel?* his questioner had asked him again and again. How did Henry Salter know about the farms near Metz? How did he know of shipments in Nice? How had Henry learned that Powell Manufacturing & Munitions was selling to Germany? *How?*

He told them he didn't know any answers and didn't know what a pimpernel was. They'd hit him then, hard, so hard and so frequently he'd blacked out and awoken, groggy and hurting, in the cell. In the pocket of his coat he found an éclair he'd taken from the breakfast table and wrapped in paper. It eased his hunger, but then he grew thirsty, and there was no water in the cell. He wanted to take off the badge number—762—that had been hastily stitched over his suit's left breast pocket, but he knew they'd beat him again if he did such a thing.

Fatigue eventually carried him into a dream. He was running up the Bundesallee and turning east on the Ku'damm, his school knapsack over his shoulders. As he approached his father's store, he saw smoke funneling out through boarded-over windows. Flames streamed from his family's apartment above the store. He ran, faster now, crossing to the north side of the street. Uniformed men laughed and jeered as they pounded more nails into the planks they'd used to block the doors and first-floor windows. They were laughing and drinking beer and throwing the empty bottles into the flames. He screamed at them, loudly as he could, but they only laughed more loudly. Two of them picked him up and—*one, two, three*—tossed him like a sack of grain against the warm stone wall. He landed, stunned, but then looked up at the flames and turned and ran. And he awoke, kicking at the air of his cell, tears in his eyes.

A guard opened the door, pointed at him, and pulled him along the hallway to the small hot room, where he stood facing a man behind a desk. Previously, the man had been wearing a badly cut black suit and a black tie with a large stain across it. The man's white shirt collar had been blackened with dirt and sweat where it met his long and very thin neck. The man had a bulbous nose and didn't wear eyeglasses, though when he read his notes, he'd hold them close to his face. On this visit the man had been transformed.

He no longer wore his black suit. Instead, being on foreign soil, he wore the uniform of the SS. It fit the man perfectly, had been carefully pressed, and was cinched at the waist by a black belt that shone in the light. Here was an officer of the Geheime Staatspolizei, the Gestapo. David buttoned his suit coat and tried to meet the man's eyes but couldn't raise his own above the uniform, with the black cross at the throat.

"I am Unterscharführer Kruger," his interrogator informed him in German. "Would you tell me how you answered the guard in our language?"

David pretended not to understand, though he blinked when he heard the man's rank, which sounded quite elevated.

Kruger walked toward him, and David's hands began to shake. He further lowered his eyes, until his vision was filled with two enormous black boots. He tensed as Kruger repeated his question in crude French. He replied softly, "The guard asked me a question in German. He asked if I wanted a drink of water or wine. I said water."

"But you didn't say the word *eau*, did you? You said, *'Ich hätte gerne ein Glas Wasser.'* Why did you do that?"

"He asked me in German, I thought he had no French."

"How were you able to do that?"

"I take German in school."

"Which school do you attend?"

"I have a tutor—Monsieur Kisling."

"How does he know German?"

David knew he'd have to be careful answering this question, as he'd been careful in answering it the last several times he'd answered it. "I don't know."

"Is he German?"

"I don't know."

"Is he Polish?"

"I don't know. We just do my lessons, and one of my lessons is the German language. But Monsieur Kisling says I'm very bad at the German."

"I doubt that," said Kruger. "I doubt that very much."

"It's true!"

The high black boots stepped closer. He could smell sausage and beer on the man's breath.

Kruger said, "You have a faint accent, and it isn't French or English. It's Prussian. But I don't care about fine distinctions. I know you're German, and I think you're a Jew. Do you admit that you're a Jew?"

"No." David shook his head solemnly. "I'm Lutheran. I've never been to synagogue."

"Lutheran, are you?"

"Yes, sir."

The black boots stepped away from him. As David raised his eyes, he saw Kruger motion to the guard at the door. "Administer the test on this Jew."

The guard took hold of David's shoulders. "Let down your pants," the guard said in German.

David caught himself before reaching for his belt. He waited, pretending not to understand.

Kruger moved his head side to side. "Let down your pants," he said in French.

The previous beatings had taught him that to resist would be painful and pointless. So he unbuckled his belt, unbuttoned his trousers, and let them down.

Kruger pointed at him, and in French: "Underwear."

With index and thumb around the waistband of his cotton boxer shorts, David pushed them down to his knees, sighing as he did. Knowing they could see his circumcised penis, he couldn't prevent his knees from trembling, couldn't avoid Kruger's gaze.

It was no surprise when Kruger stared at his penis in silence, then looked him in the eye, shook his head, and said, "You didn't tell me the truth."

"But I *did*. In America, most boys are like me. You can ask my mother and father. They'll tell you. Have you spoken with them?"

Kruger laughed maliciously and said to the guard, "Send him with the others, to Le Bourget."

The guard took his upper arm and pulled him to his feet and out of Kruger's presence. In the corridor they passed the cell. He looked in, but the other men and boys were gone. The corridor turned, and turned again. Out through a heavy door, and sunlight caused him to squint and shield his face with his free hand. Alongside the building where he'd been kept was a truck with a barrel-shaped metal cover over the bed. The guard led him to the rear of the truck, where he could see inside. Standing, for there wasn't room to sit, were the men and boys from his cell, with perhaps a dozen others. He didn't see how they could make room for him. But the guard lifted and thrust him against the wall of flesh at the back edge of the truck. He put out his hands to give himself some space between himself and the men and boys around him, but he smashed into them just the same. Behind him the door closed, and he stood with the others in darkness.

"What is Le Bourget?" he asked aloud.

The men remained quiet. A stocky boy next to him, perhaps sixteen years old, said, "A railway station."

David turned and looked at the boy. He could see the face: it was dark like his grandfather's had been. The boy's breath was sour, and he spoke with a German or Austrian accent. David bowed and turned away, as best he could in that close space, and yet again he spoke. "I'm not an enemy of anyone. Why would they send me to a railway station?"

"Why do you think?"

"I really don't know," he said.

The boy with the sour breath whispered, "They will put us on trains to Poland."

73

After their visit with Sturmscharführer Hanover, Henry and Laura arrived home with no one following them. Henry gave the taxi driver a one-hundred-franc note, and Laura used his shoulder for support as they walked up the steps to the front door.

In the foyer, stepping out of her heels and walking barefoot on the cool marble, she greeted Frau Kisling and embraced her, leaning over and weeping on the petite woman's shoulder. Her housekeeper's round form and rosewater scent soothed her, and she was able, with some effort, to dry her eyes. Frau Kisling told her they were safe and that David would return very soon. But she didn't believe anyone's assurances.

Henry stood in the open doorway. "I'm going to have a look around the neighborhood and the *seizième*," he told them. "Please stay here, darling. I don't trust the Germans around you."

"But is it safe for *you*?" she asked.

Henry shrugged and went out, closing the door behind him.

"Don't go!" Laura called after him.

But he didn't return.

After a moment she left Frau Kisling and went upstairs to David's bedroom. She lay on his bed and breathed the scent his hair and skin had left on the goose-down pillow. There was sweat, and oil, and a fresh smell like soap. Would his scent be the only part of him that would remain in her life? She shuddered and looked up at the white plaster ceiling and the cove molding, as he must have done on hundreds of occasions, trying to think as he thought. *If I were David,* she asked herself, *and decided to sneak out of the house late at night, where would I go?*

Only one place seemed likely.

In the early evening, she left for La Pomme, though Henry hadn't returned. She didn't leave a note for him and asked the Kislings to keep her destination secret. Henry shouldn't know, she explained to them. He'd think her stupid for risking her own safety. But she knew she must go. David would find her at the club, she believed with desperate certainty.

Monsieur Bellegarde welcomed her and, when she told him of David's disappearance, assured her that David would be found. She kissed the trio in greeting; she drank a whiskey. She turned from the low stage and looked out the windows at the streetlamps and the passersby. Would David see her through the glass? Would he see her blond hair and pearls, recognize her, and come into the nightclub?

Summoning hope, she'd sing for him tonight, and perhaps he'd hear her. She turned her back to the room and faced the trio as she sipped her martini and assumed the role of la Perle. She smiled and strode across the stage. When the trio nodded its readiness, she turned to the room. At the table nearest the stage was Frederick Abendroth, the German businessman who'd paid her such compliments and attention before the war. Tonight he was transformed. Instead of his customary suit, he wore the uniform of the Gestapo.

He appeared larger than ever. In the sweep of the stage lights, his high forehead shone and the buttons of his sharply cut wool jacket glinted. Although his legs were crossed almost delicately, the pose showed off his polished boots. Now it was clear his claiming to be a businessman had been a ruse. Fear slipped into her heart, and yet she was so confident onstage that her movements and voice remained natural. When her eyes met his, she smiled. For he could help her.

74

David was as hungry as everyone else. He couldn't leave the room, and even if he did, there was little food in the camp by the Bourget railway station.

In his years traveling alone, he'd never been as desperate for food as he was this evening. Ignoring Herr Mandelbaum, the old man with whom he shared a small room on the building's third floor, he looked out the window and saw a few rooftops but no recognizable landmarks. His whereabouts were unknown to him. He feared he'd never be found.

He and the other men and boys from the truck had been herded into Vue de Bourget, a new but unused apartment building of five stories that was made of dun-colored brick and that bordered a small courtyard filled with yellowing grass. The rooms were small and had floors of concrete and no furniture. In the day the sun beat through the windows and the building grew stifling, but at night it was cold, and there were no blankets or extra clothes. Extremes of temperature made many sick. His nose began to run uncontrollably, and in the morning he coughed himself awake.

Here, prisoner gossip was the milk of life. It ran through the small rooms, along the straight corridors, and out into the yard. He couldn't avoid talk of trains filled with men and boys like him. He heard that if he were sent east on one of these trains, to a *Konzentrationslager*, he must escape or he'd die. For the camps and the ghettos in Germany and Poland were hell, and nobody survived. *Nobody.*

That's what the other prisoners had told him. And each inmate assumed the purpose of this camp was to evaluate who'd remain in France and who'd be sent away. In order to remain here, in relative safety, they reasoned they needed to exhibit their health. Many did push-ups and sit-ups in their rooms, or outside in the sunshine when they were allowed access to the building's interior courtyard. Yet in order to have health, one had to have nourishment, and there wasn't enough food for everyone.

The prisoners residing on different floors of the building were released, in shifts, out into the courtyard in the middle of his first day at the camp. Herr Mandelbaum, who had tremors caused by God knew what, grew progressively weaker due to his refusal to eat. He could hardly get down the steep staircases at each end of the floor's hallway. David helped him down and helped him back up forty-five minutes later. The Germans had organized the handing out of vegetable broth and stale bread. David obediently stood in line, received the end of a baguette and soup that sloshed around an old ceramic bowl, its thin cracks forming a spider's web across its base. He went off to the side, behind other, taller prisoners who were standing, and lifted the bowl to his mouth, drinking the broth quickly. He ate the bread in three large bites and set the bowl in the grass. Then he asked to borrow Mandelbaum's spectacles and olive raincoat.

The old man shrugged and removed his eyeglasses and took off his coat, revealing a short-sleeved white shirt and arms whose skin hung loosely off the bones. His flesh was patterned with wine-colored age spots, and David felt that by donning the coat and by putting on the old man's eyeglasses, he was draining the last of the man's strength. David brushed his hair forward, over his forehead, and insinuated himself into the line. Despite the awkwardness of having to decipher the world through lenses ground for Mandelbaum's myopia, he straightened his back and pretended at being a man, rather than the boy who'd already been served lunch. The women handed him another bowl of soup and the end of a baguette. The woman ladling out the soup gave him a lingering look, perhaps indicating she'd caught on to his scheme or warning him not to try it again. But he would try it again, at dinner (if there was dinner), or at lunch the next day. In fact he'd keep doing it until someone stopped him. He returned to Mandelbaum, who took back his coat and spectacles without a word. When the soup ran out, at least twenty men and boys had eaten nothing. The women showed them the empty pots and promised more tomorrow. David was too hungry to feel pity for those who hadn't eaten, and he wasn't ashamed of his attempt to survive. That was his first—maybe his only—duty.

The guards, holding pistols and rifles, began shouting at the prisoners to return to the building. Nobody argued with them. David helped Mandelbaum up the staircase and along the hallway to their unfurnished room.

As soon as they sat on the concrete floor, the boy with the sour breath—whom he'd met on the truck ride to the camp—appeared at the doorway. With him were two other boys, and all of them weighed far more than David or Mandelbaum.

"We saw you," the boy said. His face was dark and his head enormous. His arms and shoulders were large like Mr. Henry's. "We saw you take more soup than anyone else."

David looked at the floor. Saying anything would be a mistake.

Another boy, with a long, narrow face like a rat, stepped toward him. "You eat twice, someone else doesn't eat at all."

"I'm sorry," David replied meekly.

"Yes, you should be," said the third boy, who had a thin mustache. "You took two meals, and I didn't get any."

The boy with the sour breath came into the room, the other boys behind him. They surrounded David and began kicking him. He curled up so their feet would land on his back or his legs, but they weren't interested in those parts of his body. One of the boys took hold of his arms, the other his legs, and they pulled, opening him up, exposing his stomach. The boy with the sour breath brought back his leg as if he were going to kick a football, and landed a sharp blow at David's stomach.

Air rushed up his throat, and he tried to breathe but suffered another kick to his stomach, and another. He felt himself weakening. He could no longer resist the boys. The large boy kicked and kicked until David vomited on himself, until his stomach was empty and his two helpings of soup and two pieces of bread ran in half-digested streams down his throat and chest.

Then, laughing brightly, the boys let go of him and left the room. He gasped for air and turned on his side, crying with pain. His insides burned so hot he wanted to die. And when the pain began to lessen just a little, he smelled himself and removed his suit coat and shirt, then rubbed them against the wall in a feeble attempt to clean them. But it was cold, and he had to put the shirt and coat on again. At last he lay on the concrete floor, his face wet with tears. In the corner he noticed Mandelbaum, watching him with weak eyes.

75

Henry returned home in the darkness. Another night when no man watched them from across the street. In the foyer he removed his suit coat. His shirt was damp from walking all day in the heat. He needed a bath and rest. Hungry, not having eaten all day, thirsty for water and wine, he walked into the kitchen. Frau Kisling hunched over the stove, stirring a pot of tomato sauce. It was a scene of comfortable domesticity, but he couldn't enjoy it. "Is Laura upstairs?" he asked.

Startled, Frau Kisling looked up at him. "You are home. Would you like something to eat?"

"Yes, I would."

"You didn't find our David?"

"Not yet."

Nodding, as if she'd known his search would be unsuccessful, she opened the oven door and removed a cast-iron pot with a heavy lid, lifting and setting it on the stove.

"Frau Kisling?"

"Yes?"

"Where is Laura?"

"She is out."

"Out where?"

"She is working."

"At La Pomme?"

"Yes."

"But David's missing. How could she go to La Pomme? How could she sing and smile at the patrons?"

Frau Kisling turned to Henry and brushed her hands against her olive green housedress. "Miss Laura told me that David had left this house in order to visit La Pomme. She decided to go there and wait for him, in case he finds her there."

Henry shook his head and muttered to himself, "David has been caught. I don't know how to pretend he's all right."

Frau Kisling responded only by setting out a plate with roast pork and asparagus. Henry ate quickly, hurried up the stairs, bathed, and dressed. Then he walked out into the night, smoking as he walked to the place Victor Hugo, where he'd find a taxi that would take him to see Laura and to wait for David. Hopeless futility, he knew, but he was tired and could think of no other way to find his son.

76

By the time Henry arrived at La Pomme, Laura had finished the first few songs and was at the marble-topped table nearest the stage. A man with blond hair was sitting with his back to him, talking with Laura, pouring her champagne. She was smiling and laughing as if she'd not a care in the world, as if her son hadn't been lost. Anger rising and not recognizing the man from the back of his head, Henry marched toward the table. He was going to push the man aside and take Laura home. But then she looked up, her eyes warning him though her smile remained like that of a statue, and turned again to the man. Henry stopped, looked more carefully. Now he could see the man in profile. It must be Abendroth, the German, who'd returned to court her with more insistence, more certain of his success, now that he wore the uniform of a senior officer of the Gestapo.

Henry stepped backward, slowly. From the rear of the large room he saw Laura reach for Abendroth. Saw the Nazi's hand close around hers.

He held himself, checked his outrage, and knew that Laura, smart girl, was asking a favor of the occupier. He feared the price of success.

77

Laura worried her plans would be ruined when Henry saw her and recognized Frederick. But he caught her eye, her unnatural behavior and glacial expression, and her hand on Frederick's. He knew that she wouldn't betray him. So with his dark form leaving the club, she could smile at Frederick and tell him about her son who'd gone missing, who might have been picked up and taken somewhere, she couldn't imagine where, by Frederick's *organization*.

"On which night did he fail to come home?" Frederick asked her, a Gauloise between his lips. His face had become flushed red with the warmth of the room, the Veuve Clicquot, the attentions of la Perle, and the authority his uniform gave him.

"Last night."

He nodded. "The Wehrmacht's first night in Paris."

She ignored the noise of chairs being slid back, of patrons, having seen her obvious affection for this Gestapo officer, leaving La Pomme. She knew that Monsieur Bellegarde would have liked to ask Frederick to leave, but he wouldn't dare. Frederick could have him killed, and they all knew it. "Yes, Frederick. He tried to come and see me sing, but he didn't make it here. I went home and to bed, and in the morning he was gone. It was a terrible shock. I didn't think I could sing again. But I thought maybe, if I did, he'd hear me, he'd find me here. But"—and here her smile at last faded, and she puffed out her lips and cast down her eyes—"he hasn't returned. I don't know what to do. I'm not sure that I can sing anymore. It hurts, you see," she told him, hand on her chest. "It hurts to live when my son is lost."

His eyes remained for an indecently long moment on her breasts. Her low-cut black dress revealed much of them, and she wore no brassiere. She leaned a little to one side, revealing a bit of pink, and then straightened.

"Do you have any influence, in your *organization*?" she asked in the breathy voice of la Perle.

His eyes rose to meet hers. He thrust his chest forward, exhaled smoke upward, and nodded. "Of course," he said. "I command most of Paris, you understand? My rank is *Obersturmbannführer*."

"So much responsibility," she said, admiringly. "You must be too busy to worry about my son."

"No," he said, stubbing out his cigarette and smiling at her. "I can help a good friend."

She allowed her face to reflect a bit of his smile. "Really? You might help me?"

"I will help you," he promised. "If your son is held by my *organization*, as you call it, then I will return him to you."

"Oh, Frederick," she cried, leaning forward and kissing his lips, lingering there for a moment while forcing herself not to blanch, and kissing him a second time, before sitting back into her chair. "If you help me, if my son is returned to me, I'd be very grateful."

He silently drank his champagne and watched her. She didn't know what to do. She felt that she was about to cry, but she didn't want him to see her without the mask of la Perle. She'd remain strong; he wouldn't wait much longer to make his request.

And he didn't.

As he leaned toward her and spoke into her ear, she listened carefully and nodded. She explained that she'd married but that if he could keep their secret, then she could as well. "If you find my son," she whispered, "I'll meet you wherever you'd like. You must know that I'm attracted to you. If I hadn't been engaged, I'd have expressed my feelings two years ago. You feel it, yes?"

"Definitely," he said, smirking and raising his chin. "And if I can arrange for your son's return," he said, "shall we say eight o'clock tomorrow, at the George V?"

"Yes. If my son is returned to me, I will be at the hotel."

As she stood and climbed onto the stage to begin her second set of songs, she nearly toppled over. It wasn't the drink she'd shared with Frederick; it was the oddity of his confidence. She went to the piano and picked up Étienne's glass of emerald-colored absinthe. Sipping it, buying time before she had to turn and face the man who'd taken her son, she harnessed every bit of good breeding, every ounce of self-control, every ability she had to dissemble. Yes, she saw now, it had been Frederick who'd ordered the taking of her son. How else could he know he'd find David, and so quickly that he'd made plans to meet her at the George V at a certain time the following night?

As she turned around, she again wore the mask of la Perle. She was hard and brilliant, glamorous and free with her favors. When her eyes met Frederick's, she winked at him and then looked at every other patron in the room before returning, eventually and warmly, to him. But under her enchanting mask she burned with an essential question. Had Frederick ordered the taking of her son only to get her into bed? Or was there a darker reason, to do with Henry and his safety?

78

Shortly after sunrise the next morning, the guards shouted at the prisoners on the third floor to leave their rooms immediately, and to go down the stairs and outside, into the courtyard, for an important announcement. Mandelbaum put on his glasses and got to his knees. Having nothing to hold onto as he raised himself, he reached toward David.

David looked out into the hallway, saw the nearest guard at least ten meters distant, and returned to the cell. He grasped Mandelbaum's large bony hand, and pulled him up. Then he ran from the cell, leaving the old man to descend, unaided, the narrow staircase at the end of the corridor.

He felt weak with hunger and hoped there would be breakfast. But he didn't see the stout women who brought the soup and bread. There were only guards, perhaps a few more than usual.

"Form a line!" the guards shouted at them.

They stood shoulder to shoulder, the line stretching from one end of the courtyard to the other. Now there were so many prisoners that a second line formed, and this was where David contrived to be. Next to him came the boy with the sour breath, who'd attacked him last night, as well as his friends, the rat-faced boy and the boy with the mustache. It was as if they wanted to underscore their own strength by drawing a comparison to his weakness.

Two men, one wearing the white coat of a doctor, the other a Gestapo uniform, walked slowly past each man and boy in the first line. The doctor looked carefully at each of them, saying to the guard either *"ein"* or *"zwei."* The guard, who carried a clipboard, scribbled the prisoner's badge number and either *one* or *two* next to it. Whenever the guard with the insignia said *"zwei,"* a few of the Gestapo walked over to the man or boy, took hold of his arms, and pulled him across the courtyard to the far corner of the space. After two or three men and boys had been chosen as *zwei*, it was clear to everyone that to be *zwei* was very bad. Each of the men chosen was old, feeble, crippled, or all three. The boys were scrawny or sickly. They stood in the corner of the courtyard, sneezing and talking among themselves. One man lost his temper and screamed at the guards, denouncing them as monsters. Immediately the space around him cleared, and the other prisoners lowered their eyes. A rifle butt to the head silenced him, and he collapsed onto the grass and lay immobile.

When the guard with the insignia had finished with the first line, the remaining men and boys from that line were told to go to the corner opposite those who were damned. Then the guard started with the second line, where David stood with the boys who'd attacked him. After wiping his nose with his hands, he drew himself up as tall as he could, lifting a little in his shoes, filling his chest with air to appear larger.

Mandelbaum was the first in this row to be labeled *zwei*. David watched him shuffle to the corner of the damned, but felt little sorrow. Mandelbaum had lived to be old, but he, David, was young and deserved to live awhile longer, even a great while longer. He pushed his chin forward and up and waited for the doctor to reach him.

As the doctor approached, the boy with the mustache turned and punched him in the stomach. He hadn't expected it, hadn't tensed up. Almost falling over, he gagged and tried to breathe evenly. It was all he could do to remain standing and not to cry. The doctor stared at him a long moment, and then said to the guard with the clipboard, *"Ein."*

In a moment his line was broken up the way the first had been. He went to the corner with the others designated *ein*, the fortunate, joining the rat-faced boy and the boy with the mustache, and stood there quietly, watching the guard with the clipboard double-checking the prisoner badges against his paperwork, before the old and sick were surrounded by guards and pushed out through the high courtyard gate to certain doom.

The door remained open. The guard with the insignia walked to the middle of the courtyard and addressed the elect, David's group.

"Prisoner seven hundred sixty-two," the guard said, in German. "Come forward."

None of them moved forward. Some bent their heads to read the number stitched onto their clothes. All were terrified.

"Prisoner seven hundred sixty-two!" repeated the guard.

David knew his number by heart, knew they were calling him. He stiffened with fear and willed himself to disappear.

"It's you," said the rat-faced boy.

"It's him!" cried the sour-breathed boy, pointing at David.

"No," David told him in a whisper. "You're mistaken."

"I'm not mistaken. It's you. You have to step forward, you little *Saftsack*. You're going to die."

"Please," David begged, his legs almost buckling, his chest hot with fear. "Please, say no more."

But the rat-faced boy ignored him and raised a hand. "This is the one you're calling! Here, next to me!"

He couldn't escape.

"Come forward," the guard said, meeting David's eyes.

He was damned.

"Please, sir," he said to the guard as he left the line and walked across the yard. "Please, let me remain here, in this nice place. I can work, I'm not sick."

"This way," the guard said and pointed toward the gate. "You must leave."

He began to cry. "But I don't want to go east."

"You must leave," the guard insisted. "Now!"

"I can't leave. I can't!"

The guard with the insignia turned and inclined his head toward the other guards. They were enormous and took hold of David. He fought them off, bit one of them, and for it received a harsh slap across the side of his head. He kicked them, he punched the air, but they found his arms and legs and tightened their grip on him, at last carrying him out of the courtyard as if he were a rolled-up Oriental rug. He faced the ground, which bobbed up and down with each step taken by the guards. He saw the ground change from the courtyard of grass to sand and then to asphalt. The guards stopped and righted him. He stood. Instead of the frightening truck he expected to see, there was a large black Mercedes-Benz.

"I don't understand," he said.

"You're free," one of the guards told him. "You won't be so lucky next time."

"But why?"

"You have a powerful friend," the guard explained, pushing him toward the car.

He decided to go quietly. Surely, the Gestapo wouldn't transport a prisoner to the railway station in a beautiful car. He climbed into the large back seat, and one of the guards climbed into the back seat via the other door. The driver put the car in gear, and they left the prison. Around them were all the things he hadn't seen for what seemed like days: trees thick with summer leaves, the whitewashed buildings with their roofs, the great plazas and squares, the monuments and fountains. He stared out the window in wonder. Everything shone in the sunlight. As the car moved through the maze of streets, the spire of the Eiffel Tower moved slowly, as if floating in the blue sky, a symbol of something, perhaps of triumph.

79

Henry heard the pounding on the front door of the house in the rue Dosne. "I'm home!" came the voice he most wanted to hear. "I'm home! Let me in!"

Setting aside the bank statements he'd been studying in the library, he charged into the foyer and opened the door. As David wrapped his arms round him, Henry saw both a large Mercedes-Benz rolling away from the house and a man with a sidearm watching from the doorway across the street. But in that moment, all that mattered was that David had been returned to them. He lifted up the boy, holding him close, his eyes suddenly teary, and brought him inside, closing and locking the door behind them. "Thank God," he said. "Thank God you're here."

"David!" Laura called as she and Frau Kisling entered the foyer together. "My darling!" Her cheeks had reddened, and her eyes glittered with happiness. "My son, my baby," she said.

Henry set David on the floor and let go, and the boy ran toward her, nearly toppling her over, so athletic was his embrace. "Miss Laura," he said, pushing his mouth against her neck, kissing her as she kissed the top of his forehead. "I thought I'd be sent east."

"No, sweetheart. You're safe—that's all that matters now."

David turned and addressed all of them, even Herr Kisling, who'd descended from the third-floor bedroom, where he must have been taking a nap, his hair standing up at every angle. "They sent the men who were old and sick to the train station. I saw them do it."

Henry watched Herr Kisling's face darken as the old man pointed at David. "We should not speak of this. It is too awful."

"But Herr Kisling," the boy said, "you don't understand. They take people to Le Bourget train station and send them east, to Poland."

"I do understand, young man. I understand much too well. For they took my daughter, Tabitha, from the school where she taught maths, and they . . ." He faltered.

David appeared to understand. His face lost its happiness. "I'm sorry, Herr Kisling. I'm very sorry."

In response the older man looked at his wife, withdrew a crumpled handkerchief from his back trouser pocket, and dabbed his eyes.

Henry wished to be sensitive to the Kislings' distress, yet he wanted more information from David. "How can you be sure the prisoners were going east?"

David looked at him, his eyes darker and less childlike than before his abduction, eyes that Henry had seen on the *Île de France*, before David had been allowed to become a boy again. "Everyone knew what was happening. It was whispered about, and then it wasn't whispered anymore."

"No!" Herr Kisling said, holding up his hands and looking at Henry and David. "You must not speak of it, do you understand? My family, my friends were forced into ghettos, and they are dead. You must not speak of these things."

"Shouldn't people know about them?" David asked his tutor, challenging him today as he had during his lessons. "Shouldn't we talk about it and embarrass the Gestapo?"

Herr Kisling shook his head, his eyes never leaving the boy's. "They're monsters, David. Instead of shame they feel pride. Don't you see?"

Henry glanced at all of them, noticing for the first time what David's absence had done. Laura seemed to him as beautiful as always, yet there were dark patches below her eyes. The Kislings were haggard, their faces heavily lined. It was a great relief to all of them that David had returned. Now, they might eat.

Standing there in the foyer with the others, David lowered his eyes. "I'm sorry," he said to Herr Kisling. "I shouldn't have mentioned the trains and the ghettos."

Herr Kisling watched him to see if he'd say more, as he often did. Henry knew that David had a way of speaking a few words too many. But now the boy's exhaustion showed in his slumping shoulders and his tired face. "After I take a bath," he said to Frau Kisling, "may I have something to eat? I'm so hungry I can barely stand."

Frau Kisling nodded vigorously. "Of course, David. I will make you an enormous lunch. You will eat like Solomon!"

Henry watched David trudge up the wide staircase to the second floor. And soon, those in the foyer could hear the sound of a door closing upstairs and then water running through the pipes in the walls to the tub in the bathroom.

Frau Kisling looked at her husband, expecting some word from him.

Herr Kisling touched Henry's shoulder and looked at each of them in turn. His voice was low as he spoke. "I've seen my friends dragged from their homes and shot in the street. I've lost my daughter and everything else except my wife. Henry and Laura, do you understand? The Nazis will take everything from us. Yes, David was lucky this once. But next time there will not be sufficient luck for him, for any of us. We used all of it today."

Henry nodded and put an arm around Laura. His chest tensed. He knew that Frederick Abendroth's interest in her would create their only chance of escape.

80

As if by silent agreement, Henry followed Laura into the library and closed the door. He went to the desk, poured two glasses of whiskey, and handed one to her.

After drinking it in one motion, she inhaled deeply. Yet she didn't meet his eyes, and he knew why.

She wonders if I'm questioning her love, he thought, *and wondering if she'll sleep with another man.*

"I ought to send word," she said, "to the George V."

He went behind the desk and sat in the chair, facing her. She stood with the glass in one hand and her other across her stomach, as if she might be ill.

He said, "What will you tell Abendroth?"

"I'll say I've reconsidered and can't meet him at the hotel."

"No." Henry shook his head. "You can't reconsider. You owe him, and you can't refuse. *Obersturmbannführers* in the Gestapo don't make requests."

"Are you suggesting . . . ?" She left her question unfinished.

His face warmed. "No, I'm not," he assured her. "My plan was to get us out of Paris just after the Germans arrived, when they weren't in control of the roads. But David's time in the camp, and Abendroth's demand, have changed things. We must escape tonight."

Her eyes widened. "*Tonight?* How?"

"I've made arrangements," he promised, speaking in a low voice and as calmly as he could. "But if we leave this minute, the man watching the house will see us. I'm fairly sure he's Gestapo or working for them. But if we leave after dark, along the roof, we'll be invisible. We'll make it to the place Victor Hugo and be driven out of the city. The difficulty is . . ."

"Frederick Abendroth."

"Exactly. When he arrives at eight o'clock, the sun won't have set. We can't possibly climb onto the roof without notice."

She shook her head. Nervous, she walked in a circle around the room. "I don't understand. Why are you talking about the house? I'm to meet him at the George V."

"You mustn't go to the hotel. You know what he'd do there."

She stopped. "But what's the difference if I see him here or there? And if I see him here, what will you . . . ? I don't know what to do, Henry. I don't see a way out."

He nodded, silently agreeing with her. For there *was* no way out, short of an act which two years ago he wouldn't have countenanced. But circumstances had changed. He'd changed. His first inkling of the change had been his surprising request that David steal the old woman's pin on the *Île de France*. That had been the beginning of a willingness to act in ways outside the usual moral standards. And now, less than two years later, he would attempt to commit himself—and Laura and Frau Kisling—to the ultimate transgression. The strangest thing, the biggest surprise, was that he felt no regret for the decisions he'd made. Each had seemed right. "We have a way out," he said to Laura, "but it's very dangerous. At least we'll have a chance to survive."

Watching his eyes carefully, she set her tumbler on the desk. He poured another ounce of whiskey, and she took it up and drank it quickly. "Tell me," she said. "I don't care how dangerous it is. I'm not going to be anyone's mistress."

This was said strongly enough that he knew she'd accept his plan, no matter the risks to herself. And it was filled with obstacles with little in the way of contingency. Either it would work, or it wouldn't. And if it didn't work . . . he couldn't bear the thought. He leaned over the desk and held open his hands, as if he were a magician showing her the secret to a card trick. "Send word to Abendroth. Tell him that David and I are away, picnicking in the Bois de Boulogne, and ask him to come here."

Her astonishment showed on her face. "But I don't want that man in our house."

"It's the only way," he told her. "David and I will be at a café on the place Victor Hugo with Herr Kisling. Frau Kisling will be in the kitchen and will offer to serve him a drink and something to eat."

"But, Henry," she said, "Frau Kisling is a Jew, and . . . she might be hurt."

"I understand. But that's why she will take care of Abendroth."

"What?" Laura couldn't believe her housekeeper would lift a finger to hurt anyone, though God knew she had one towering reason to hurt a Nazi. "She couldn't, she wouldn't."

"She can, and she will," Henry insisted. He reached forward and poured himself another whiskey. "This must work. It must. Or we won't survive."

Laura trembled at the bleakness of this statement. She knew it was correct. She went over to the window and looked across the street. There, the man watching the house seemed to smile at her. Quickly turning away, she returned to the desk and looked at Henry.

"The stationery is here," he said, pulling open a drawer. "Write to Abendroth, and take it to the hotel. I'd do it, but they'd stop me." He finished his drink, stood, and looked at her. "Now is the time. When Abendroth fails to leave our house, we'll be marked forever. We must leave, and we must leave immediately after Frau Kisling does her work."

She sat in the chair facing the desk, as if suddenly weak. "So it's really happening. We're going to run away with David and the Kislings. Will we survive?"

He breathed deeply. "I hope we will. But we can't sit here and wait for them to line us up against a wall. They'll have to catch us first."

"Will they, do you think?"

"No, they won't," he said, though he knew, and knew that she knew, that their survival depended to a large degree on chance, on luck. On their not having used their allotment of it.

81

In the gray afternoon Laura left the house in a pink-and-green floral-print dress, a broad-brimmed straw hat, and sunglasses. Without turning her head toward the man watching her from across the street, she took in his appearance.

He had the face of a teenager, with pimples and proud eyes. In his plain gray suit he seemed harmless, yet beneath the soft wool, he stood so upright she thought he must be a member of the German military. He smoked and watched her as she walked away from him, up the street toward the place Victor Hugo. For a moment she feared that he'd follow her, perhaps force her into Frederick Abendroth's hotel room, leaving Henry's plan in ruins. Yet he remained at his post.

As she hailed a taxi, a faint rain began to fall. She wondered if the thick clouds over the city were an omen of the night to come. So much could go wrong. So much would, she feared. But did she have a choice? She knew enough of men to make this prediction: if she were to yield once to Frederick Abendroth, he'd want her as a constant presence in his life in Paris. Always he'd have something to trade for her affection—her life and the lives of her family. So she'd come to believe that Henry's plan was the only solution. She just wished that Henry could work the plan instead of her grandmotherly housekeeper. But of course Frederick's guards, or even Frederick himself, would search the house before he took her upstairs to one of the bedrooms. There wasn't anywhere for Henry to hide. But Frau Kisling? She hoped the

German would be blinded by lust and would regard the older woman as a harmless servant.

Near the Champs-Élysées she stepped out of a taxi and walked with feigned confidence through the misting rain and into the lobby of l'Hôtel George V. Her stomach turned when she thought of Frederick reading her note, of herself welcoming him to her house and her bed.

She carried her letter to the reception desk and left it for Herr Abendroth. Without further explanation, she turned and walked out of the hotel, trying to keep her eyes in front of her, seeing many uniforms and fearful that he'd hear her shoes clicking against the marble and somehow smell her perfume. Had he already arrived at the hotel, and would he force her into an upstairs room? She tried to breathe evenly and made for the door. Another moment, and she was outside in the rain, climbing into the waiting taxi. Her hands shook until she passed l'Étoile. She could think only of the night, and Frederick, and Frau Kisling.

82

The afternoon lasted but a short time. All members of the household packed essentials, which for Herr Kisling meant his Goethe and Rilke, his Mann and Schiller, and two changes of clothes. Henry rolled back the Persian rug in the library and withdrew the money he'd hidden under the loose floorboard, having already spent the rest of the funds—those he'd hidden in his suits and the many other hiding places—on the evening's transportation. Some of the money he kept on his person; the rest he hid in a picnic basket under plates, cutlery, and a ham. Other than this ham, they brought none of the food they'd purchased. More than what was in the basket would indicate flight. And there would be plenty to eat once they reached their destination, he promised.

By seven o'clock the rain had stopped. The city lay warm and unsettled under a layer of thick clouds. It was dusk but still light. Herr Kisling, David, and Henry left the house in the rue Dosne for the last time. Each wore a suit and a good pair of shoes. The man across the street studied them carefully but didn't move toward them or the house. To him, their departure was fortuitous, for it cleared the way for the *Obersturmbannführer* to enjoy his time with Henry's lover. And the two men and the boy appeared to be peaceable, doing nothing more than walking to a picnic dinner in the Bois de Boulogne.

Even with the terrible events of this month, Henry believed that Paris remained as beautiful as ever. It was possible, he knew, for many people to forget about all that was happening, but he couldn't. His family might not live through the night. They might be shot in the street. Or worse. And as they entered the place Victor Hugo, he could hear but not see the German Army marching along the nearby rue Copernic. Death and life mixed street by street, person by person. Life would smile on him tonight or cover him with an eternal cloak of darkness. But he'd made all the choices he could make. He was helpless and couldn't do more. Now fate, luck, and Frau Kisling's skill at dissembling would be brought to bear.

After the short walk they came to the Café du Futur on the place Victor Hugo. Inside, they took a long rectangular table in back. Henry ordered a double whiskey for himself and a glass of raspberry soda for David. Herr Kisling asked for a bottle of white burgundy. The older man sat down with a grimace, eyes watering. When Henry had presented his plan, Herr Kisling had agreed without complaint. He saw no alternative, and his wife insisted. They hadn't been able to save their own daughter when they'd lived in Berlin. They'd do what they could to save Laura. Yet, Herr Kisling told Henry, in the rush of preparing for tonight, he hadn't felt the full weight of what might happen to his Greta. Now the possibility of losing her to the same kind of men who'd taken his daughter overwhelmed him. Henry had grasped the older man's stooped shoulders and told him that they must live with hope, even when doing so seemed impossible. Herr Kisling could only frown silently.

Earlier that afternoon, when their makeshift family had been in the kitchen, Henry had set a small glass vial on the marble countertop. Within it was white powder that might have been sugar, except that it caught the light differently than sugar did. This substance was luminous, as if a deadly light came from within it.

"What is it?" David asked, reaching toward the vial.

"Poison," Henry said, catching his hand.

Herr Kisling leaned forward and peered at the white power through his eyeglasses. "Cyanide?"

Henry nodded.

"I've never seen it before."

"That isn't very much," David said. "I doubt it would kill a chicken."

"It would kill a horse," Henry told him.

David gazed at it with new respect. "Where did you get it?"

"A helpful chemist near the Sorbonne."

Then David pulled away and asked, "But how do you make anyone eat it? Do you think the Gestapo will be hungry?"

"No, but they'll be thirsty."

"How do you know?"

Henry laughed. "It's warm outside, they'll be wearing uncomfortable uniforms. And I've never met a uniformed man who doesn't like a drink."

"But what if they decide *not* to have a drink?" David asked. "What if they want Frau Kisling and Miss Laura to have a drink with them. Then what?"

Henry picked up the vial and placed it in Frau Kisling's small hands. "Then the plan doesn't work."

David's eyes widened. "But what happens?"

None of the adults moved. All were silent. Eventually David had understood, and his face had turned white.

The time in the café passed with awful slowness. After their drinks they grew hungry and ordered a modest dinner of sandwiches. When the food arrived, only David ate heartily. Henry and Herr Kisling managed only a mouthful or two and then drank more of the burgundy. Henry smoked.

They considered the slender Laura and the terrible officer of the Gestapo, and the diminutive, almost frail Frau Kisling, who remained the sole obstacle to the officer's having Laura. Everything depended on the sleight of hand the older woman would endeavor.

331

83

Frau Kisling looked through the open doors to the patio and the fading light. Darkness would soon arrive, as would the Gestapo. The air was warm and gray under the clouds and very still, and she wished that what might be the last evening of her life had been fair, with sunshine and a pleasant breeze. She felt herself perspiring in her housedress and knew that nervousness and fear made her unnaturally irritable and uncertain.

When the Nazis arrived, she'd have to work against her impulses. She must be the efficient *Köchin*, interested only in making sure her mistress's guests had enough to eat and drink. If they noticed her and thought her dangerous, the plan would fail. And God knew what would happen to her and to Laura. In German, she said under her breath: "Greta, you must be calm, efficient, and without curiosity. You must be as bland as a loaf of bread." But she knew this would be difficult. She wasn't good at dissembling, and her nervous energy had never made her less than obvious.

After taking down a crystal tumbler from the cupboard and setting it on the stone countertop, she took a bottle of chambord and poured half a glass. She didn't smoke but wanted to. She couldn't read or think about anything except how and where and when she'd poison a man. How was it possible? She spent her days going to the market and the boulangerie, cooking and listening to mystery stories on the wireless, and playing Doppelkopf with her husband. Now she'd attempt murder.

Her beloved Max and Henry and Laura feared that she couldn't do it, but she knew, oh, she knew she could.

She'd come to think of Laura as her younger daughter, and she'd willingly put herself between Laura and the Gestapo. She'd have done the same thing for her only child, if she'd had the chance. But they'd taken Tabitha from the Jewish high school where she'd taught, and there'd been no word, no explanation given by the Gestapo or the city government of Berlin. Her daughter, she knew, had died. Somewhere in the city or possibly in the countryside, and in a horrible way. A wave of deep sadness came over her as she recalled Tabitha's oval face and curly black hair. How she longed to embrace her daughter just once more! Shaking away this recollection, she decided that today she'd seek her revenge. But resolve didn't make her undertaking easy.

Sighing with momentary doubt, she went into the library and took hold of the heavy wireless, which she carried with her to the kitchen and set on the counter. In the pantry she put on a blue apron with large pockets. Then she went outside and stood on the patio, sipping her drink, watching the beautiful lilies and box hedges fade slowly into the night. Tucked into her brassiere was the vial of cyanide.

84

Wearing a modestly cut light-brown dress, Laura paced the second-floor hallway. From one end, where the master bedroom had been prepared with fresh linens for Frederick Abendroth's visit, past the bathroom, in whose cabinets she and Frau Kisling had stowed their bags, and on to David's bedroom and the room where her Louis Vuitton trunks were stored. And back again, each of her footsteps causing the parquet floor to creak. But she didn't notice the sounds of the house. She stood for a moment at the doorway to the master bedroom, admiring the painting of Mont Sainte-Victoire to the left of the armoire. Knowing she'd never see it again, she admired the shape of the gray mountain rising above the greens and yellows of the fields and trees, and over the mountain a shimmering blue sky. She wondered if she'd see the real mountain from their hiding place, which Henry hadn't disclosed to her. Of course if the plan failed, her family might go, but she'd be killed in this very house.

Images, dozens of them, troubled her. Images of Henry, of her own parents' faces when she'd told them she wanted to sing in Saint Paul, of David's smudged cheeks the first time she saw him on the *Île de France*. Soon there would be another face, that of Frederick Abendroth, a man hard as stone but at same time oily. The image of his lips against hers made her wince. The thought of his pressing his rough wool uniform, with the hard buttons, against her brown dress and her soft skin, of his unfastening his large belt buckle and pulling his awful uniform down to his knees in order free himself, made her shiver.

As she went down the stairs, she understood there was no way out. The man across the street wouldn't allow her to leave until Abendroth had his reward, and perhaps not then. And who was to say that if she and Frau Kisling tried to gain entrance to the house behind theirs, the Germans hadn't stationed another man along the rue de la Pompe? If she believed in a god, she'd have asked that god to take the cup of suffering from her. But there wasn't anyone to ask, no one to ease her worry that the plan would fail and she'd fail, that Frau Kisling would be killed, and that Henry and David would be found at Café du Futur and put to death.

A knock at the door made the entire house go still.

85

Laura and Frau Kisling, standing by the kitchen island, stared mutely at each other, stricken. They lowered their eyes, and Laura turned to go along the hallway to the foyer.

"Laura," Frau Kisling said.

"Please don't say more. I can't bear it."

The older woman nodded. Laura went over to her, leaned down, kissed both her cheeks, and left the room.

She wiped her eyes as she went through the foyer and reached the door just as it was struck again, sharply and insistently. Fixing a smile to her face, she drew the lock and opened the door. What remained of her confidence immediately faltered.

Obersturmbannführer Frederick Abendroth, standing in the exterior lights, was flanked by two brutish-looking guards. Both were barrel-chested giants, with the straps of machine guns looped around their shoulders and pistols in their right hands.

How, she thought in a panic, *could Frau Kisling deal with three men? It's impossible. The plan has failed.* She wanted to send word to Henry, but there wasn't a way. She'd suffer this cruel man alone. Frau Kisling would die. Life had tilted against them, and she'd be lucky to survive the evening. As hopelessness filled her, she gripped the doorpost for support.

Abendroth must have found the gesture charming. He removed his cap, with the leather band and swastika insignia, and tucked it under one arm. He smiled at her. "Good evening, Laura. May I come in?"

To this question that wasn't a question, she nodded, not trusting herself to speak. She stepped back and to the side.

"*Danke*," he said, as he and his men entered the house.

Their presence made her so cold that she shivered. They seemed out of place in the pretty foyer, with its white walls. She could smell their boot polish and sweat.

The first guard looked around the foyer, and the second closed and locked the door behind them. Both wore uniforms similar to Abendroth's—gray and black with high leather boots and holsters attached to wide belts. They had very short hair that made them resemble aggressive fighting dogs. Next to them she felt like a slender reed that they could bend in whichever direction they wanted. She felt increasing anxiety at having to submit to all three of them. But they didn't touch her, none of them did. Not yet.

The first guard walked along the hallway toward the kitchen. Noise came from within: glasses being set on the stone countertop. The guards raised their guns and aimed toward the interior of the house.

"I'm alone, except for my housekeeper," she said, able to speak only out of necessity. "Madame Kisling, who is in the kitchen, is preparing drinks for Frederick and me. And you, if you're permitted."

The first guard went quickly along the hallway. A moment later Laura heard him speaking in German to Frau Kisling. She expected shots or the sound of the enormous man clubbing her dear friend. But then she heard the guard climbing the staircase. The floors upstairs creaked as he walked from room to room, opening wardrobes and perhaps looking under beds. Then more steps as he climbed to the Kislings' room in the third-floor attic. Through all this Abendroth watched her with a vague smile that was incongruous with his cold blue eyes. Her gaze mostly on the floor, she waited for him to do something. Yet he didn't move, only breathed quietly, his long-fingered hands at his sides.

When the first guard returned to the foyer, he looked at Frederick and nodded.

"Now we have our drink," Abendroth said to her, his voice having changed from the solicitous one he'd used at La Pomme to something else entirely. Now she heard a man used to giving orders and to having his orders obeyed. His voice filled the foyer like a foul odor and left no room for questioning or argument. With an unhurried but firm gesture, he extended his hand and touched the small of her back. "We will go into the kitchen."

Shuddering visibly, she forced herself not to pull away from him. He noticed her response, and his face tightened with determination. He nodded toward the kitchen, and she nearly skipped forward, away from his hand. It wouldn't be the last time he touched her tonight, she knew, and she tried to prepare herself for the sensation of his skin against hers. Before entering the hallway she looked back and saw the second guard unlock the door and go outside and wait on the stoop, his head turning side to side as he watched the street. No one could leave. Nobody could get into the house to save her.

86

She followed the first guard into the kitchen, the sound of his steel-toed boots in front of her and Frederick Abendroth's behind her. The first guard walked out into the courtyard. There he took up a post by the table. Though he didn't sit down in one of the cushioned wrought iron chairs, he lit a cigarette.

"We have whiskey," Laura said when she and Abendroth stood by the island countertop. "But we also have champagne."

For a moment he stared at Frau Kisling. She was at the sink, wearing an apron and scrubbing a skillet. Laura held her breath, releasing it only when Frederick looked down at the marble countertop, where stood a half-empty whiskey bottle and the unopened Veuve Clicquot chilling in a silver bucket filled with ice. "Champagne!" he told her. "We must celebrate."

She looked at him quizzically. "What . . . ," she began, then hesitated.

"Your son," he reminded her. "He is found, is he not?"

She managed to nod.

"And we must toast the success of National Socialism."

She blinked and looked at the narrow back of Frau Kisling.

"And the leadership of the führer," Abendroth continued, his voice rising with excitement. "And the betterment of France and the unity of worthy races."

As if she hadn't heard him, she asked Frau Kisling to open the champagne. The older woman turned and lifted the bottle from the silver bucket, unwrapped the foil at its neck, and slowly withdrew the cork. An innocuous gunshot sounded: *pop!* Then she moved to the right, obscuring from the eyes of Laura and Abendroth the two wide glasses, into which she poured the effervescent liquid. A few seconds later, she picked up the glasses and set them on the center island, pushing the one in her left hand to Abendroth and the one in her right to Laura.

He raised his glass and smiled at Laura. "Congratulations on regaining your son."

"Thank you," she said, taking her glass and drinking deeply, still avoiding his eyes, not tasting any adulteration of her drink. Her stomach reacted unfavorably, and she swallowed twice to keep her nausea at bay. She was thinking of the failed plan. How stupid they'd been, to believe it would work. Even if Frederick fell ill, the guard on the patio wouldn't let Frau Kisling out of his sight. And had she been able to add cyanide to Frederick's glass? He seemed perfectly healthy. It would happen, then, wouldn't it? He'd drag her into the bedroom she'd shared with Henry and force himself upon her.

"Music?" Abendroth said. "Is there good German music?"

He'd noticed the wireless on the counter. Frau Kisling gave a faint nod and switched it on. She turned the dial past the news programs, both those from the BBC and those now managed by the Nazis in Paris, in favor of a station playing waltzes from the Strausses. She raised the volume almost to an excessive level and then returned to scrubbing the skillet that had been soaking in hot, soapy water.

Frederick watched her. He didn't seem to know if her playing the music so loudly was meant to mock him or because she thought he'd like it that way. A moment later his eyes shifted to Laura.

She looked at him and for the first time noticed his tongue.

"The sounds of Vienna," he said, the dark-red muscle running along his teeth. "Now part of the Reich, of course. But really it's always been German."

She found the music overpowering, its forced gaiety disturbing. Better would have been Piaf's weary voice in "*Mon Dieu*," or the *Lacrymosa* from Verdi's *Requiem*. For she felt that she'd die when he took her upstairs, that she'd never again kiss David's soft cheeks. She couldn't let this Nazi have her, and yet she must. There was no choice to make. To steel herself, she asked for more champagne.

"Yes, *Liebling*. Of course you may," he said, taking the bottle from the silver bucket and refilling her glass and his. "Peter," he called out to the courtyard. "A glass for you?"

"*Ja, mein Herr.*" The guard came in from the darkness of the patio.

"Another glass," Laura told Frau Kisling.

The older woman methodically dried her hands, forcing the young soldier to wait, and then took down a third glass from the cupboard. Then she again moved to her right, hiding her hands and the glass from them. Laura thought she saw her housekeeper reach quickly upward to her chest but couldn't be sure. A few seconds later Frau Kisling handed a glass of champagne to Peter, eyes always on her work, never on him or Abendroth or even Laura. For this, Laura was grateful. A plaintive glance from her housekeeper, and she might have confessed all and begged for the older woman's life.

"Take it, Peter," said Abendroth. "You've worked hard today."

The boy—Laura realized upon looking at his face in the light that he was a boy, possibly younger than twenty—lifted the glass and drank quickly, in a single gulp.

"*Sehr gut, mein Obersturmbannführer*," he said and gave a slight bow.

"*Exzellent.*" Abendroth nodded. "Now, *die junge Frau* and I will go upstairs."

Trembling, Laura put both hands around the stem of her glass. "May I take this with me?"

"We will take our glasses," he agreed and carried the bottle as they walked into the hallway. "Please, Laura, show me to your bedroom. You needn't fear me. I have only tenderness for you."

"I'm nervous, Frederick," she said, hiding her repulsion at what he'd do to her. "We hardly know each other."

"*Liebling*, I have known you for two years. There was a time I saw you almost every night. If you think about it, you will see that we are old friends."

87

As she climbed the staircase, she told herself not to react if—when—he touched her again. She mustn't tell him no, mustn't avoid his hand. Each moment she expected to feel his long fingers. She thought she'd scream if they grasped her. And then he'd hit her, and then . . .

But his hands remained around his glass and the champagne bottle. Yet she felt his eyes upon her, and this sensation made her squirm. She reached out and steadied herself by holding the railing but kept going. At the top of the stairs she turned and walked along the hallway to the large bedroom. At the door she stopped and looked back at him.

He grinned and pushed past her, his uniform brushing, scratching her shoulder. Standing in the middle of the room, he admired its size and leaned close to examine the painting that might be a Cézanne. Then he moved alongside the bed, set his champagne glass and the bottle on the nightstand, where Henry used to put the novels of Dickens, Stendhal, and Balzac, and unbuckled his wide black belt. He rotated his head, the way an owl does, unnaturally to the side and almost around to his back. This time there was no smile. His expression hardened, and his pupils dilated with arousal. "Come in, *Liebling*, and close the door. We will enjoy ourselves, the way the French do these things. And maybe we will do this again, another time. *C'est bien?*"

She shut the door, but not all the way. Coming from downstairs she could hear the *Kaiser-Walzer*.

He waved her into the room. "Closer, *bitte*."

She remained where she was, her eyes on the serene painting. She tried to become entranced by its beauty, yet her mind remained entirely connected to this awful event. He took her reticence for shyness. He must have decided to give her another moment to prepare herself. But he wouldn't allow a significant delay. He unbuttoned his jacket and threw it across the overstuffed chair. Through her peripheral vision she saw his undershirt, and the slight belly his uniform had disguised. He'd gained weight over the past two years. Too much drinking, probably. The image of that belly resting on hers caused her to shake.

"Closer," he repeated, his voice louder, rougher.

She took a step forward. He could almost reach her.

He held out his hand. "Now."

She sighed and walked forward and took his hand, which was damp from the champagne bottle or from nerves. He smelled of sweat and damp wool. At last she raised her head. His eyes narrowed as he leaned down to kiss her. She remained immobile. His lips met hers, and the shock of his mouth caused her to draw back.

He grabbed her by the shoulders and brought her close to him. If a kiss could be a jab, this was. His mouth pushed against hers, forcing hers open. Rather than drawing away, she allowed him to kiss her, though her tongue remained as far back in her mouth as possible.

His kisses ended abruptly. He pushed her down on the bed and lifted her legs until she was lying lengthwise on the mattress, the hem of her silk dress gathered about her knees. He examined the scoop neck and turned her onto her stomach. "There are no buttons."

She said, "It has to be lifted off."

"You do it," he ordered.

"No."

"As you like." He rested a knee on the edge of the bed and turned her onto her back. Then he grabbed at the silk and pulled it down, the threads coming undone and the fabric tearing. He folded it downward until her neck—encircled by her string of pearls—and her cream-colored brassiere filled his vision. After touching her neck, he ran his fingers down to the brassiere. He pulled down the left cup and touched her breast, rubbed his index finger over her stiffening nipple. Her reaction came from fear rather than desire, but he seemed to believe she'd betrayed her lust. Leaning forward, he rested partly on the bed and partly on her. He kissed her other breast and sucked on the nipple, and knelt over her and lifted the hem of her dress until he could see her panties. After pushing them down to her knees, he stared for a moment in silence.

88

She writhed meekly but kept her mouth shut. It would do no good to resist or scream.

Frederick got onto the bed, his face hovering above her crotch, his warm breath against her. He placed his long-fingered hands on her upper thighs.

Then he coughed once, drew in a ragged breath, and attempted to breathe again. His head turned scarlet and then purple. Veins rose in his forehead. He coughed again, but wasn't able to expel air from his lungs. His shoulders and arms tensed and shook. His blue eyes showed confusion and alarm, before rolling up under his eyelids. Then his head descended, but much too quickly. It crashed into her pubic bone, hard enough to hurt her. A warm river of foamy saliva ran from his mouth and along her thigh.

She looked up and saw Frau Kisling in the doorway. Quietly, she pulled herself out from under the heavy and unmoving body of Frederick Abendroth so she could close her legs and swing them off the bed. She wanted to scream, for what he'd have done to her and for what Frau Kisling had done to him.

Frau Kisling looked at her with narrowed eyes, her nostrils flared. "We must go now."

Laura needed to be sick, yet feared making a noise. "The man on the patio?" she whispered.

Frau Kisling shook her head. "He's gone, like this one."

Averting her eyes from the bed, she hurried into the bathroom, used a towel to wipe the almond-scented saliva off her thigh, and took her leather valise from the cabinet. Then she pulled up her brassiere and put on a simple black summer dress, stepped into black flats—the only pair she owned—and waited at the bottom of the narrow staircase leading to the attic rooms. Frau Kisling removed her valise from the cabinet and led Laura up to the third floor. They moved silently as a whisper, forgetting neither the guard outside the front door nor the man across the street. Eventually the guard at the door would come into the foyer and call for his superior officer. Hearing nothing but music on the wireless, he'd bound up the stairs and find not only Abendroth but them as well—if they delayed. And if they made any noise, the man across the street would notice them, and they would be surrounded and killed on the roof.

They opened the doors of the attic room and went out to the small balcony. Oxygen filled their lungs and steadied them. Edging past the potted flowers, Laura looked down and saw the uniformed man directly below. He was standing, smoking, joking with the man who usually stood in the doorway across the rue Dosne. Frau Kisling followed her eyes and nodded with relief. With both men directly below them, they'd be more difficult to see.

Laura went first, placing a foot on the wooden step stool they'd placed there earlier, and climbed up to the edge of the mansard roof. She grabbed hold of it and moved from the stool to the smooth tiled roof. It would have been simple, had she not been so nervous and almost in a state of shock, and if she hadn't had her bag hanging from her shoulder. But after a moment of struggle, she made it up onto the roof and set down her bag. Then she leaned down, took hold of the valise that Frau Kisling lifted toward her, stepped back, and waited.

Frau Kisling climbed onto the stool. Laura crouched and watched Frau Kisling reach upward, breathe heavily for a few moments, and then, in one motion that seemed almost effortless, grunt and grasp the roof and pull herself over, with Laura holding the small woman's shoulders.

Laura stood and embraced her quickly, before they walked south along the roof. She noticed the lights around the neighborhood, but most of her attention was on the obstacles before her. Glass skylights they might fall through and many chimneys. At last they came to the end of the row of houses. Below them lay the rue Dosne as it turned east toward the rue de la Pompe.

89

The rope tied to the last chimney was coiled around and around. It was where Henry had promised it would be, where he'd placed it the night before. The plan had worked, thus far. But Laura began to fear it would be their ruin. Frau Kisling, when she tried to lower herself off the roof, wouldn't be strong enough to brake her slide down the rope. But this was what they'd do, whether or not it ended in death. She embraced Frau Kisling once again. "Thank you," she said.

Frau Kisling patted her arm. "I'll wait for you in the street. If it's safe, you come down."

The older woman looked over the edge, held the valise out over the flagstones below, and dropped it. When it landed, there was only a muffled sound. The street was empty; nobody saw the bag.

Frau Kisling took the rope in both hands and gripped it in front of her stomach. She stood at the edge of the exterior wall, leaned backward, and began to rappel down the side of the house. This technique lasted only a moment. Laura watched from above as the older woman slid quickly down the rope, her dress catching and tearing against the wall. Yet she held on to the rope and reached the flagstones, falling onto her side but getting up again and waving.

Laura stood at the edge of the roof and dropped her valise. Without looking down, she gripped the rope as tightly as she could and stepped over the edge. Her fingers burned, yet she held on, willing herself toward Henry and David. Half walking, half sliding down the side of the house, she twice passed over a window and made sure not to kick it or break the glass. The rooms inside were dark, except one bedroom that was empty of people. The skin of her hands seemed to stick to the rope until nothing but bone remained. When she landed gracefully on the flagstones, she let go of the rope and looked at her palms in the light of a streetlamp.

She saw torn flesh and blood welling up through cuts in her skin.

"Please, go into my bag," she said to Frau Kisling, "and take out the green blouse at the top."

"No, no, it's much too nice. I have something." The older woman opened her own valise, took out a cotton nightgown, and tore strips from it. "Your hands," she said.

Laura held them out, as if she were a child.

Frau Kisling wrapped speedily. "I have nothing to fasten the cloth, so make a fist. Yes?"

"Yes."

They walked—nearly ran—up the rue de la Pompe and then east along avenue Bugeaud until they reached the well-lit place Victor Hugo. Across the street was Café du Futur, where their family waited. Soon, they knew, the murder of Frederick Abendroth would be discovered, and the hunt for them would begin.

90

Henry lurched up, pushing so hard against the table with his waist that Herr Kisling's wine sloshed out of its glass. All turned toward the door. The older man stood and extended his hand to his wife.

"*Mein Gott,*" he said, eyes wet. "I thought, I thought . . ."

"I am here," she said and wrapped her arms around his large belly. "I am here."

He kissed her narrow cheeks, and both of them wept.

Henry looked at Laura. What had happened to Abendroth? Her figure was so lithe and vulnerable beneath her summer dress. Had Abendroth touched it? Had he forced himself onto, into her? Henry felt weak and ill. But his eyes found hers, and she very slightly shook her head, a message intended only for him. And then she smiled with evident relief, and David got down off his chair, went to her, and hugged her tightly.

But Henry knew that soon the place Victor Hugo, and all the streets in proximity to the house in the rue Dosne, would be filled with Gestapo and possibly with Wehrmacht and gendarmerie.

"We must leave," he told them. He took out his money clip, his thumb pressing against the words inscribed on the silver—*Go Far*—and set several francs on the table for their food and drinks. "First the Kislings, then the rest of us. The cars should be waiting around the corner to the left, in the rue de Sontay. In the morning," he said with a nonchalance he didn't feel, "we'll breakfast together."

"Where are we going?" David asked. "To London? New York?"

"You'll know tomorrow," Henry assured him.

"But how will the Kislings know where to go?"

"I've told Herr Kisling of the hiding place."

David looked at his tutor and then at Henry. "Is it nice? Will I be able to play outside?"

"Yes and yes," Henry assured him, curtly this time, strained by the boy's questions. "But tonight we must leave. And if our plan fails and we have to hide somewhere other than the place I've discussed with Herr Kisling, we must agree to meet in this very café, on this very date, two years from now. Yes?"

"Yes," they repeated solemnly.

"But why discuss these things?" he asked them. "We'll have breakfast tomorrow morning, all together. So au revoir, not adieu."

A few more kisses, a last hug, and the Kislings left the café. As Laura wiped her tears, Henry and David noticed her wrapped hands.

"The rope hurt me, but I'm all right," she explained.

"Did Frau Kisling kill the man?"

"Shh, David. We'll talk later."

Henry looked around. A few patrons were watching them, had overheard some of the conversation. He didn't care. "Ready?" he asked them.

Laura and David nodded.

They went out of the café and walked to the left, to the corner and the intersection with the rue de Sontay. The first car had already taken the Kislings into the night. The second car, a black Mercedes-Benz, idled quietly. Atop each headlamp was mounted a small German flag—a black swastika within a white circle on a field of red.

91

When David saw the car, he stopped and grabbed hold of Henry's suit coat. "No, no, it's the Gestapo."

"I arranged for the car and the flags," Henry assured him in a calm voice. "I want everyone to think it's the Gestapo, but it will be us. All right?"

David loosened his grip.

"You have to trust me, David."

A man of perhaps sixty years of age opened the driver's door and stepped out of the car. He wore a gray suit, a white shirt, and a gray tie, and his hunched back was evident as he opened the car's rear door for Laura. They climbed inside, the three of them sitting in a row on the soft leather seat as the older man took Henry's picnic basket and Laura's bag and stowed them in the trunk.

"See," Henry told his son, "this man is going to drive us out of Paris, through the Bois de Boulogne. But we must leave now, before they begin searching for us."

The boy gripped his hand. "Yes, we must leave."

David looked forward at the older man, who'd climbed into the driver's seat. He slid closer to Henry on the seat as the big German car moved with a heavy elegance away from the curb and turned west along the avenue Bugeaud and then left in the rue de la Faisanderie before proceeding south, all the way to the place Tattegrain, and then turning right into the avenue Henri-Martin.

After a while they passed through the porte de la Muette and angled northwest along the route de la Muette-à-Neuilly. The few cars Henry saw were filled with others who braved the curfew and, upon seeing their Mercedes-Benz with its flags, sped quickly by. Three trucks of German soldiers passed them as they drove through the Parc de Saint-Cloud in the rue de Versailles. The soldiers recognized the make of the car and the flags and saluted.

Their driver honked in feigned support.

On into the darkness the older man drove through the maze of streets that wound through the woods west and southwest of Paris, on small arterials rather than the main roads, toward their destination that was south of Orléans. They left behind the city's beautiful monuments and cathedrals and parks, and with those things, the innocence and promise Henry had felt upon arriving in France. *How much has changed,* he thought, and worried anew about the overwhelming responsibility of caring for a child in wartime. *Now, nothing is certain, not even our lives. We must rely on the last of our money and the kindness of people we don't know.*

The car moved on through the vast darkness.

Outside the village of Ablis, where they expected to turn directly south, they came to a checkpoint set up by the Wehrmacht. Without warning, klieg lights lit up the Mercedes-Benz, blinding them.

The driver braked, for through their squinting eyes they saw a metal barricade stretched across the road. Large trucks lined the edge of the asphalt.

Henry took David's hand but could think of no words to comfort him or Laura. Before the soldiers raised their weapons and fired into the car, he'd tell them he loved them. And then it would be over, he was certain, the pain intense but brief.

The driver put a black cap on his head and cranked down his window as the car slowed and then stopped near a cluster of four German soldiers. He nodded to them.

In the back of the car, Laura leaned forward in an attempt to shield David with her body, a final but futile effort to protect him.

Henry sat as regally as he could, eyes in front of him. Everything would turn to dust, he knew. His heart went cold.

The old man began speaking to the Germans, angrily and loudly and in their language. Though Henry understood few of the words, he recognized the man's fluency and native intonations. The soldier closest to them took a step back from the car but held out a hand, saying "*Ausweis*" and "*papiere.*"

The old man laughed mockingly but reached over to the front passenger seat for a thin sheaf of papers clipped together. He handed them out the door to the waiting soldier and said gruffly, "*Und seien Sie schnell dabei!*"

Henry saw the soldier was young, blond, cherry cheeked, and uncertain of the status of the passengers in the Mercedes-Benz. He nodded respectfully to the old man driving the car and huddled with the three other soldiers, who held their flashlights above the papers and read them, assessing them for accuracy.

Two minutes went by. Three.

The old man called to them. "*Genug!*" He honked the horn once, twice.

Henry saw one soldier shake his head and make a chopping motion, while the other three nodded theirs and pointed north, in the direction of their superiors in Paris, and in Berlin. The four soldiers returned to the Mercedes-Benz. One of them, the one who'd made the chopping motion, shined his flashlight into the left rear window, illuminating Laura. She held up a hand to shield her face, but the soldier must have seen her blond hair and pale skin, must have satisfied himself that she was German as the papers attested. He grunted something to the young soldier with the cherry cheeks.

That soldier shouted a command. In an instant, one of the trucks started its engine and dragged the barricade to the side, allowing just enough space for the large Mercedes-Benz to pass. He then handed the sheaf of papers to their driver, who grumbled and eased the car forward, showing no fear, only anger and annoyance.

"Thank God," Henry said when they were through and once again were hurtling south through the gloom. "Thank God."

The driver removed his cap and shook his head and chuckled, "*Satanés Allemands.*"

Laura comforted David, whispering to him, assuring him that they were safe, though Henry knew no such thing, not here on the road in the *zone occupée*. He longed for a place of safety where they could live and not continually wager their lives, but he didn't know if they'd find it in France.

After a while, David's fright waned. He bent over until his head rested on Henry's leg, and he soon fell asleep.

Laura reached over David and touched Henry's sleeve. He took her bandaged hand in his and held it gently.

"Is it a secret?" she whispered. "Where we're going?"

He laughed quietly. "No, darling. Not anymore. You remember Madame Bernard, the woman who let us the house—the woman I called from Nice?"

"Only vaguely. We never met her."

"True. We never met her. But several weeks ago, I contacted her again, and arranged for sanctuary with her sister Françoise Bernard at her house near Châteauroux, in the *zone libre*. I had to pay most of the money I'd saved since we came to Europe to buy this car, to obtain false papers, and to get us out of Paris, but I could trust no one else."

She watched him for several minutes before asking, "How do you know we can trust Françoise?"

"Oh, darling. Nothing is certain—not in war. But I learned the family is Jewish. Their relatives in Vienna have been murdered. In return for that confidence I let them know that we'd made David our son and the Kislings our friends. Madame Bernard relayed this information to her sister, and the reply came two weeks ago. Françoise would take us in, if we needed to flee Paris. Americans and Jews would be difficult to hide, but I'm told she has a private estate, that her servants are loyal and hate the Germans, and that the Wehrmacht has remained far from Châteauroux. I think we'll be safe," he assured her. "We'll live just outside the great storm."

"For how long?" she asked.

He shook his head. "For as long as we can. Maybe until the war ends."

And so they rode on through the night, unsure of the future, but hand in hand. Despite all of it—the war, the occupation, the danger that he knew would follow them, his heart beat with optimism and his chest warmed with love for Laura and David. He understood that if he hadn't worked as a spy and written his newspaper articles, he'd never have wagered his life on anything important. Tonight, he wanted to shout that they'd escaped, and that while many had died, they still lived.

Not even Laura could see him in the darkness, but if she could, she'd have seen his eyes brighten and his mouth form a faint smile.

92

They arrived in Châteauroux without incident and before sunrise.

Laura noticed that it was warmer, one hundred fifty miles south of Paris, the air fragrant with lime trees and lavender. She rolled down her car window and smelled the country as their driver took them along a route known only to him. Just south of the town, whose buildings appeared gray in the early dawn, they turned onto a narrow gravel road that led up and around a sharp bend and eventually to the summit of a low hill.

The car slowed as they approached a country house with a single-story center and two-story wings. It wasn't enormous, but she knew it would fit all of them. When the car stopped, she climbed out. In the faint light the house appeared to be the color of a peach, with terra-cotta tiles and a chimney at each end of the center portion. Having feared a cold and dank castle, she breathed more easily. David, sleepy and subdued, followed Henry out of the car.

She waited as the driver opened the trunk and removed their luggage. He carried her bag up to the front door, then turned back to her, smiled, and tilted his head toward the house.

Henry and David took up the remaining bags and returned to the car for the picnic basket, where Henry had hidden bundles of franc notes. From inside the house, she heard a woman's musical voice, which carried through the open windows. This woman, she knew, had saved them.

Standing quietly, she closed her eyes. Her heart grew calm here in the country. No soldiers or taxis, no signs or streetlamps, no surveillance. Around them were the untroubled fields, the neat vineyards, the faint birdsong. Inhaling, she opened her eyes and walked with Henry and David up to the house, where they were greeted by their landlady, Françoise, earthy and still cherubic in her early sixties.

We'll be able to live here, she decided as Françoise led them into the front hall. *We'll be able to disappear.*

Yet worry intruded upon this hopeful peace.

In the late afternoon she tried to rest in the upstairs bedroom of the wing where Françoise had put them. The house was spacious and bright, and the lady had endeared herself to David by giving him a raspberry tart she'd baked that morning. But Laura's composure was troubled, for the Kislings hadn't arrived.

Over lunch she'd spoken of their fate with Henry and David. They'd taken a different route, she'd suggested wistfully; they'd be here soon. While David spoke of the Kislings as if they'd gone away on holiday, she feared they'd been caught and somehow connected to Abendroth's murder and then shot quickly and without ceremony. She sighed and hoped that her missing family members had found a hiding place in an unoccupied part of the country, that they'd survive and reach this fine country house or, if that proved overly difficult, that they'd meet again at Café du Futur on the place Victor Hugo, when the war ended.

Lying quietly, she thought of the path she and Henry had taken. They'd left America, where their lives had been stifled by her parents and by social convention. France had given them freedom but at last eroded their safety. Now freedom, too, had evaporated before the German tanks like water on a hot day.

Had she returned to America, she wouldn't listen anxiously for approaching footsteps or fear her family would be taken in the night. Yet a life in Saint Paul would have been narrower. She'd eventually have married a man she didn't love, while aching for the man she did, diminishing every part of her life. If she'd not become a singer at La Pomme, she'd never have become the woman she'd meant to be. Her life would have been contained on all sides, like a tree that would be cut whenever it began to grow too broadly or too tall. And without David in her life, she might have believed that she didn't have enough love for a child.

Yes, she thought. *I've chosen well.*

The essence of her time in France was that she and Henry had been able to live as they wished. They'd been able to love each other and the boy who'd become their son. They'd steeled themselves against evil. Within them they'd discovered a natural goodness that surprised them. They'd done and learned more than if they'd remained in America. Yet she felt no antipathy for her country. It was just that she loved her life with Henry and David more.

She closed her eyes. Through the open window she heard David playing in the vineyard to the east of the house. From downstairs came Henry's voice: pleasant, calm, warm.

Now she heard an engine outside, its noise overwhelming the birdsong and David's games. A farmer on his tractor, she assumed. But the noise grew high pitched, and gears were shifted. She got out of bed and went over to the tall window, concerned their escape had been discovered. Along the gravel drive a pewter-colored Renault approached the house, dust rising in its wake.

The car stopped, and the engine was shut off. For a moment, nothing happened.

She held her breath. Her chest burned with worry.

The rear doors of the Renault opened, and a little unsteadily, out climbed the Kislings. They stood gazing at the rolling hills lined with vineyards, at the wide-open sky, touched in the distance by silky clouds, at the large stone house before them.

A middle-aged man dressed in a loose-fitting blue suit climbed out of the car, went around to the back, and removed Frau Kisling's valise from the trunk. Her husband took it from the man, who shook hands with both of them, climbed back in, started the car, and went down the winding drive, the sound of the engine fading.

In the silence, a boy's excited shout: "Herr Kisling! Frau Kisling!"

From her place at the stone house's upstairs window, Laura watched the Kislings turn in the direction of the vineyards. She saw their faces brighten as they moved quickly, despite their exhaustion, toward the boy, who ran from between two rows of green vines and out into the drive, where he nearly leaped into their arms. They bent over him, hugging and kissing him, touching his black hair, his smooth face. David's voice rose in rapid cadences, his words filled with relief and joy.

She heard the heavy oak front door open and Henry's voice joining David's, delighted and comforting to the older members of the Kislings, who'd loved and cared for them, defended them, risked everything for them. After he embraced the older couple, Henry took the valise from Herr Kisling and led them into the stone house, their voices sounding below her perch on the second floor, enlivening the house with the familiar sounds of her family, the one each of them had chosen, a modern family.

A new warmth spread through her body, a surprising blend of love and security and, most importantly, happiness. As she turned from the window and strode toward the hallway and the stairs that would take her to those she loved, she couldn't help but smile at her good fortune.

ACKNOWLEDGMENTS

The author wishes to thank the entire team at Lake Union, especially Danielle Marshall and Chantelle Aimée Osman, for their enthusiasm and support for this story. And to Charlotte Herscher for her suggestions to improve the manuscript.

Thanks, also, to the Carleton *Voice* for publishing the first two chapters of this novel, in slightly different form and under the title *The Boy and the Pin*, in the summer 2021 issue.

And thank you to Megan, for your support and understanding of my writing, no matter how distracted it can make me.

ABOUT THE AUTHOR

James Tucker is the author of two acclaimed mysteries: *The Holdouts* and *Next of Kin*, an Amazon Crime Fiction Bestseller and recipient of a *Publishers Weekly* Starred Review.

In 1944, a fighter plane flown by James's grandfather was shot down over France, landing in a farmer's field near Châteaudun. In 2002, the author visited that field, along with the man and woman who saw the crash. On that warm afternoon nearly sixty years after his grandfather's death, James found pieces of the plane still in the field. For him, France, sacrifice, and freedom have always rhymed.

James grew up near Minneapolis, attending Carleton College and the University of Minnesota Law School. Formerly a lawyer, he's an executive at a Fortune 40 company. In his free time, James enjoys skiing, tennis, and travel. He and his wife, painter Megan Rye, live with their family near Minneapolis.

For more about the author, visit https://jamestuckeronline.com.